PRAISE FOR *THE LAUGHING DEAD*

"Turn on the lights and check your locks before settling down with Jess Lourey's latest thriller. *The Laughing Dead* is a tense, twisty read that will grab you by the throat and won't let go until you race to the very last, spectacularly creepy page."

—Melinda Leigh, #1 *Wall Street Journal* bestselling author

"Writing from multiple perspectives, Lourey weaves an intricate tale of despair and hope, leading to an explosive and gripping climax that had my jaw dropping to the floor."

—Yasmin Angoe, author of the Nena Knight trilogy and *Not What She Seems*

PRAISE FOR *THE REAPING*

"Mystery and horror mix in a creepy novel whose suspenseful ending hints at a very special sequel."

—*Kirkus Reviews*

"*The Reaping* is so much more than a mere thriller. There are complex characters, unpredictable settings, and a mix of supernatural and mystery elements that drive this tale to a unique finale."

—Bookreporter

"There are just some books—or series—that grab you and don't let go, and this is one of those."

—*Madison Daily Leader*

PRAISE FOR *THE TAKEN ONES*

Short-listed for the 2024 Edgar Award for Best Paperback Original

"Setting the standard for top-notch thrillers, *The Taken Ones* is smart, compelling, and filled with utterly real characters. Lourey brings her formidable storytelling talent to the game and, on top of that, wows us with a deft stylistic touch. This is a one-sitting read!"

—Jeffery Deaver, author of *The Bone Collector* and *The Watchmaker's Hand*

"*The Taken Ones* has Jess Lourey's trademark of suspense all the way. A damaged and brave heroine, an equally damaged evildoer, and missing girls from long ago all combine to keep the reader rushing through to the explosive ending."

—Charlaine Harris, *New York Times* bestselling author

"Lourey is at the top of her game with *The Taken Ones*. A master of building tension while maintaining a riveting pace, Lourey is a hell of a writer on all fronts, but her greatest talent may be her characters."

—Danielle Girard, *USA Today* and Amazon #1 bestselling author of *Up Close*

PRAISE FOR *THE QUARRY GIRLS*

Winner of the 2023 Anthony Award for Best Paperback Original

Winner of the 2023 Minnesota Book Award for Genre Fiction

"Few authors can blend the genuine fear generated by a sordid tale of true crime with evocative, three-dimensional characters and mesmerizing prose like Jess Lourey. Her fictional stories feel rooted in a world we all know but also fear. *The Quarry Girls* is a story of secrets gone to seed, and Lourey gives readers her best novel yet—which is quite the accomplishment. Calling it: *The Quarry Girls* will be one of the best books of the year."

—Alex Segura, acclaimed author of *Secret Identity*, *Star Wars Poe Dameron: Free Fall*, and *Miami Midnight*

"Lourey conveys the edgy, hungry restlessness of teen girls with a touch of Megan Abbott while steadily intensifying the claustrophobic atmosphere of a small 1977 Minnesota town where darkness snakes below the surface."

—Loreth Anne White, *Washington Post* and Amazon Charts bestselling author of *The Patient's Secret*

"Jess Lourey is a master of the coming-of-age thriller, and *The Quarry Girls* may be her best yet—as dark, twisty, and full of secrets as the tunnels that lurk beneath Pantown's deceptively idyllic streets."

—Chris Holm, Anthony Award–winning author of *The Killing Kind*

PRAISE FOR *BLOODLINE*

Winner of the 2022 Anthony Award for Best Paperback Original

Winner of the 2022 ITW Thriller Award for Best Paperback Original

Short-listed for the 2021 Goodreads Choice Awards

"Fans of *Rosemary's Baby* will relish this."

—*Publishers Weekly*

"Based on a true story, this is a sinister, suspenseful thriller full of creeping horror."

—*Kirkus Reviews*

"Lourey ratchets up the fear in a novel that verges on horror."

—*Library Journal*

"In *Bloodline*, Jess Lourey blends elements of mystery, suspense, and horror to stunning effect."

—*BOLO Books*

"Inspired by a true story, it's a creepy page-turner that has me eager to read more of Ms. Lourey's works, especially if they're all as incisive as this thought-provoking novel."

—Criminal Element

"*Bloodline* by Jess Lourey is a psychological thriller that grabbed me from the beginning and didn't let go."

—*Mystery & Suspense Magazine*

"*Bloodline* blends page-turning storytelling with clever homages to such horror classics as *Rosemary's Baby*, *The Stepford Wives*, and *Harvest Home*."

—*Toronto Star*

"*Bloodline* is a terrific, creepy thriller, and Jess Lourey clearly knows how to get under your skin."

—Bookreporter

"[A] tightly coiled domestic thriller that slowly but persuasively builds the suspense."

—*South Florida Sun Sentinel*

"Set in an idyllic small town rooted in family history and horrific secrets, *Bloodline* is *Pleasantville* meets *Rosemary's Baby*. A deeply unsettling, darkly unnerving, and utterly compelling novel, this book chilled me to the core, and I loved every bit of it."

—Jennifer Hillier, author of *Little Secrets* and the award-winning *Jar of Hearts*

"Jess Lourey writes small-town Minnesota like Stephen King writes small-town Maine. *Bloodline* is a tremendous book with a heart and a hacksaw . . . and I loved every second of it."

—Rachel Howzell Hall, author of the critically acclaimed novels *And Now She's Gone* and *They All Fall Down*

PRAISE FOR *UNSPEAKABLE THINGS*

Winner of the 2021 Anthony Award for Best Paperback Original

Short-listed for the 2021 Edgar Awards and 2020 Goodreads Choice Awards

"The suspense never wavers in this page-turner."

—*Publishers Weekly*

"The atmospheric suspense novel is haunting because it's narrated from the point of view of a thirteen-year-old, an age that should be more innocent but often isn't. Even more chilling, it's based on real-life incidents. Lourey may be known for comic capers (*March of Crimes*), but this tense novel combines the best of a coming-of-age story with suspense and an unforgettable young narrator."

—*Library Journal* (starred review)

"Part suspense, part coming-of-age, Jess Lourey's *Unspeakable Things* is a story of creeping dread, about childhood when you know the monster under your bed is real. A novel that clings to you long after the last page."

—Lori Rader-Day, Edgar Award–nominated author of *Under a Dark Sky*

"A noose of a novel that tightens by inches. The squirming tension comes from every direction—including the ones that are supposed to be safe. I felt complicit as I read, as if at any moment I stopped I would be abandoning Cassie, alone, in the dark, straining to listen and fearing to hear."

—Marcus Sakey, bestselling author of *Brilliance*

"*Unspeakable Things* is an absolutely riveting novel about the poisonous secrets buried deep in towns and families. Jess Lourey has created a story that will chill you to the bone and a main character who will break your heart wide open."

—Lou Berney, Edgar Award–winning author of *November Road*

"Inspired by a true story, *Unspeakable Things* crackles with authenticity, humanity, and humor. The novel reminded me of *To Kill a Mockingbird* and *The Marsh King's Daughter*. Highly recommended."

—Mark Sullivan, bestselling author of *Beneath a Scarlet Sky*

"Jess Lourey does a masterful job building tension and dread, but her greatest asset in *Unspeakable Things* is Cassie—an arresting narrator you identify with, root for, and desperately want to protect. This is a book that will stick with you long after you've torn through it."

—Rob Hart, author of *The Warehouse*

"With *Unspeakable Things*, Jess Lourey has managed the near-impossible, crafting a mystery as harrowing as it is tender, as gut-wrenching as it is lyrical. There is real darkness here, a creeping, inescapable dread that more than once had me looking over my own shoulder. But at its heart beats the irrepressible—and irresistible—spirit of its . . . heroine, a young woman so bright and vital and brave she kept even the fiercest monsters at bay. This is a book that will stay with me for a long time."

—Elizabeth Little, *Los Angeles Times* bestselling author of *Dear Daughter* and *Pretty as a Picture*

PRAISE FOR *SALEM'S CIPHER*

"A fast-paced, sometimes brutal thriller reminiscent of Dan Brown's *The Da Vinci Code*."

—*Booklist* (starred review)

"A hair-raising thrill ride."

—*Library Journal* (starred review)

"The fascinating historical information combined with a storyline ripped from the headlines will hook conspiracy theorists and action addicts alike."

—*Kirkus Reviews*

"Fans of *The Da Vinci Code* are going to love this book . . . One of my favorite reads of 2016."

—*Crimespree Magazine*

"This suspenseful tale has something for absolutely everyone to enjoy."

—*Suspense Magazine*

PRAISE FOR *MERCY'S CHASE*

"An immersive voice, an intriguing story, a wonderful character—highly recommended!"

—Lee Child, #1 *New York Times* bestselling author

"Both a sweeping adventure and race-against-time thriller, *Mercy's Chase* is fascinating, fierce, and brimming with heart—just like its heroine, Salem Wiley."

—Meg Gardiner, author of *Into the Black Nowhere*

"Action-packed, great writing taut with suspense, an appealing main character to root for—who could ask for anything more?"

—Buried Under Books

PRAISE FOR *MAY DAY*

"Jess Lourey writes about a small-town assistant librarian, but this is no genteel traditional mystery. Mira James . . . flees a dead-end job and a dead-end boyfriend in Minneapolis and ends up in Battle Lake, a little town with plenty of dirty secrets. The first-person narrative in *May Day* is fresh, the characters quirky. Minnesota has many fine crime writers, and Jess Lourey has just entered their ranks!"

—Ellen Hart, award-winning author of the Jane Lawless and Sophie Greenway series

"This trade paperback packed a punch . . . I loved it from the get-go!"

—*Tulsa World*

"What a romp this is! I found myself laughing out loud."

—*Crimespree Magazine*

"Mira digs up a closetful of dirty secrets, including sex parties, cross-dressing, and blackmail, on her way to exposing the killer. Lourey's debut has a likable heroine and surfeit of sass."

—*Kirkus Reviews*

PRAISE FOR *REWRITE YOUR LIFE: DISCOVER YOUR TRUTH THROUGH THE HEALING POWER OF FICTION*

"Interweaving practical advice with stories and insights garnered in her own writing journey, Jessica Lourey offers a step-by-step guide for writers struggling to create fiction from their life experiences. But this book isn't just about writing. It's also about the power of stories to transform those who write them. I know of no other guide that delivers on its promise with such honesty, simplicity, and beauty."

—William Kent Krueger, *New York Times* bestselling author of the Cork O'Connor series and *Ordinary Grace*

THE BLACKTHORN WOMEN

OTHER TITLES BY JESS LOUREY

BLACKTHORN BOOKS

Twice in a Blue Moon

STEINBECK AND REED THRILLERS

"Catch Her in a Lie"

The Taken Ones

The Reaping

The Laughing Dead

MURDER BY MONTH MYSTERIES

May Day

June Bug

Knee High by the Fourth of July

August Moon

September Mourn

October Fest

November Hunt

December Dread

January Thaw

February Fever

March of Crimes

April Fools

THRILLERS

Unspeakable Things

Bloodline

Litani

The Quarry Girls

SALEM'S CIPHER THRILLERS

Salem's Cipher

Mercy's Chase

CHILDREN'S BOOKS

Leave My Book Alone! Starring Claudette, a Dragon with Control Issues

YOUNG ADULT

The Verdant Cage

NONFICTION

Rewrite Your Life: Discover Your Truth Through the Healing Power of Fiction

Better Than Gin: A Coloring Book for Writers

THE BLACKTHORN WOMEN

A NOVEL

JESS LOUREY

Previously published as *The Catalain Book of Secrets* in 2014 by Toadhouse Books. This is a revised edition.

Published by Thomas & Mercer, Seattle

www.apub.com

EU product safety contact:
Amazon Media EU S. à r.l.
38, avenue John F. Kennedy, L-1855 Luxembourg
amazonpublishing-gpsr@amazon.com

ISBN-13: 9781662535260 (paperback)
ISBN-13: 9781662535253 (digital)

Cover design by Richard Ljoenes
Cover image: © lavendertime, © Master1305, © Alexander Y, © LightField Studios, © RidiUmbrella / Shutterstock

Printed in the United States of America

For Erica Ruth, forever generous with her courage, her compass, and her magic

Time makes more converts than reason.

—*Thomas Paine*

Trust your instincts.

—*Your mother*

Part 1

The Curse

The Blackthorn Book of Secrets: Blue Glass

Store spells in blue glass. Its powerful magnification and healing properties make it sacred. Once, only women were allowed to touch it. The world might be a better place if that were still the case, but people forget about its holy nature and pour anything into it: liquor, bile, cheap perfume. Its purpose is holier than that. Never forget.

Also remember that the heart is like blue glass—a vessel for magic, hope, and dreams. It's at its weakest when it's empty; deny it its due and it'll break on a turn; fill it with chance and light and it's indestructible.

Chapter 1

Ursula

The snake lay across Ursula Blackthorn's workshop doorstep, fat and lazy as spilled sin.

She paused, and she was not a woman easily deterred.

Nearly sixty years on this earth had taught her to take what she wanted. The attention of a man she fancied, the run-down family mansion she'd bought for a song, a fair price for the medicines she brewed out of her workshop . . . if she desired it, she claimed it.

Only snakes made her flinch.

Which was unfortunate, because her hometown of Faith Falls, Minnesota, was infamous for an event the locals had come to call "the snakening." No one could predict when it would strike, but it always started the same way, with an early spring that blew into town hot and jittery. The US Geological Survey would begin to measure unusual Richter readings in the area. Shortly after, tens of thousands of red-lined garters would unravel from a massive ball and writhe up to meet the sun.

The sight and sound were bad, but the smell was worse.

Scientists called the phenomenon "a sporadic emergence from underground hibernacula attributed to anomalous thermoregulatory behavior." Locals viewed it as an inconvenience that didn't outweigh the bucolic charm of their river town. The superstitious called it bad luck.

Ursula didn't believe in luck, but she had a good reason to be wary of the creatures. Her first snakening, when she was just a child, had been the worst day of her life. Something terrible had happened to her father, Charlie Tanager, after sunset. The snake currently lying on her doorstep brought fragments of that night back: a beer glass embossed with a twelve-point buck, the terrible quiet after violence, the way Charlie had looked at her and her mom, his breath rattling in his chest as he roared:

Every time the snakes rise, I'll be there to steal your power. Your children will pay, and their children, forever down the line. Not one of you Blackthorn witches will find a better man than me. Not one of you can stop me.

Take it back, Charlie Tanager! her mother had screamed. *Take that curse back!*

Fear carved itself into Ursula's bones that night, a terror that lingered as she waited for her father to return as promised to seek his vengeance. But years passed, and Charlie Tanager never showed. Then came the next snakening many years later. Her daughters were teenagers. She'd jumped at shadows those awful days, certain she'd spotted her father in a crowd, in passing cars, in the face of every man who looked at Katrine and Jasmine too long.

But then the snakes slithered back into the earth, and not a single Blackthorn had been hurt. Ursula began to think maybe Charlie wasn't returning, ever. She'd been foolish to waste so much time worrying. That's when she really started to claim her life. Stopped asking for permission, started taking up space.

That didn't mean the red-lined garter currently lying on her studio doorstep hadn't jolted her with a sharp shock of fear. She'd been heading out to do some late-night work when she'd spotted it. Her heart was still dancing from the fright.

She glanced over her shoulder at the gorgeous Queen Anne mansion, now totally renovated, then back at the snake all lit up by the blue moon. The garter was the length of her forearm, its glossy black body striped with vivid red and gold. Just a snake, not an omen. *You're being silly, Ursula. This is August. Far too late in the season for the snakes to rise. Charlie's not coming back.*

Still, she was careful to step around it, and she muttered a protection spell as soon as she was inside her workshop. It should have soothed her, but unease continued to cling to her ribs like damp wool. She lit every lamp in the workshop, flooding the place with honey-colored light, then pulled over a chair to reach the high cupboard where she kept tools she rarely had a use for.

She went straight for the obsidian bowl. She filled it with rainwater from the jar by the window, water she'd caught three nights ago, during the tail end of a summer storm. She scattered in crushed rowan berries and a pinch of powdered bone—stag, not human—then dipped in her fingers to ripple the water. Closing her eyes, she began the incantation. The basin vibrated faintly against the workbench as the surface darkened, and the smell of worms and soil rose into the room.

She glanced down at the water, which had become a moving image. There was the town of Faith Falls, framed in twilight, the river glinting like molten pewter. From its banks, a black tide began to swell. Snakes, more than she'd ever seen, their bodies a knotting, writhing mass. The image shifted, closing in on a figure standing among them. Charlie Tanager's face bloomed out of the murk, grinning with a mouthful of yellow teeth.

His eyes fixed on hers as if the vision was a window.

The whisper came next, sliding from the bowl and into her ear: *Every time the snakes rise, I'll be there.*

She staggered back, heart hammering, then hissed a banishment spell. Charlie's face blurred, but his grin lingered a moment too long, and in that moment she knew that nothing would stop him this time.

The only question was, Which one of the Blackthorn women would he destroy?

At least Katrine was safe, halfway across the world.

Chapter 2

Katrine

The Volkswagen Beetle's dome glided alongside the prairie grass like a giant scoop of French vanilla ice cream. The car was a rental, the smallest in the SIXT stable, and it contained everything Katrine Blackthorn now owned: a laptop, two suitcases filled with clothes and lotions and makeup and jewelry, a box of records and notes, and a framed newspaper article.

She'd started out the evening by parking in the far corner of the rental lot and huddling inside the car, worried that jet lag, the witching hour, and a habit of driving on the opposite side of the road would do her in. A sleepless hour had passed like water dripping as she'd stared at the Beetle's cloth ceiling, focusing on an oily stain the size of a quarter. She couldn't seem to swallow past the thickness in her throat. When she could no longer abide being motionless, she'd propped up her seat, twisted the key in the ignition, and pointed west.

The familiar scent of a Minnesota summer night began to seduce her once she passed the Minneapolis city limits. The peppery spice of corn silk. The clean warmth of wheat waving in the evening breeze. The elemental freshness of lake water. The smells reminded her of sailing on a tire swing over the Rum River, the sweet, glittery crunch of watermelon rock candy, and her first kiss, stolen by Kyle Hansen during the middle school version of homecoming. She'd been thirteen, wearing corduroy pants and a flowing blouse that felt pretty. He was two years older. They stood outside the school gym, Prince's "Little Red Corvette" reaching them through the walls. Something sharp and golden lit up inside her when his sweet-apple-wine lips met hers.

The memory brought unexpected tears. She swiped at them and rolled up her windows to fade the smell of her past, then jabbed at the radio until she located NPR. The soothing monotony of the newscaster's voice steadied her. Even so, her hands looked odd on the steering wheel, and she had the distinct feeling of staying in one spot as the road rushed past, a toy car on a child's movable track. When the radio produced more static than words, she switched it off, afraid to search for other stations, to stumble across a song that would trigger more tears.

An hour out of the Cities, her head began to baby-wobble. She needed to stretch her legs or she'd fall asleep at the wheel. She exited the interstate, taking the Saint Augusta ramp so fast that she almost squashed a leopard frog hopping across the road. She slammed her brake pedal to the floor. The pickup driver behind her was forced to swerve, honking and flipping her off as he squealed past. She ignored him, stepping out to transport the amphibian to the far ditch.

Frogs. She'd always felt a connection with them, been compelled to save them. Maybe she was hoping one would turn into a prince.

She laughed at the thought.

Or at least made the dry sound that passed for laughter these days.

She returned to her car and drove a few blocks to a gas station, planning to splash some cold water on her face. All four pumps were open, so she topped off her tank and went inside to pay. The place was empty except for the attendant behind the candy-laden counter. She tried to catch his glance, to feel real, to be seen. He never glanced up from his cell phone. On impulse, she walked to the coolers and grabbed a frosty root beer before approaching him, feeling disassociated from the cold bottle in her hand.

He still didn't look up. The tears were returning, but then the shiver of a million fingers tickled her skull as she felt what she called intuition. The attendant wasn't ignoring her. His furrowed brow, drawn mouth? He was a man in crisis.

"I'm sure whatever it is, it's going to be fine," she said. She wanted to comfort the worry in his belly.

"What?" His head shot up, his expression a paint-bucket blend of surprise and fear. When he laid eyes on her, he did the same double take most men did, and then his face slipped back into confusion.

Katrine blinked rapidly, her eyes blurry from forty-two corrugated hours without sleep. She'd been born with the same flashes of insight as any other woman, nothing more. But growing up, her mom, Ursula, had liked to tell her she had Blackthorn magic. Specifically, she'd tried to convince Katrine that she could read minds. All that make-believe had ever gotten her was dumb stares like the poor gas station attendant was giving her. She wanted to make a joke to break the tension (*For my next trick, watch me pull a foot out of my mouth*), but what could she say? So she settled on, "Nothing. Keep the change."

She slid him a twenty, her last, and hustled out the door, not bothering with the bathroom. She had only jingle left in her purse, no paper, and a credit card that'd sidled past its limit two weeks earlier. She'd called in a favor to buy a plane ticket out of London, a kindness she hoped she'd be able to repay. In front of her glowing computer, searching for a flight, she'd told herself that it didn't matter where she went, as long as it was *away*. Since the moment she'd discovered Adam's betrayal, her world had become a pulsing black, accented by the red of fear. She'd been too tired to shop for groceries. She'd stopped going to work. Her friends were worried about her, pleading with her to leave her flat, grab a cup of coffee, meet them for lunch, smile, shower. (*Hey, think how much money I'm saving on water,* she'd said. No one had laughed.)

Muscle memory had begged her to return to her life, but she was stuck.

She'd been abandoned. She was alone, unmoored.

And that's when she realized she had only one choice.

She had to return to the town that she'd abruptly left fourteen years earlier, a place where she'd never known her father—not even his name—and where she'd grown up in a haunted Queen Anne perched atop the only hill for miles, complete with a witch's workshop in the rear.

Ready or not, Faith Falls, here comes Katrine Blackthorn.

Chapter 3

Ursula

After seeing that terrible image of Charlie Tanager in her scrying bowl, Ursula had stumbled outside, desperate to cleanse herself. There was nowhere better than her garden. The nighttime scents here were heaven, sweet as basswood honey, and she might as well harvest some moonflower pollen, given tonight's rare lunar event. She finished with one white bloom and moved to the next, cupping the sparkling flower firmly, its petals reflecting the starlight. When she tapped it over the blue decanter, the pollen tinkled like a thousand fairy bells when it landed.

Sweat trickled down her neck beneath her long braid as she worked, curling the short gray-black hairs around her ears into question marks. At one point, she whispered a quiet blessing, equal parts hope and fear. She knew Charlie could take any shape he wanted and might very well be watching them right now, biding his evil time until the snakes rose. There was no point in alerting her mother, Velda, who'd taught her in the long silent years after the first snakening that speaking a curse aloud only made it bite deeper. Telling her sisters, Helena and Xenia, would only cause them worry. Her daughter Jasmine wouldn't believe her and refused to let her share "witch nonsense" with Tara, her granddaughter. For the second time that night, Ursula gave thanks that at least Katrine was far away.

Ursula rubbed her hand across her forehead, leaving a streak of dirt-stained dew. She realized she had only one option. Until she could find a way to defeat Charlie's curse, telling anyone would only spread panic, and panic was the quickest way to open the door for him. So she would keep the secret locked behind her teeth, guard the ones she loved, and figure out a way to make sure he came only for her.

After all, she was responsible for what had happened to him that night.

Her knees creaked as she adjusted her weight. She'd been out here for hours. All the flowers had been groomed, and it would be four more weeks until she could return to collect more pollen, unless an early frost snapped the blossoms before then. She held the decanter up to the moon. The flower dust mottled the sides of the cobalt glass and settled on the bottom in a soft coating of pure sweetness, shuddering in the moonlight.

She'd been tending this garden, tucked between the Queen Anne and her moss-covered workshop, for more than half her life. Her grandparents had lost the homestead in the stock market crash of 1937, when it was sold at public auction for a fraction of its worth. The majestic house had passed through many hands after that. By the time Ursula stumbled across it during one of her runaway nights—not knowing at first that it used to belong to her family—it'd been divided into four apartments rented by coeds attending the local community college. The grass had gone to seed. The front porch was showing the wear of kegs, high heels, and neglect.

Despite its decay, from that first moment she set eyes on the Queen Anne, Ursula loved it. She chattered on about it so much that Velda finally revealed who'd built it. After that, Ursula went out of her way to be near the Blackthorn estate, lolling on the front porch as a kid and squirming into house parties when she hit her teens in the '70s, smoking dope and yelling to be heard over Creedence Clearwater Revival.

Then she went away to college and forgot about the house, and Faith Falls.

When she returned two years later, a steel-forged woman already bearing life's scars, the only thought that brought her peace was the notion of living in the old Queen Anne her grandparents had built. By then, the house was abandoned, the cost of upkeep and heat proving too much. Its glorious wraparound porch had begun to sag, the tiny oriels in the turret broken accidentally or by vandals and boarded over, the luscious burgundy paint peeling.

To most townspeople, the lines of the house began to appear ragged, like a photo unfocused at the edges. Occasionally, someone out walking their dog or jogging past would pause on the cracked sidewalk in front, puzzling over whether it was a trick of their eyes or something about the paint that gave the grand old home a blurry look. Soon, though, they'd forget why they were standing there and move on, certain they'd lost something, checking their pockets for keys, wondering if they'd turned off the oven, running through a list of their ballerina dreams.

Ursula had no trouble seeing the house. And she intended to make it her own.

She worked long hours marketing her elixirs during the day and crafting them in her one-room apartment at night, saving every penny she didn't absolutely need until she had enough for a down payment and renovation materials. Then she began the painstaking process of remodeling the Queen Anne's interior, which was more neglected and abused than she could've imagined. She started by stripping dirty white paint off original crown molding, digging out the hand-carved banisters from the attic and restoring them, and peeling away flowered wallpaper, first alone and then while heavily pregnant and, finally, with newborn Jasmine cozied to her chest.

The house began to purr and preen.

One day, she'd been refinishing a piece of hardwood floor. She was laying heavy on the sander, sweat running down her back, melding her shapeless dress to her like a second skin. She was going at a particularly rough spot when her damp hands lost control of the machine. It careened into the nearest wall, tripping a switch. A thick maple panel slid open with a whoosh and an exhalation of air that smelled of salt and roses, revealing a small alcove.

Heart fluttering, she reached in.

The hidden space was empty except for a book so thick that she couldn't hold it with one hand. The cover was worn brown leather that felt warm to the touch, like an elephant's skin, *The Blackthorn Book of Secrets* embossed on it in delicate gold script.

She opened the book with shaking hands. The paper inside was linen and the secrets handwritten in fine, scrolled black calligraphy. No author was credited, though it looked to Ursula like at least two different types of handwriting were in the book, along with a third hand that'd drawn vibrant flowers, vines, and plump vegetables at the edges.

She tried to start at the beginning but a different page fell open, and the silky promise of answers pulled her in. She lost a whole day to the book, reading about spells and potions, and barely put a dent in it. Magic was familiar to her—every Blackthorn woman was born with some—and so she accepted the book as she had accepted the house. It was a sentient thing, powerful and independent. She told no one about the *Book of Secrets*, vowing to open it only when she had a question or needed help, and went back to refurbishing the Queen Anne.

While she finished up the inside, she hired a local handyman to scrape paint the color of a smoker's teeth from the exterior. He tinted the turret and first and second floors a rich maroon and the third story malachite green. The recesses and trim were painted cream except for the many window frames, which he shaded the turret's malachite green on the outer rim and deep purple on the strip closest to the window.

It took two years, but when Ursula was done, she'd reclaimed the storybook house of her imagination. It was in focus for the first time in a half century, a crisp form against the plum-and-cream of a dusky sky. People commented on what a beauty it was, so well preserved, so pristine. *Of course*, they whispered, *it must be terrible to heat in the winter, those old houses always are, and thank goodness it isn't my problem.*

Ursula chuckled. She could laugh now that she had the Queen Anne.

With the house restored, she tackled the garden, reclaiming an overgrown tangle of animal waste, crabgrass, and cigarette butts that abutted the Rum River near the twenty-foot waterfall that'd given the town its name. She tilled it until freshly turned soil was as deep and soft as velvet, crawling with plump earthworms, swollen with minerals.

The garden cottage was her final project, the building little more than an oversize shed and draped with thick, spongy moss that gave off the intoxicating scent of petrichor no matter the weather. Rather than disturb the drowsy moss, she instructed a carpenter to build it up from the inside using wood and stone.

The result was a garden bungalow straight out of a fairy tale.

The inside became a rustic but sturdy laboratory, the walls lined with bottles, books on alchemy, glittering charms, tables strewn with herbs, and containers of sweet oil that undulated even when the bottles were still. The smell was of humid earth and exotic plants, sewn together with a chemist's tang.

She divided her days between the garden and the cottage, her sweet, serious Jasmine at her feet playing with hand-sewn dolls or chewing sticks and tasting plants. The baby would reach up with chubby hands when she was hungry, and Ursula's face would break into a surprised smile every time, as if she'd forgotten she had a child.

On either side of her property, bland colonial ramblers sprang up, so Ursula hired the same handyman who'd painted the mansion to build a six-foot-tall cedar fence to shield her garden. She grew no vegetables, only herbs and flowers, spicy bright things that winked and flirted with the sun but worshipped the moon.

When everything on the property was ready, she invited her beloved twin sisters to live with her, whippet-thin Xenia driving the moving truck and comfy, sunny Helena steering their cornflower-blue minivan. At the time, Ursula was eight months pregnant with Katrine, father unknown, even to her.

"The Blackthorns are back in town," people whispered.

It was funny because their mother, Velda, had been around for well over half a century. She'd just done an exemplary job of massaging the town's memory. And of course, Ursula had been back for more than two years, quietly building her nest. But the four women in Faith Falls together for the first time in more than a decade had created a critical mass, dipping the townspeople a little too deeply into the muddy gray puddles of their lives. This was the way of all small towns, forever. Too much brightness reminded people of what they didn't have, and so they fought to extinguish it. The whispers of witchcraft, so prevalent immediately after Eva and Ennis Blackthorn had built the Queen Anne and then disappeared, began to recirculate.

The twins ignored the rumors and even talked Ursula into letting Velda visit, and the Blackthorn women carried on with their lives.

Men and women came and went from their bedrooms.

Ursula's daughters, Jasmine and Katrine, grew.

Then Jasmine closed her mother out and Katrine moved away.

Ursula waved the thought off like a mosquito. She refused to give that sort of negativity a place to perch. Instead, comforted by the embracing sweetness of moonflowers and the familiar rhythm of her backyard oasis, she pushed one hand into the rich soil. The earth's pulse caressed her fingertips as she searched downward. Her stretching fingers passed earthworms and beetles and plunged through the crust into the first level of the water table. She let them dance there for several seconds before yanking her hand back, startled by the sound of a car.

In a town of not even ten thousand people, traffic at this hour was as rare as a police siren. She shook the dirt from her hand, grabbed the blue decanter by its neck, and stood. The glass hummed.

"Oh, you old knees," she whispered down at her legs. "What am I going to do with you?"

But then she sensed something that made her shoulder blades draw up. She cocked her head, searching with the antenna of her intuition. She sniffed to be sure, but there it was: a hint of sandalwood and cucumber.

And just like that, the only silver lining in Charlie Tanager's imminent return was gone. Katrine was driving home, straight into his snare.

Chapter 4

Jasmine

Jasmine Blackthorn's white curtains fluttered with the breeze, carrying the honeydew-scented predawn August air. She watched the cloth inhale and exhale, inhale and exhale beneath the light of the blue moon. A nightmare had driven her out of bed, a terrifying dreamscape where she and her daughter, Tara, were being chased by an unseen man. She'd woken up with a scream on her lips and lain there, panting, for several minutes.

She got up only when she could no longer stand the empty spot in her bed.

Up until three months ago, Dean would've been sleeping next to her every night that he wasn't on the road. That was before he'd left her, walked away from their perfect life and their perfect house. She'd immediately upped her dosage of antidepressants. The meds silenced the whisper that'd always helped her to choose the perfect ingredients for her roasts and cakes and sense just what temperature and how much time were required.

She *craved* the deadening.

She'd been surprised at how quick the separation from her gifts had been. It took three weeks of the medication, the glass-smooth capsules sliding down her throat, through her stomach, and into her blood, where they cloaked every bit of bright-blue alchemy, leaving a brownish-gray sludge that washed out in her urine, stinking of forest decay and ink. If any power remained, any of the cellular keys to the great Blackthorn mystery she'd been born into, the cotton of the drug stuffed her brain and absorbed her juices, making it impossible to concentrate on it.

In that way, the pills allowed her to live in the world like a normal person. The mental scaffolding she'd built over her past was shaky, but she balanced on it as best she could, fighting not to look down. The work had its rewards. Her husband, for one. No way would stable, normal Dean Moore have married a Blackthorn in her full power. Few men were that brave. And Jasmine and Dean's daughter, Tara, would've been ostracized if her mother were still a Blackthorn in name or deed.

Jasmine vividly remembered her first day of ninth grade, when she graduated from the shelter of middle school to the jungle of Faith Falls High. Only a hallway separated the schools, but still, she'd been so excited to start a new chapter that she'd gotten up early that day to curl her hair and apply makeup. It all went to pot when Heidi Baum convinced a boy to dump a bucket of water over Jasmine's head on the way in. Then a ring of teenagers circled her, pretending to be screeching flying monkeys until her mascara ran with her tears.

Wicked Blackthorn witch! Wicked Blackthorn witch!

Katrine had barreled through all of them and led Jasmine away, but the damage had been done. Jasmine wasn't funny, pretty, or popular enough to shake the witch label, and so she decided to do the best she could to make herself invisible. It helped, but the teasing continued throughout her school years.

She was a Blackthorn, after all.

She would fight to protect Tara from ever having to bear the weight of that name, just as she'd fought to protect Katrine by casting that final spell before forsaking her magic, the spell that'd banished her sister to the other side of the world.

She sighed, missing Katrine with the same powerful ache that visited every day, but content in the knowledge that she was safe as long as she stayed in London, away from Faith Falls.

She would protect Katrine where their mother, Ursula, could or would not.

Chapter 5

Katrine

Because Faith Falls had been settled in a river valley, the first visible landmark was the soaring steeple of Our Lady of the Lakes. The spire had been a point of pride with the Catholics who'd built it with tithe money to show the Lutherans who was closer to heaven; unfortunately, the church itself was embarrassingly modest, and so the whole structure looked like an upended turtle struggling to maintain a giant erection (which the Lutherans were quick to point out, privately and in more colorful terms; you couldn't beat a Lutheran for body-part euphemisms). Katrine had had friends from both affiliations growing up and never understood the earnestness of either.

Have I really been gone for fourteen years?

She shook her head. Thinking about all that time passed made her feel like garbage. She'd considered visiting, had promised her mom and Jasmine that she'd visit for Christmas, or a birthday, but something always came up. As she tried to get a bead on the exact reason she'd never returned, not even for a single visit, her thoughts grew slippery, and she was left wondering what she'd been trying to remember.

She continued to drive into the valley beneath a sky turning a murky lavender, more of the town coming into view. She noted the box stores and fast-food restaurants now ringing the edges of Faith Falls like tinfoil jewelry on a queen, the new mobile home park that pocked the south side, the bland housing development sprung up next to the river. She held her breath until she was through the haunted Pappas Sanitorium neighborhood, something she and Jasmine had done since they were girls to keep the bad luck at bay.

When she reached the heart of the old downtown and saw it hadn't changed a bit, she was caught off guard by a powerful sense of relief, an alien emotion this past month. She felt like she could finally draw a deep breath. It was funny because Faith Falls had smothered her when she was growing up. It was a flat dead-end, a nowhere town that'd remained stubbornly outside the flow of life. A fear of the suffocating smallness must have been what kept her away.

So why did those restraints suddenly feel like an embrace?

On a whim, she twisted open her soda, the sharp kiss of released carbonation loud inside the VW. She hadn't drunk a root beer since high school, hadn't even known she'd missed it. It tasted like caramel and a good joke as she motored down River Street, three blocks of old-fashioned sleeping storefronts, wide sidewalks, and knee-high brass sculptures of beavers. Bradley Willmar, owner of Willmar's Apothecary, had convinced the chamber of commerce to install the sculptures to liven up downtown back when Katrine and Jasmine were in high school. The Rum River was thick with beavers, and reminding folks of them would add to the village's charm, he'd argued.

It was no coincidence that his drugstore, in the family for four generations, was planted in the middle of River Street, with Hobbes Theater on one side and Belinda's Boutique on the other. Across the boulevard was an office shared by an accountant and a chiropractor, Juni's Salon, Ragged Cover Used Bookstore and Coffee Shoppe, and Farmers & Merchants County Bank. Turned out brass beavers didn't affect the business prospects of a single one of them, for good or ill.

Katrine had worked at Hobbes the last two summers of high school, ripping tickets and scooping popcorn. She'd loved it. She'd watched every movie that came through for free, sometimes twice, and would sneak Jasmine in on slow nights. The two of them had been nearly inseparable before she'd moved. She tried to remember what else had been important to her back then, what made her heart race and lit her eyes, but she'd been a firefly in her youth, soaring from one petal to another.

Introspection hadn't been her game. She'd left that for her sister.

She scanned the streets for a familiar face, but of course no one was out at this hour. For a second she thought she spotted a man in a cowboy hat disappear down an alley, but that was bananas. Minnesotans didn't wear cowboy hats. Exhaustion must have been playing tricks on her eyes.

She steered toward the river, turning without thinking, until she spotted it, the house built by her great-grandparents, the beautiful, restored, dignified old Queen Anne.

Looking at it, Katrine felt as empty as a fresh-dug grave.

Chapter 6

Ursula

"You sure you don't need anything?"

"Mom."

It sounded like a four-letter word the way Katrine said it, and Ursula felt the sting.

She closed Katrine's bedroom door and stood on the other side, unable to shake the image of how tired Katrine looked. She'd walked past Ursula, heading straight to her bedroom to collapse on her childhood bed a few hours earlier, her lovely cheekbones sunken, gray dust coating her skin, her green Blackthorn eyes dimmed. The child couldn't possibly know Charlie was back, or even what that meant. All she knew of her grandfather was that he'd disappeared when Ursula was young. That meant she'd come home for a different reason.

But it didn't make any difference why she was here, did it?

She was now directly in danger's path.

Mom.

It hurt Ursula's heart, the way Katrine uttered it. That, coupled with last night's vision in the scrying bowl, was too much, and so she decided to soothe herself the only way she knew how.

By visiting her latest lover.

She'd been thirteen when she lost her virginity, fourteen when she started sleeping with men twice, sometimes three times her age. Velda hadn't noticed.

Her current paramour was a plumber who lived on the south side of town. After remaining outside Katrine's door for another few minutes to make sure her daughter didn't change her mind about needing something, Ursula drove to his house and watched him and his wife through their bay window, the light of the TV flickering across their faces as it delivered the morning news. He was a potato-faced man, she a kindhearted woman who wore her marriage like an old sweater. When the wife went upstairs—hopefully to shower and get ready for the day—Ursula left her car to tap on the glass.

The plumber's head jerked toward the window. His eyes widened when he saw Ursula, traveled in alarm to the stairs his wife had gone up, then landed back on Ursula. She didn't move. He met her at the front door.

"What are you doing here?" His voice was a heated stage whisper.

She grabbed his hand and pulled him toward her car. This was their fourth meeting; the first had been when he'd stopped by three weeks earlier to fix the water heater, and the second and third were when he came over to do "follow-up work." She'd chosen him by the same criteria that she chose all her men: They were already taken and so there was no risk of a relationship, and they'd cheated on their partners before. He tried to pull away from her now, but she placed her hand on his crotch, squeezing hard. His shoulders softened.

"Fine, but hold up. I need to tell Myrna I've got an emergency call."

He slipped back into the house, exiting a few minutes later with his plumbing tools in hand. Ursula was leaning against her car.

"Can you at least hide, for Christ's sake?"

She stared at him coolly. "If you didn't want this, you didn't have to come out."

He glanced over his shoulder, then back at Ursula. His expression blazed with a particular heat she'd become accustomed to in the eyes of other women's husbands. "I'll meet you at the north edge of City Park."

She beat him there, yanked open his pickup door when he arrived, and climbed on top. She changed his radio to an oldies rock station before unzipping his pants and guiding him out. She wasn't wearing underwear. Her movements were confident and aggressive. She rode him with her eyes closed, imagining he was someone else, until the wave of pleasure began to build in her stomach, reaching lower and spreading out, until it overtook her.

Her peace was complete, but temporary. Always temporary.

She climbed off without so much as a goodbye, leaving the plumber with his mouth and pants open. There was nothing more to be had from this man. She would end their trysts the way she always did, by giving him a potion that would reignite his love for his wife, turning it into a consuming passion where the only way he could earn respite was to treat her like a queen.

Despite getting what she'd wanted, Ursula returned home feeling even more restless. Her daughter had been gone for too long. The woman sleeping upstairs felt like a stranger. So she paced her bedroom, ears tuned to the slightest sound from Katrine's direction.

It wasn't until her sisters began clattering in the kitchen below that she finally left her room. The sight of Helena and Xenia bustling around loosened her chest.

Though twins, they couldn't have been more opposite in appearance. Where Helena was round and soft, Xenia was lean as a jaguar. They both had shoulder-length hair, but Helena's was thick, blond, and curly, and Xenia's was black and straight as a sword. Their personalities were equally dissimilar. Helena was the type of gardener who couldn't bear to pull any of the tiny shoots when they first sprouted, even if they were suffocating each other, but Xenia gutted them without a second thought.

Despite their vast differences, they could be picked out as Blackthorns from across a crowded room. It was in their quiet confidence, not the slightest hint of apology in the swing of their hips.

"Was that Katrine I saw walking up the drive a few hours ago? If so, she looked like a ghost who didn't know she was dead yet," Helena said to Ursula by way of a good morning. She stood at the island at the center of the Queen Anne's grand kitchen, its cupboards painted a deep purple that accented forest-green wallpaper, the countertops maple butcher block, the fixtures bright copper.

"You don't have to be so dramatic," Xenia cut in, reaching behind her sister to grab the coffee beans from the cupboard. "She was just tired."

"*Dead* tired," Helena corrected. She was using a metal spatula to coax divinity off parchment paper. She waved the spatula in the air when Ursula glanced at the candy. "Don't even tell me it's too humid to make divinity. We need it for the clarity it provides. Soothing, too. See the soft blues and greens I chose?"

Ursula sighed, her love for her sisters a constant. She'd raised them, after all.

An old thought, one she hadn't considered in decades, flitted across her brain: Would her sisters still love her if they knew what happened that night with Charlie Tanager? She stuffed the black idea back into whatever hole it'd crawled out of. She'd figure out how to handle Charlie on her own, and soon, before he had a chance to so much as *look* at either of her girls. In the meanwhile, she had a more pressing problem. "What do I do about Katrine?" she asked simply.

"Return that rental car," Xenia began.

"Then throw her a welcome home party," Helena finished.

"I don't—" Ursula started, but before she could complete her sentence, Helena tossed a puff of divinity into her mouth. The sweetness melted into her tongue like an answer. Such was Helena's gift.

"Who wants to tell Jasmine Katrine's back?" Xenia asked.

"You don't think she already knows?" Helena opened a glass-faced cupboard to grab a coffee cup.

"There's a lot that girl doesn't know since she started medicating." Xenia reached over and chose a kiss-shaped candy, a wisp of seafoam green, and popped it into her mouth.

"If she needs the medication, she should have it," Helena said. "Shouldn't she?"

"Of course," Xenia said agreeably. "Except she isn't depressed, not in the way she thinks. I'll call her. Let her know Katrine's home."

"Maybe we could invite her over for dinner? And Tara?" Helena had a habit of ending her sentences in questions, especially when she was talking to her twin, the shadow to her light.

"And Velda," Xenia said, already dialing.

Ursula clenched.

"And Velda." Helena reached into the cupboard for pecans and brown sugar. "I'll get started on the patience candy."

Chapter 7

Katrine

Katrine guessed that her beloved aunts were downstairs right now worrying, and that Ursula was wishing she could brew her a potion, but Katrine couldn't find it in herself to either sleep or leave her childhood bed. Her body was jittery, humming with electricity under the mariner's compass quilt, her thoughts racing around her skull like a caged fox.

Did I leave London too soon? Could Adam and I have made it work?

They were a fool's thoughts, she knew that, which was why she didn't fight when the sharp, clean scent of sage pulled her attention outside to the whispering banks of the Rum River trailing behind the house, where she and Jasmine had spent summers back when the earth was a softer place for children. Pigtailed and freckle-faced, they played at rock skipping, toad hunting, flower picking, daring each other to swim out to the middle, where the current shot swift and silver. Playing chicken drop, they called it.

Katrine always ventured out the farthest, would let the river's force whisk her to the rocky whorls. She wouldn't dare it in spring, when the water was so high that it rushed the banks, but if the summer had been dry, she'd let the river propel her to the edge of the falls the town had been named after.

"You're going to go over!" Jasmine would squeal every time, shadowing her along the bank, her colt legs poking out of her shorts as she darted downstream.

Katrine dared not open her mouth or the river would rush through her, embracing her inside and out. Instead, she'd flash Jasmine a thumbs-up, feet poised forward so she could bounce off rather than crash into rocks. Her target, a low branch ten yards on the safe side of Faith Falls and the last stop before going over, rushed to meet her.

Each pass, she had one chance to catch it.

Every time, she did.

The rapids would gnash their teeth in a thunder of frustration, but Katrine ignored them, towing herself along the branch until it was shallow and calm enough for her to stand.

"Goll, you're crazy!" Jasmine complained one day.

Katrine laughed when she reached the riverbank. She stood, her breath short from the work of it, and shook herself like a dog. The sun warmed her summer-brown skin, and her heart thumped pleasantly. "It's fun. You should try it one of these times."

Jasmine was the older of the two, a rule-follower since she was born, according to their aunts. Her constancy shaded Katrine like an umbrella, protecting her from critical eyes and giving her the confidence to skin her knees and pop up to try again, to ring doorbells and run on a dare, to make up ghost stories featuring fairy princesses and hook-handed pirates, to wear too-short dresses because she liked the feel of the breeze on her thighs.

Even at a young age, Katrine recognized what a gift her sister gave her.

Still, she couldn't help pushing Jasmine to lighten up.

"At least swim with me," Katrine begged. "We can walk back up to where it's shallower."

Jasmine shook her head, shoving her toe in the mud. "I don't want to."

"We could make a Popsicle raft and float a frog down on it?"

Jasmine's eyes widened before she erased the expression. "You wouldn't."

"I might."

"You'd *never* hurt a frog. Everyone knows that. Anyway, I'd tell Ursula." They'd always called their female relatives by their first names, even their mother. *Especially* their mother.

"Would not," Katrine said, rolling her eyes. "Anyhow, I wasn't going to float a frog for real. I just wanted you to stop being such a chicken and do the drop."

Jasmine stuck her tongue out. "There isn't time. Ursula's taking us to get our hair done for the dance. Remember?"

"I prolly remember better than her."

But Jasmine was off, grabbing the empty picnic basket before striding upstream toward the house. She'd basically lived in the kitchen since she was old enough to walk, asking Ursula what she was stirring or Helena why she boiled toffee longer than caramel. She had baked her first pie at seven, an apple tart with homemade crust that tasted like autumn and cured Xenia's allergies.

For today's picnic, Jasmine had packed creamy egg salad sandwiches dotted with bright dill and celery, spread on homemade wheatberry bread and complemented with a side of crunchy salt pickles that she'd canned herself. The meal had been the perfect mix of textures and flavors, and eating it made Katrine feel precious. As a bonus, while she was chewing, she recalled where she'd left the amber ring she'd lost over a week ago. She often wished she possessed a powerful talent like her sister's, but she'd been born without.

Katrine skipped along the bank behind Jasmine, listening to the song of the river, watching water bugs slide and skate across the surface. Her nose itched, and she wondered what it would feel like to be able to fly. "I know you think the same. She's already forgotten about our haircut."

"What?" Jasmine had stopped and was scowling.

"I was agreeing with you," Katrine said. "I think Ursula has long forgotten about us. She has that client coming over tonight, and you know how she gets with new clients. Always in her workshop."

Jasmine shoved her fists onto her tiny hips. "You stop that, Katrine Blackthorn."

"Stop what?"

"Believing you know what I'm thinking." Tears gleamed in Jasmine's eyes, escaping the sheltered pool around her heart. "If Ursula isn't waiting for us, Helena will drive us. We'll still get our hair done."

Katrine shrugged. It didn't take a mind reader to know that her sister was worried their mother would let them down. *Again.* Ursula tended to her daughters like the sun cared for the planets—distantly, almost as an afterthought, by nature of gravity rather than intent. Katrine knew Jasmine felt it like a new hurt every time their mother chose a customer over them.

"I don't care about any *fucking* haircut," Katrine said, trying out the swear for the first time. She'd wanted to shock her sister out of one of her sad tempers, but once the f-bomb passed her lips, she thought she might like to try it on for size more often. It tasted delicious and bitter, like dark chocolate.

But Jasmine was gone, running toward the house. Katrine held back, searching for the translucent red river agates that always cheered her sister up. Her fingers grew muddy digging for the stones, and she bent more than one fingernail back trying to pry them loose from the earth. When she had a handful, she rinsed them in the river and took off toward the house.

The water burbled its approval.

◆ ◆ ◆

At some point, the cushiony claws of exhaustion coaxed adult Katrine from the river memories and into a deep sleep, pulling her down, through the mattress, outside the room of musty wallpaper and crown molding, away from the high school yearbooks, a treasure box brimming with smooth stones, bits of colored glass, a dusty bird's nest.

She found herself in a hallway, being chased by a faceless man.

She screamed herself awake, ripping open her eyes and embracing the merciful light of day, realizing she'd gone from a girl who'd play chicken with waterfalls to a woman afraid to leave her bedroom.

She needed Jasmine.

The Blackthorn Book of Secrets: Sisters

There is no single element on this earth that will double your magic like a sister. If you can, keep one close at all times.

Chapter 8

Jasmine

Yesterday's nightmare of being chased had burrowed deep into Jasmine, clinging to her like smoke. She couldn't scrub it off. Not with hot water, not with distraction, not even with reason. After completing her day's work, she found herself staring out the kitchen window obsessing over it as she prepared supper. The shadow of Our Lady of the Lake's spire stretched across the yard like a finger pointing at her heart.

She sought distraction in the reassuring safety of her planned neighborhood. This area had defined the edge of town after World War I, row upon row of tiny, identical bungalows ordered from the Sears, Roebuck catalog and erected for the newly hired employees of the Pappas Sanitorium. Each house had a tunnel connecting it to the hospital so the workers could reach their job no matter the weather.

Constantine Pappas, the visionary behind the sanitorium and its surrounding neighborhood, had arrived in America from Greece in 1918, oblivious to the war, following a black-eyed girl with hips like a lyre. The affair didn't last long, but he stayed where he'd landed—New York. The woman with dark eyes turned out to be one of many beauties he fell hard for, but he had the good fortune to impregnate only a wealthy socialite whom he met while cleaning the elevator of the New York Hilton. She encouraged his dreams, including his passion for architecture. They drove west to Minnesota, the land of cheap real estate, mosquitoes, and abundant water.

The Pappas Sanitorium was born.

Pappas's tuberculosis center filled quickly and stayed at capacity for many years, ownership handed from him to his sons, then his grandson, who saw the sanitorium go from tuberculosis center to mental health facility to—finally—a vast, empty building as state funding disappeared. A handful of businesses had made motions to buy it in the years since, and there'd even been talk of turning it into condos, but the building remained empty, enticing generations of Faith Falls' teenagers to sneak through the shattered windows into the abandoned sanitorium's creepy passageways, where they drank sweet liquor and smoked stolen cigarettes.

Before Jasmine and Dean moved into their Pappas bungalow, she'd ordered him to brick over their basement tunnel entrance and to put up a fence so she couldn't see the sprawling, decaying asylum from their backyard. She'd had bouts of curiosity about what lay inside the facility—she'd heard rumors of patient rooms still decorated with family photographs—but the antidepressants shushed those thoughts.

They also gave her access to the normal, regular world of Faith Falls, which she craved like oxygen. She'd joined the local homeschooling group—the Kitchen Table Scholars—and learned how to educate her daughter, ferried her to Immanuel Lutheran Church on Sundays and Wednesdays and music lessons on Tuesdays, did accounting work around her daughter's schedule, and provided Dean updates when he was home from the road.

She'd completed most of an accounting degree before Tara was born, toting her preternaturally quiet newborn to her last semester of classes. She would arrive early and sit in the back. Some of her teachers didn't even notice she had an infant tied to her chest. With her CPA license in hand, she ran a profitable business out of the converted front room of her beige bungalow, balancing books and completing taxes. She'd earned a reputation as being reliable.

As a woman who *didn't* cling to nightmares all day long.

The phone screamed at her, pulling her out of her reverie, the unexpected trill turning her breasts cold. She tugged her white cardigan tighter and rested the knife she'd been using to mince garlic. She was preparing chicken alfredo, Dean's favorite. He preferred the store-bought version, but she'd discovered that if she added a sprinkle of sautéed garlic to the generic sauce, he couldn't tell the difference and she could sneak in a bit of flavor for her and Tara.

It wouldn't matter, of course, since he wouldn't be joining them, hadn't eaten a meal at his own table in three months. It was her unhappiness, he'd said. He couldn't take it anymore. She'd protested, explaining that she had everything she wanted. He'd shaken his head, his solid brown eyes so deep and sad. And then he'd left.

Jasmine had told Tara that her dad would be traveling more and so she wouldn't see him as often. To everyone else, she pretended everything was fine, that her husband was simply away on a regularly scheduled route.

The kitchen phone kept ringing.

She rinsed her hands under warm water, waiting for it to stop.

Besides chicken alfredo, she was preparing his favorite sides: crisphead lettuce with ketchupy Western dressing and uniformly square garlic croutons and fresh-baked Pillsbury breadsticks. She didn't know why she was doing it. The house smelled like canned bread, a one-dimensional imitation of the hand-kneaded loaves she used to make. She'd even picked up a frozen cheesecake for dessert.

Heidi Lewis, née Baum, gone from chief bully in school to friend-adjacent in adulthood, had dropped off Tara only a few minutes earlier. Should Jasmine have invited her in? It'd taken years of hard work and personal sacrifices to win Heidi's confidence, but it'd been worth it. Heidi hailed from the most powerful family in town—her mother a Gottfridsen—and had a daughter Tara's age. So what if Heidi had majored in terrorizing Jasmine in high school? Befriending her ensured Tara's popularity. Jasmine drove their daughters to religion class, and Heidi drove them home. With both girls starting viola, the routine had transferred to those lessons as well.

Even though it was only two nights every other week that Tara wasn't with her, Jasmine was afraid that the mooring that was Tara would cleave from her if she didn't watch over her child, as if without active attention, her daughter would float off into the ether. Jasmine reminded herself that there was more to her than being a mother, and when the day came for Tara to move out and on, she'd try her best to remember what that was.

The ringing, blessedly, stopped as the machine clicked over.

"Jasmine? It's Xenia. You're probably busy, but, well . . . Katrine is back in town. Can you believe it?" A dry chuckle. "We'd all love to have you and Tara stop by tomorrow for supper. Dean too, if he's home. No need to call, or to bring anything. Just show up if you can make it."

Jasmine was shocked by an unexpected electric surge of betrayal, but that jolt quickly gave way to a single, agonizing drumbeat: Her sister was back in the spiderweb.

She returned to her cutting board and took up the chef's knife, mincing the already tiny garlic flecks until they became juice and the board was etched with grooves.

Chapter 9

Tara

Tara's stomach knotted when her mom began brutalizing the garlic.

She wished she could talk to her, but Jasmine shut down when Tara got too near anything real. But Tara, like all children, paid attention, and this was what she'd gathered through eavesdropping and assembling the puzzle pieces.

Growing up, her mom had had one best friend in the world: her sister, Katrine.

Then something terrible had happened to Jasmine.

That awful thing had somehow sent Katrine across the globe and driven Jasmine to antidepressants. It was also the same reason Jasmine wouldn't talk to Tara about her Blackthorn gifts, wouldn't even acknowledge that Tara might have some. Might have *a barrelful,* in fact, enough for her to know things about people that they didn't even know about themselves. Enough to know that her dad had moved three months ago. Enough to know that if her mom didn't soon open the door on her heart and release the secrets that were poisoning her, her magic would be gone forever.

Tara had been studying her mom since her dad had left, noticing her jerky movements, the way she snapped and then apologized, how she forgot what she'd gone into a room for. Even now, as Tara watched her cook, she understood that Jasmine was strung as tense as piano wire, so taut that she didn't even notice Tara on the other side of the breakfast nook.

When the phone had rung, they'd both jumped. Tara itched to answer it, but she knew she'd learn more by observing her mom.

Jasmine had stood rock-still.

When the ringing ended, Jasmine had exhaled a shaky breath.

Then Xenia's message had played out, and Jasmine began to obliterate the garlic.

Tara, though, had turned to stone. *I finally get to meet Katrine.*

Chapter 10

Ursula

Ursula washed the lunch dishes, watching the woman standing in her backyard through the kitchen window. The woman had been reaching toward the cool doorknob of Ursula's cottage but stopped, and now her hand dangled in the air. It looked like she'd dressed up for the visit: slouchy suede boots, a matching skirt, and a navy-blue blouse. At her wrists and neck, chunky plastic jewelry deflected the sunlight.

Ursula *should* help prepare for tonight's party, but Xenia and Helena had taken over, as they usually did when it came to family. So Ursula might as well head out back to do her job.

Make medicines.

She'd first discovered her gift when she was six years old. It'd been one of the many days her parents had kicked her out of the house. At the time, Velda was hugely pregnant with Xenia and Helena, uncomfortable as a grounded moon.

You're always underfoot. Go find something to do. I don't want to see you again until it's dark, her mother had said.

Ursula started to cry, her fingers kneading the hem of her paisley dress before she remembered that both habits made Velda angry. She wiped her face and straightened her clothes. The day was hot. She decided to go swimming. She played her favorite game in a shallow bend in the river, the one where she pretended to be a fish with a whole school of friends. Some of the imaginary fish were six years old, like her. Others were older but still played close. All of them enjoyed the rainbow feel of cool water on hot skin.

She was smiling when the rock sliced her foot.

She paddled to shore, stepping tenderly on her bleeding heel when she reached the bank. That's when she spotted it: The field horsetail lining the river's edge had morphed from its normal green to a bright blue.

Her curiosity getting the better of her, she plucked some leaves, smelled them, rubbed them in her hands, and then—quickly, before she changed her mind—shredded a bit and patted it onto her wound. The bleeding slowed and then stopped. On her walk home, every plant that could help her shone the same blue—willow bark for the pain, juniper berries for an antiseptic wash. She giggled as she limped home, gathering all the blue-washed herbs in the pockets of her summer dress.

She discovered that with practice, she didn't need to be experiencing the pain to identify which herbs would heal. She began haunting the local library, devouring botany books. The more she learned, the more she collected plants and seeds against future possibilities.

When she got good enough, she started charging for her services.

Today's well-dressed visitor had arrived at the back gate as they all did—tentatively—and had made her way to the cottage. Ursula recognized her as Diane, owner of Faith Falls' only Vietnamese restaurant. Probably she'd overheard customers talking about the witch's workshop, and the spells that could be purchased there. Most of the Blackthorn marketing was hushed word of mouth.

Would Diane have the courage to approach the Queen Anne once she realized there was no one in the cottage?

Turned out she would.

Ursula waited several beats after the knocking before she opened the mansion's back door. The restaurateur stood there, a scared animal ready to bolt, her eyes on her feet.

"Hello," Diane whispered.

Ursula continued to dry the plate she'd just washed. "Can I help you?"

Diane still didn't look up. Ursula had never met the woman before, not formally, but she read her name tag when she picked up the occasional to-go order. She let the silence grow heavier than Diane's fear. It took less time than she'd guessed before the woman dragged her gaze up. Her eyes widened.

Ursula knew how she looked. Hair down her back in a single braid. Blackthorn eyes as green as jade in a face that was plain but strong. A body that was beginning to sag but still curved like a fertility doll. And something more, something that made most folks shiver like the devil had just said their name.

Diane took it all in, and then her story poured out.

She and her husband had fled Vietnam after the war. She'd concealed all her jewelry in her youngest daughter's diapers and managed to keep it hidden on the long journey to America. Her husband had brought them to Minnesota, where he sold her precious gold to buy a restaurant in a river town where everyone looked the same. She was proud of her cooking and her ability to honor the principle of five elements in every dish—five spices and five colors corresponding to five organs, senses, and elements. Her specialty was *lẩu canh chua*, a bright, sour soup simmering with slivers of shrimp and crab, cheerful pineapple floating against deep-red tomatoes, bamboo shoots, and a hint of tamarind paste.

Her English was good enough for her to converse with her regulars, both the people she cooked special dishes for and those who came for her fire-engine-red sweet-n-sour pork. She didn't tell them the latter was not a Vietnamese dish; they liked knowing only what they knew. She smiled when she talked, a big toothy grin, and to all her customers, she was cheerful, forever happy, the perfect hostess.

On the surface, it was true.

Underneath, though, she was restless. Her daughters were ungrateful, her husband sullen, her son lived across the country, but that wasn't why she was dissatisfied. She recognized that she was lucky to be alive, and not a day passed where she didn't thank Jesus Christ for her family's safety in their new country. The reason she was unhappy in her belly?

It was because she'd never sung in public.

Ursula had no problem keeping a straight face when Diane revealed this last part. She'd learned long ago not to guess what people carried in their secret soul.

Diane kept talking. She'd saved for years, it turned out, stealing pennies here and there to purchase her own home karaoke machine. Her husband mocked her, asked why she'd bought something she wasn't going to use. Her daughters played around with it for a few weeks but soon grew bored. None of them knew that she stole downstairs when they were asleep, mouthing the words to "Dancing Queen" with headphones cupping her ears. Lip-synching made her whole body hum, but it was just practice for the day when she was brave enough to pick up the microphone at the VFW on Karaoke-n-Taco Tuesday.

But she feared that day would never come, not in this lifetime. She suffered from crippling performance anxiety that prevented her from singing out loud even in the privacy of her own basement. She'd resigned herself to a lifetime of disappointment before she overheard two customers mentioning a woman named Ursula Blackthorn between mouthfuls of chicken chow mein and shrimp noodle salad. They said Ursula could cure anything. Diane had moved in closer, pretending to wipe a soy sauce bottle over and over again.

"Just ask Brenda," the chicken chow mein woman said smugly. "She couldn't lose that last ten pounds until she visited the Blackthorn witch.

Said she got a powder that tasted like bat crap, and the fat melted right off her tummy."

"Maybe the bat poo made her too sick to eat?" the shrimp salad customer said, dabbing at her chin.

Chow Mein rolled her eyes. "It wasn't *real* bat shit." She paused, fork in hand, an expression of concern crossing her face. "At least I don't think so. Besides, Brenda ate like she usually eats. And look at her now!"

"Maybe I should get her to make me a potion to cure me of marrying losers. Did I tell you what Tony . . ."

But Diane had already moved on, heart hammering, head swimming with musical notes and shimmering applause. She'd hurried to her husband, telling him she needed to run to the store for more vegetables and would be gone for the rest of the day. He pursed his lips, his sign that he'd heard her. She dropped her apron and raced to her minivan. She turned the key in the ignition and reached for the radio knob, glancing around to make sure no one was watching before she mouthed along with the last half of "Girls Just Want to Have Fun."

And she'd driven straight here, to the Blackthorn mansion.

Her speech over, she drew a shuddering breath, her gaze still locked on Ursula's. "Please. You can help me?"

Ursula absolutely could. It was her bread and butter. And if she was quick, and she always was, she could give this woman what she needed and still have plenty of time to get cleaned up for Katrine's party tonight.

Ursula smiled. "I have just what you need." She'd just stepped out of the house, already planning which ingredients she'd grab, when she stumbled.

"Are you okay?" Diane asked her, grabbing her elbow.

"Fine," Ursula said, straightening. "Just tripped over a loose stone."

She hoped that was true. But hadn't she felt something the moment she'd stepped outside the Queen Anne's protection? Couldn't she smell it on the air, like beetle shells? If she'd thought for a minute that she could let down her guard with Charlie Tanager back in town, she'd been wrong. She managed to keep her eyes trained ahead as she led Diane down the path to the cottage, but she suddenly felt like her skin was made of eyes.

The Blackthorn Book of Secrets: Stage Fright

Each great dream carries with it an equally powerful fear. This is the natural balance of things, as every front requires a back. The danger comes when a person confuses the fear for the dream and spends more time imagining and planning for the bad than the good.

A balanced tincture of yellow jessamine, peppermint oil, and lunar caustic, with 190 proof Everclear as the solvent, will dissolve this fear and anxiety.

(If you find yourself short on materials or time, you can eliminate the jessamine, peppermint oil, and lunar caustic.)

Chapter 11

KATRINE

The small bonfire, set off from Ursula's garden, crackled in the starry night. Beyond it rested Ursula's work cottage. Behind that, the river gossiped and crooned, trying like a child to gain Katrine's attention, but she was too deep inside herself to notice.

Her grandma, Velda, had arrived first and empty-handed, exactly as she always did. Her once jet-black hair was now a glorious gray, her petite form barely brushing the surface of the Queen Anne's wraparound porch, but she was as magnificent as Katrine remembered her. Never one to show up without male company, Velda had arrived with a man she introduced as Audish Hartshorn Buckley, whose name was larger than he was. The way he introduced himself to everyone, Katrine could tell he was a new companion.

Ursula's lips had disappeared into a tight cut across her face when she laid eyes on Velda, so Katrine guessed their relationship was the same as it'd always been. Her twin aunts, Xenia and Helena, who'd hugged her more times than she could count since she'd left her bedroom, had seemed happy at Velda and Audish's arrival because it meant they could get the party started. The party of six, warm from wine and food, sat around the fire in a companionable silence.

Audish, who'd said few words all evening, was the first to break it. "How long will you be staying in Faith Falls?" he asked Katrine.

Her response was prickly. "I don't know."

"Honey, you don't have to know," Helena said hurriedly, always the first to smooth over any tension. "You can stay as long as you want. This is your home."

"It's quite the house," Audish said absently, studying the grand old Queen Anne through the fire's flicker. "Velda, your parents built it?"

"Eva and Ennis Blackthorn," Velda said.

Audish sat up. "Tell me everything."

Katrine felt herself lean forward, too. The only one who didn't seem suddenly invested was Ursula, whose eyes glittered across the fire.

If Velda noticed, it didn't stop her from launching in.

Her parents, Ursula and the twins' grandparents, had moved to town in the 1920s. Where exactly Eva and Ennis Blackthorn hailed from had never been clear. Some said New Orleans, others said Boston, but whatever the city, everyone knew they came from money. Eva had been a stunning woman with green eyes, black hair, and skin the color of fresh cream. She threw elaborate parties and organized town dances and the annual mummers' parade. Her homemade spirits were legendary, and a charming rumor began to circulate that her mulled hard cider was so delicious that it could turn back time, though surely only those who drank too much believed it. She welcomed enough people from every class into her home that gossip against her was impossible to sustain. Ennis was a solid man, his magnificent handlebar mustache his only remarkable trait.

They wanted a large house to entertain in. Like many of the homes constructed by wealthy Midwesterners in that period, theirs was a solid, drafty, rambling Queen Anne–style Victorian.

"I spent my first years in that mausoleum," Velda said, tossing her chin at the house. "My parents traveled, bringing back new styles, felted and feathered homburg hats, mah-jongg tiles and lotus-patterned silks from China, scarlet lipsticks from Egypt, mohair club chairs from New York. One year, after a particularly long absence, they brought back a daughter. Me." Her voice was bitter. "I was as pretty as a doll and just as biddable. People begged to hold me, would brag for days if they could coax a laugh from me. That's what Eva told me later."

Katrine found herself hanging on Velda's every word. She'd heard the story many times, but still, it captivated her. Her grandmother was impossible to ignore.

"What happened to your parents?" Audish asked.

Velda cut her eyes to the side. "Died. Car accident."

Xenia abruptly changed the subject. "You can help us out at Seven Daughters while you're home, Katrine," she offered, putting the focus back on her niece. "We need extra hands this time of year. The tourists are crazy about Helena's chocolates."

Helena beamed with pride. "They come for your dresses, Xenia. They just buy the candy so I don't feel bad."

Katrine knew they were both being too humble. She was familiar with her aunts' wares from when they'd sold them out of the back of the Queen Anne. Helena's candy, though she claimed nothing more than exquisite flavor, carried a quiet magic: dark lilac-petal chocolates that revealed true love, peppermint leaves that eased the sting of guilt, lavender-honey truffles that lulled the eater into sweet, dream-filled sleep, each crafted with the precision of a jeweler. Xenia's dresses worked their own sorcery, every seam and drape transforming the wearer, highlighting their strength and beauty no matter their body type.

"I'd love to see the place," Katrine said.

"You've never been inside?" Audish asked.

She shook her head. "Helena and Xenia opened it after I left. Haven't been home in years."

"Well, then Seven Daughters is as good a place to start as any in reacquainting yourself to the town," he said. "It's the only business that seems to be riding high, no matter the economy."

"I'm sure the store is great," Katrine said, frowning. "When it comes to working there, though, I don't know that I'll be around long enough for that."

"Still too cool for Faith Falls," came a voice from the side of the house.

Katrine turned, a tentative smile shaving years off her face. "Jasmine?"

The sky snapped as her sister stepped into the firelight. A teenager stood at her side, looking so much like a Blackthorn that she could only be Tara. Both had Helena's curly blond hair, but the firelight hollowed their cheeks and flickered on their lean frames, bringing to mind Xenia.

They also both had the jade-green Blackthorn eyes.

Katrine realized it was the first time these seven Blackthorns had been together: Velda, with her glamour; Ursula, who concocted potions; Xenia, the maker of dresses; Helena, the candy crafter; Katrine, whose only talent lay in escaping; Jasmine and her forsaken cooking; and Tara, the wild card.

If Katrine had glanced over at Ursula, she would have seen her mother's hands gripped in fists so tight her knuckles had gone white.

"We can't stay long," Jasmine said. "Dean's waiting for us."

Something false clung to Jasmine's words, just beyond Katrine's reach. She stood and moved toward her sister, her step hesitant but lighter than it'd been since she'd arrived. She didn't know who she wanted to hug first, Jasmine or Tara, and the palpable strength of her love for both overwhelmed her. She stopped, indicating the covered dish in Jasmine's hands. "Please tell me that's your apple cake."

She hadn't known how much she'd been craving it—moist, packed with morsels of still-warm fruit, the cream cheese frosting laced with cinnamon and nutmeg. It amplified gratitude, and the one time Katrine had taken a second helping, animals were drawn to her like she was a Disney princess. She hadn't tasted it since high school.

"Pie," Jasmine corrected through tight lips. "This is my daughter, Tara, by the way."

The girl studied Katrine with steady eyes. She was fourteen, all elbows, knees, and front teeth, but she stood with her back straight, a student of life already. Katrine nodded at her, a tiny smile flickering at the corner of her mouth. This was the first time she'd laid eyes on her niece. The girl was a beauty. "Pleased to meet you. The photos your mom sent don't do you justice."

The girl blinked solemnly.

"Dean's a trucker. You probably forgot that," Jasmine said. "Anyhow, he's only home until tomorrow morning, and we can't stay very long." Her words rushed out. "We only stopped by to say hi. I'll leave the pie on the counter."

"You can eat the pie with us," Ursula called from beside the fire. Her words were neutral, neither a command nor a request.

Unable to stand the distance a moment longer, Katrine stepped forward, her arms outstretched. Her need to be held by her sister left her breathless. This was what she'd come home for. She felt it like truth.

Yet Jasmine rejected the embrace, shoving the cold and heavy pie plate into Katrine's open hands. Confused, Katrine reached out mentally to connect to her sister. It was no use. Jasmine was closed off.

"At least stay for a piece of pie, Jazzy," Katrine said. She was surprised to hear she was begging. *Come on, let's do the chicken drop together. Please. I feel safe when you're with me. Let me in.* The words bounced back at her unheard, tinkling to the ground like broken glass.

"Please, Mom." Tara tugged at Jasmine's hand but couldn't drag her eyes from Katrine.

Jasmine pursed her lips and turned her back to the family, striding toward the house. "Fine," she called over her shoulder. "But like I said, we can't stay long."

They all followed except Ursula, who murmured about needing to tend the fire.

Helena's jittery energy was palpable once they reached the contained space of the kitchen. Katrine saw Xenia put out a hand to calm her sister. "What kind of pie is it?" Xenia asked, striding to the cupboard to grab clean dishware and forks.

"Cherry," Tara offered. "Right, Mom?"

Katrine accepted a plate. She found herself salivating, remembering the amazing food her sister had concocted throughout her school years. Jasmine's roasted garlic soup had brought neighbors over to see what smelled like heaven, her fresh bread was so soft it invited naps, and her casseroles were gone before most potlucks began.

Her food didn't just taste good; it *healed.*

Katrine dug into the sweet wedge, perfect round balls of cherry oozing out the sides. As she lifted the fork to her mouth, one bloodred circle broke loose and rolled across her plate, leaving a viscous fuchsia trail. She chewed, her eyes widening in surprise. The words passed her lips before she could weigh them. "This tastes like shit."

Helena stepped toward Jasmine and then stopped, likely halted by the grim light of satisfaction in Jasmine's eyes.

"I know someone at the newspaper," Jasmine said, not responding to Katrine's comment. "I could help you get a job."

Then she took Tara's hand and dragged her daughter out of the Blackthorn house.

Chapter 12

Katrine

Katrine found herself standing outside Seven Daughters the next morning.

She didn't know what exactly had brought her downtown in the first place. She'd woken with a hangover and wasn't sure if it was from the wine or the cherry pie. She had no plan, no desire or aversion when she thought of working for her aunts. It'd be the route of least resistance, putting in time at Seven Daughters, protected, outside of life's current. She craved easy. But it would mean more hiding, and she was starting to grow sick of herself. She needed to revive her heart, even if the spark was only a rekindled love of writing. Otherwise, she'd lose herself.

She was just about to knock when a police car rolled by. She didn't recognize the cop behind the wheel, but she felt the familiar cold squeeze to her guts. Ursula had taught her daughters to avoid the Faith Falls police, said they couldn't be trusted.

"Oh man," Katrine said out loud, shaking her head. "Can't believe that old brainwashing still has a hold on me." The sound of the Seven Daughters door opening drew her attention. To her surprise, a tall, awkward boy of sixteen or so with eyes like a baby wolf stood on the other side.

"Hello?" he said tentatively. "We're not open yet."

"Hi," she said. "I'm Katrine Blackthorn. Helena and Xenia are my aunts?"

"They're running errands." He stepped aside to let her in. "I'm their assistant, Leo. Is there anything I can help you with?"

Katrine realized the boy had something about him, something that pulled her out of herself and made her want to engage, despite the pain Jasmine's icy reception had planted inside her. It might be the way it'd only taken him a single blink to look at and talk to her like she was a regular person.

She stepped into the store and ran her hands over the silk of the honey-colored sundress nearest the door, so soft it felt like a living thing. Even on the rack, she could tell it would hang beautifully. Xenia and Helena must have built quite a clientele since their days selling out of the Queen Anne. "Gawd, I missed these gorgeous dresses. If only Xenia would go international."

Leo shook his head. "Xenia said she's an artist, not a salesperson."

Katrine studied the boy again. Yes, there was definitely something about him. "What errands did they say they're running?"

"Helena went to Cashwise to buy sugar. Xenia is making copies of a flyer for some classes they'll be offering here in the basement." He paused, blushing. "I've been working here all summer, and it's the first idea of mine that they took. I told them they should pass on their gifts to the people of Faith Falls. You know, teach them to cook and sew. Xenia said she'd do it, but only if she could call them 'End Times' classes. She said that the only way the people of this town would be interested in sewing and canning was if it were after an apocalypse and they had no choice."

Katrine chuckled, amazed that she still had laughter in her.

Leo ran his hands through his hair, still blushing. "Did you want to look around?"

Some part of her did, but she felt too restless. She sighed. "No, thank you. Will you just tell them that I stopped by?"

He nodded.

Goodbyes had never been her strong suit, so she turned and left the store without another word, accidentally charging into a man coming out of the building next door.

"Whoa! Sorry!" he said.

Katrine found herself immersed in soft cloth over hard flesh, the clean scent of soap, clumsiness. Catching her balance, she stepped back.

The man she'd run into was handsome in an earnest, elementary school teacher way. He had thick, curly brown hair laced with gray, though he didn't look old, maybe mid-thirties, with a strong nose and eyes so blue she expected to see waves in them.

"That was totally my fault," she said. "I should have been watching where I was walking." She felt herself shrink. There'd been a time when she'd been acutely aware of her surroundings.

"Hey, it's okay." He sounded concerned. "I just barreled out of there. Are you hurt?"

She shook her head. "You work there?" She indicated the sign painted on the window of the store he'd left, REN'S WATCHES, UNIQUE TIMEPIECES SOLD AND REPAIRED.

"More often than not." A smile crinkled the corners of his eyes. He held out his hand. "Ren Cunningham."

She nodded at his hand—it was long fingered and strong, with a contrasting delicacy that reminded her of cascading piano music—but didn't take it. "I'm sorry for bumping into you." She stepped around him and continued walking up the street, unsettled by the encounter and the buzzing it left in her stomach.

"You're sure you're all right?" he called after her.

She raised a hand but didn't turn. If she had, she would have seen him study her in puzzlement before stepping into Seven Daughters for one of Helena's Lilac Love chocolates, a sudden craving for which had pulled him from his shop moments earlier, leaving an antique pocket watch half-assembled.

Katrine continued down the street, ignoring a momentary pang in her chest, a charged sensation somewhere between leaning over a cliff and jumping across it.

Must be something I ate.

She entered the yellowed offices of the *Faith Falls Gazette*, unsure whether her sister had mentioned to the owner that she might be coming. It wouldn't matter. The newspaper either needed another reporter or they didn't. Besides, she didn't know if she even wanted to work here. She just had nowhere else to be. The place stank of ink and instant coffee. Behind the front desk, a Fleet Farm calendar was one month out of date.

"Hello, may I speak to the editor?"

The receptionist, her body perfectly suited for life in a chair, turned from the computer screen and flashed Katrine a wide smile. The nameplate on her desk read Stephanie. "You're in luck. She came back early from a meeting. Whom shall I tell her is here?"

Who, thought Katrine, years of training blooming like a rash. *Who shall I tell her is here.* "Katrine Blackthorn. I'm interested in applying for a job."

Stephanie's eyebrows shot up at the name, and she gave Katrine a full once-over. "We're a pretty small paper."

"I understand." She didn't offer any more.

The receptionist shrugged and walked Katrine back, past the particleboard desks and cheap wood-paneled walls, until they reached a door decorated with a brass plaque that read, simply, Editor. She knocked.

"Come in," called a woman from the other side of the door.

The receptionist smiled and returned to the front, leaving Katrine no choice but to enter.

Her throat locked up when she recognized the person behind the desk.

Her hair was different, done up Texas cult–style, serving as a tall, poofed stage to full lips and a nose like the tip of a paper airplane. But other than the hair and the makeup-creased wrinkles shading her eyes, she looked exactly the same as she had in high school.

Heidi Baum—now Heidi Lewis, according to her nameplate—her and Jasmine's chief high school tormentor.

Katrine was surprised by the strong reaction, her stomach muscles clenching as if she were a Faith Falls student all over again, fighting the boys who tormented Jasmine and enduring the taunts hurled at both of them: *Don't eat me, witches! Where are you hiding your warts, Blackthorn?* Or her personal favorite and clearly the result of protracted group brainstorming, *Which witch bitch are you?* She forced herself to stand straight.

"Katrine Blackthorn, as I live and breathe," Heidi said, keeping her voice level. "How are you?"

Heidi's mother was born a Gottfridsen, and Gottfridsens were Faith Falls' spine and fingers, had been since Albrikt had opened the sawmill in town 120 years earlier. Their enmity toward the Blackthorns went nearly as far back, starting as a deep friendship that went sour after Eva and Ennis were no longer around. The Gottfridsens had taken it personally, passing the bitterness down to their children in their genes along with ginger hair, a missing pinkie knuckle, and a predisposition to heart disease.

Heidi hadn't inherited the little-finger deformity, but her red hair blazed like a corona. Her and Katrine's rivalry had been legendary, both of them pretty but Katrine with the edge, winning homecoming queen to Heidi's princess, voted "most likely to succeed" to Heidi's "best smile." Heidi had had her small revenges. She'd taped KICK ME, I'M A BLACKTHORN signs to Katrine's back, told boys that Katrine was easy and girls that she was stealing their boyfriends, had even convinced Katrine that their sophomore-year picture day was actually 1950s Dress-Up Day. It'd all transpired a lifetime ago, and once the shock at running into Heidi dissipated, Katrine wondered why it'd ever mattered.

"I'm well, Heidi." Katrine turned to go. She was too numb to grovel.

"Wait." Did Heidi's voice hold a hint of urgency? "Your sister called me."

Katrine paused but didn't respond. She wondered what deals with the devil Jasmine had made to befriend this woman who'd made their school years a hell on earth. *Jasmine, who are you now?*

"She said you need a job." Heidi's voice climbed a note higher, causing Katrine to turn. The pencil Heidi was gripping made a tiny cracking sound. "Do you?"

Katrine scanned the office. The venetian blinds shading the window were dusty, and they sliced a view of the brick wall of Fenlason Portrait Studios. Somehow, the light made the sliver of an office seem smaller, barely large enough to house the desk, three file cabinets, and two chairs. The desktop was cluttered with paper, a chipped mug full of pencils, a stapler, office implements, an outdated computer. Photos of the town and front-page news spreads clung to the walls like barnacles, and a cluster of family photos were balanced on the desk and atop a file cabinet. They featured the same two girls, maybe eleven and fourteen in the most recent one. There was no photo of a man. Heidi's ring finger, which she'd worked so hard to conceal, was bare.

"For the past three years, I've been an assistant editor in the London offices of *Vogue*," Katrine said, her mouth dry. "Fashion writing wasn't my plan, but it's where I landed. Don't bother calling them for a reference because I walked out three weeks ago without notice. I can write feature articles and take my own pictures. I don't know how long I'll be in town."

Heidi licked her lips. "I can't hire you full-time, but if you want to be an on-call reporter, I'll pay you per piece. It's not glamorous, it sure ain't London, and it pays for shit. You'll cover football games, open houses, church events."

Katrine's shoulders tightened even further. "Understood."

Heidi leveled her gaze. "You can start on Friday. There's a bead shop that just opened on the edge of the Pappas neighborhood. You remember the Stearns Bank? The bead shop's there now. They plan to offer crafts classes."

Katrine automatically held her breath at the mention of the haunted neighborhood before realizing how ridiculous she was being. She wanted to call Jasmine and ask if she still practiced their ritual against bad luck, and the thought made her ache. Her sister was a stranger to her.

"The bead store is offering their first class this Friday. I'd cover it myself but I already have plans." Heidi chuckled softly. "The store opening is the biggest story I've had in weeks, probably the biggest I'll have until the snakes come back."

A picture fell from the wall, and Katrine had the oddest feeling of falling with it. When it hit the floor with a crash, she didn't jump—she'd seen it coming—but Heidi almost leaped out of her skin.

"Should I take that as a sign?" Heidi laughed uncomfortably as she leaned over to pick up the framed article.

"Did it break?" Katrine knew about the snakes. It was one of Faith Falls' many haunty stories, like the Pappas neighborhood, except real. The last snakening—the only one she'd experienced—had happened when she was about to start high school. She shuddered at the memory. Tens of thousands of reptiles slithering through the streets like water.

"What?" Heidi asked.

"The picture." Katrine pointed at it. "Is the glass okay?"

"It's fine." Heidi hung it back on the wall, adjusting the edges, then turned. "You know, my mom hates yours."

Katrine was surprised by her own bark of laughter. "The usual?"

Heidi cocked her head. "If you mean her sleeping with my dad, yeah. It was forever ago, but Dagmar's an elephant with grudges. She's been looking for a way to take Ursula down ever since."

Katrine nodded. It had nothing to do with her.

Heidi wiped her hands on each other. "So, you want the job or not?"

Katrine hesitated. Ever since that day four weeks earlier when she'd walked in on Adam, she'd been fighting the gray sloth that wanted to keep her in one spot. Thinking about her next move felt like too much of a commitment, or like admitting to failure. She had no illusions about what accepting the gig would get her. She'd still be here. Her marriage would still be over. Adam would still be gone.

"Kat? You want the job?"

Katrine leaned closer to the weak pilot light still flickering in her belly. A strong gust, and it'd be gone. She cupped her hands as if to shelter it. "I'll get you the article."

Chapter 13

Jasmine

Two days after she'd fed store-bought cherry pie to her sister, Jasmine found herself on the other side of the bricked-over tunnel entrance in the basement of her home. It was so different down here from the Queen Anne's root cellar of her childhood. That basement had been stacked with vegetables, salsas, and jellies canned by Jasmine's own hand. The single bare bulb would glitter off the jeweled purple of the grape jam, or the quart jars of tomatoes so red you'd smell summer just looking at them. Those food stores had made her feel safe and proud.

Here in her box house, the basement was instead a family room with faux wood–paneled walls and a rough carpet that smelled faintly of wet. She'd wanted the paneling to cover the bricked-over tunnel entrance, too, but Dean had broken three drill bits trying. She settled for having him install shelves in front, which she filled with porcelain knickknacks.

She normally only came to the shelves to dust, but today, a sound had brought her. It was faint but loud enough for her to hear it from the living room overhead, where she'd been ironing. At first, she had thought it was only the hum of the air conditioner working too hard, until she remembered that Dean had disconnected the wheezing AC last fall and never gotten around to hooking it back up. She'd padded down the stairs, cocking her head as she tried to figure out where else the noise could be coming from.

The closer she got to the bricked-over tunnel entrance behind the knickknack shelves, the louder the sound became. She pushed aside two porcelain piglets so she could stick her ear against the cool brick. *Yes.* A hissing, she was sure of it, like air leaving a tire.

The words the man had whispered in her ear rose, unbidden, icing her blood. *Every time the snakes rise, I'll be there to steal your power.* Quickly, with the help of decades of habit and medication, she shoved those words back in the tiny mental room where she trapped them. She wouldn't let that secret eat her, and neither would she infect anyone else by sharing it with them.

She could bury it a million times more if she had to.

Kids playing in the tunnels, that's all that noise was. It must have been, though she'd never heard any sound coming from the other side of that wall before. She made a sideways fist and pounded the brick. The sound was swallowed by the dusty stone, and as if to mock her, the hissing grew louder.

"Hey!" she yelled.

Tara came to the top of the stairs. She held a book in one hand, her finger marking her page. She wore gray sweats and a Guess T-shirt that Jasmine had bought at Goodwill. "Yeah?"

Jasmine stepped away from the wall, her heart thudding. "Nothing. I . . . I was just cleaning."

Tara shrugged and disappeared. Jasmine returned the two pink pigs to the shelf, one balancing on its two front legs with its back hooves connected in a leprechaun kick, the other a swollen, milking sow, its eyes comically wide, as if to say *How'd this happen?* Jasmine hadn't intended to collect ceramic pigs, but ever since she'd picked up a salt-and-pepper piglet set at a garage sale the year after Tara was born, Dean had decided that pigs were what he'd buy her whenever an occasion called for a gift.

And so she'd decided she loved them.

The murmuring sibilance suddenly stopped. Jasmine braced herself, but it didn't return. So why did she still feel shaky, threatened? She forcibly relaxed her posture and told herself it was okay that she'd agreed to let Katrine, Helena, and Xenia take Tara to dinner and the movies tonight. She hadn't wanted to let Helena talk her into it, shouldn't have allowed her to plead that a family night would be great fun for Tara and that it'd be good for Katrine, too. In the end, though, it'd been neither love for her daughter nor hope for her sister that had broken Jasmine's resolve. It was Helena saying that she and Dean could have a date night while Tara was at the movies.

Date night. Michelle Jakowski had used the term just yesterday, when she was telling Jasmine about her husband tramping around, looking for love elsewhere.

"Think he'll be attracted to me again if we have a date night?" Michelle had asked.

"It's worth a try," Jasmine had replied. Michelle didn't believe in divorce, and Jasmine thought that was a fine way to be.

Besides, "date night" sounded so *normal.* When she rang Dean on his cell, she'd had to cajole him, convince him that they were meeting to talk about Tara, that she wasn't expecting anything else from it. And that's why tonight, she would have a date with her husband to see if she could win him back.

The doorbell's shriek set her heart to pounding again. She forced herself to walk, not run, up the basement stairs. The front windows of the house were open to let in the sultry August breeze. The air smelled like nectar and river. She straightened her hair and opened the door.

"Jasmine! Thanks so much for letting us steal your beautiful girl." Helena beamed at her, wringing her hands in front of her sage-green pleated dress, sewn by Xenia.

Jasmine couldn't help but return a shrunken version of that smile. Helena had been a loving constant her whole life, a warm pillow of affection. Of course, Helena still relied on the magic that Jasmine had denounced, but she was her favorite aunt nevertheless. Xenia stood behind Helena, glaring over at the church steeple, and next to her was Katrine.

"We're going to have a wonderful time," Helena continued, "and so are you."

Jasmine nodded, noting that some color had returned to Katrine's cheeks, though they were far from the plump roses she remembered. She thought again of the buzz in the tunnels. It'd sounded hollow and mean. "I'm sure Tara will enjoy it," she said briskly. "PG-rated only, no pop, okay?"

Tara appeared alongside Jasmine. She'd changed into a purple terrycloth jumper, also from Goodwill and five years out of style. Jasmine could feel her daughter trembling, a horse ready to bolt. "I'll be fine, Mom."

Xenia raised her eyebrows. "That outfit ought to preserve her virginity."

Jasmine frowned. "Have her back by ten, all right?"

Tara rolled her eyes, but Jasmine could see her heart wasn't in it. She was too busy grinning at Katrine. Jasmine addressed her sister. "You go to the newspaper?"

Katrine focused her gaze, and Jasmine steeled herself for the liquid tingle of her sister's attention, but it never came.

"I'll probably do some freelancing there," Katrine said.

"Great. Heidi said she'd help you if she could." Jasmine watched for her sister to flinch at the mention of their old rival, but it never came. It annoyed her that she hadn't been able to sting her sister by befriending Heidi.

Then—realizing where her thoughts had taken her—she grew sad. She hadn't realized how much anger she'd stored up against Katrine for leaving all those years ago and for never before returning, even to meet Tara. She knew it was unfair. After all, she'd cast the spell that'd banished her. "Well, I better finish getting ready. No telling when Dean'll get home, so I have to be prepared. I'll take a hug, Tara."

Tara obliged. “Thanks, Mom,” she whispered, and pecked her mother on the cheek before leading the way down the sidewalk.

Jasmine turned without another word.

In the kitchen, she slid a cup of onions into a microwave-safe bowl, cooked them for two minutes to the second, and sprayed the air with honeysuckle air freshener to cover the scent. Her plan was to sneak them into the lasagna she was prepping for supper tomorrow, hoping against hope that Dean would be here to eat it.

Kitchen clean, she returned to her ironing, the hissing in the basement forgotten.

Chapter 14

Ursula

Ursula found herself alone.

It was how she spent most of her life, but being alone when the people you loved were together was a special kind of isolation. She'd chosen it, true. Keeping her distance from the girls was the best way to keep them safe.

And without anyone around to distract her, she had to admit she was the reason they were in danger. She was the one who'd murdered Charlie Tanager, after all.

She'd been thirteen the day Velda came to her.

Child, I need you to make me something.

Ursula's eyes had lit up behind her thick glasses, the desperation in them palpable. Her black hair was braided on each side, her purple cotton dress simple. Outside their shack, a Minnesota spring wind taunted the oak trees, slapping their leaves against the cabin. The air smelled of metal and storm. The earth had been rumbling for days, and everyone in Faith Falls knew what that meant, either from experience or from story: The snakes were coming.

Ursula had felt the recent temblors and heard the whispers about the snakes' return. But what was happening outside didn't matter. Her world had narrowed to this single chance to earn her mother's love.

What do you need me to make?

Poison.

For a rat?

Yes. A big one. But the poison can't have any taste or the animal won't drink it. Can you do it?

Ursula worshipped her mother back then. Velda didn't reciprocate. Instead, she would joke over Sanka and cigarettes that the fairies must have switched her real daughter for thick-waisted Ursula, with her glasses and hair as straight as a bone, a plain lump next to her mother's grace and style. Ursula was always within hearing distance. She'd look down at herself and know her mother was right.

But here, finally, was the moment Ursula had been preparing for her whole life: Velda *needed* her. Her heart smiled. She would make the most glorious poison for the rat, and Velda would realize that her daughter wasn't a mistake.

She flew to the kitchen and set a pot of water on the gas stove to simmer. Racing to her room after that, she riffled through the pouches of herbs she'd been collecting since she'd cut her foot on that river rock.

Velda may have noticed what her daughter had been up to, but she'd never spoken of it.

Until that day.

Ursula's breath was shallow as she pawed through her repository for a special plant, one that was a sedative in small doses. She spotted the labeled packet: *Conium maculatum*. She'd discovered the weed in a ditch last July and harvested, dried, boiled, and condensed it until it was a deadly brown paste, never imagining she'd have a use for it so soon. She also snatched an envelope of lavender to disguise the hemlock's bitter, carroty taste.

Back in the kitchen, she dipped an eyedropper into the now-boiling water, withdrew three globules, and squirted them into a spoon. Then she dropped the pea-size pasteball of hemlock into the hot liquid, followed by a sprinkle of powdered lavender and a touch of honey. The blood galloped through her veins as she mixed the concoction with a toothpick, stirring until it was a quarter teaspoon of murky liquid the consistency of maple syrup. Then she poured it into a blue glass bottle.

Here. She handed the mixture to her mother, her expression a muddle of triumph and shyness. *Pour it over cheese, or in a dish of milk, and put it near the rat's nest.*

Velda accepted the bottle, her eyes glittering with tears. She'd sent the now seven-year-old twins to spend the day and night at a friend's house. The left side of her face was a swollen tapestry of yellows and blues. Her left arm was in a sling. Her right arm shook as it held the bottle.

Mom?

He watches you sleep, you know.

Ursula tipped her head, one braid falling over her shoulder. She pushed her glasses up her nose out of habit. Her expression turned to slapshock when Velda tipped the contents of the bottle into Ursula's father's favorite beer glass, the one embossed with a twelve-point buck on its side.

Mom? No response. *Mom!*

Go to your room.

It had never in her life occurred to Ursula to stand up to Velda. Why would a bug argue with the sun? So she stumbled out of the kitchen and cowered behind her bedroom door, every nerve so tender that she was sure she'd been skinned. She tried to press herself into the door, to become part of it. Outside, the fierce wind screamed. She'd be cleaning up branches tomorrow. She wished the storm would break already.

Charlie Tanager wasn't a great father, Ursula recognized that. Some days he was a savage, other days loving, but overall, he'd been as distant as Velda. Until lately, when he'd begun paying attention to Ursula, telling her she was pretty, asking her about her day and pulling her onto his lap, even though she was more woman than girl. The new attention tasted like stolen candy. She loved to hear him say nice things in his slow drawl, sweet and lazy like Mississippi honey. What did Velda mean that he watched her sleep?

When the front door slammed, Ursula jumped, pressing her ear against the rough wood of her door. The sounds that assaulted her were not new: crashing, yelling. A popping sound. Velda's cry. Then the worst sound of all: quiet.

The silence shook her. When she couldn't stand it any longer, she snuck downstairs. Her father was at the kitchen table drinking beer from his favorite glass, the one that held the poison. He scowled at her, his face handsome and angry, his chin three days past a shave. Her mother was seated across from him, bleeding from her nose. Ursula dropped next to her. She reached toward Velda, yanked her hand back, and then rested it on her mother's knee. Velda leaned into her.

Side by side, they watched him grimace and swallow his beer, muttering about *goddamned women, should have known better* before opening another. The hiss of that second cap popping would be a sound Ursula could forever after call up at will.

The end was not pretty. Before the second glass emptied, he knew. His eyes bulged, and they landed on Velda.

Why? The single word was raw, the straight letters a plate for his fury.

Ursula didn't think her mom was going to answer. She didn't know if she'd hear her even if she did, so loud was the blood thumping in her ears.

You're a snake, Velda finally said.

To Ursula's eternal surprise, her father laughed. The sound was horrible, torn from his throat and bile-soaked. And then he lunged, but not at Velda. He came for Ursula. The hemlock had robbed him of grace, but he managed to reach her, a hand to her throat. He pressed his nose to hers, his breath a bitter cloud, his eyes growing milky with the poison. She screamed, and he tightened his grip.

You did this to me, you goddamned little witch, didn't you?

She was too scared to breathe. Her heart skipped, and the urine trickled out of her. He squeezed harder.

You'll pay for this, he said, his eyes now the yellow of pus. *I'll be back.* A fit of wet coughing overtook him, but he didn't loosen his grip or break his stare. His spittle flew, each drop landing on Ursula's face, sizzling her flesh. *Every time the snakes rise, I'll be there to steal your power. Your children will pay, and their children, forever down the line. Not one of you Blackthorn witches will find a better man than me. Not one of you can stop me.*

Thick coughing rattled him again, this time with such power that he fell to his knees, releasing Ursula. She sucked in a great gasping breath. Her heart restarted. She began to cry. The terror of what was happening exploded her, and then the loss of hope emptied her. This could not be fixed.

Velda stood to the side. She lit a cigarette, her hands shaking. *Take it back, Charlie Tanager,* she said through the acrid smoke. She could not seem to locate her mouth with the cigarette.

His laugh was dark and empty. *Take the* poison *back,* he said, collapsing onto his stomach. He clawed toward the phone, but it was clear he wouldn't make it. The skin of his hands was shriveling, revealing the rigid angles of his finger bones.

Take that curse back! Velda screamed. Her smoking cigarette dropped to the ground. A dying man's curse was a terribly strong thing.

Charlie tried to stand, lunging at the phone, but his body was overcome by spasms, and he fell back to the floor. By the time he vomited, he was paralyzed from the waist down. He yelled, but his words were gone and it was the incoherent roar of a terrified animal. Velda led catatonic Ursula into the living room and closed the door behind them. Out of sight of her dying father, Ursula became aware of the cold urine soaking her underpants.

When his screams took on a pleading tone, his garbled voice escaping in rasping gurgles, Velda led Ursula outdoors.

The spring air was preternaturally warm, but the wind that had been blowing hot all day had died down, leaving behind a path of stripped leaves and twigs. The storm had never broken. Ursula and Velda walked side by side, not touching, the dying branches crunching underfoot.

Velda finally spoke. *He was the only man who ever saw through my charms.*

Ursula was empty—of feelings, words, light—after what she'd just seen and done, so she remained quiet. Overhead, a full moon appeared. Bats swished through the evening ink. The air smelled of wild roses. The world hadn't stopped after what she'd done. How could that be?

Then the ground rumbled underfoot with such force that Ursula was thrown against her mother. When the path in front of her began to swell as if giving birth, Ursula's mouth fell open. The soil was pulsing, rising, leaves and branches rolling down the sides of earth split with the force of labor.

And then, a ball of snakes burst forth.

They seemed to be disoriented at first, but they quickly unraveled and squirmed away from their birthing. Ursula screamed until her throat was raw. Velda simply watched, letting the snakes course over her feet like a living river. Eventually, she told Ursula it was time to return to the house.

Ursula had never stood up to her mother before, but as much as she wanted to escape the snakes, she couldn't go back.

No. Ursula's voice was quiet.

What? Velda asked.

I don't want to go back. Please. Let's never go home.

Don't be stupid. Velda took a deep pull on her cigarette, her hands steady now. *And don't ever tell a soul about today. Sharing a secret makes it worse. Do you understand?*

Ursula nodded, the words branded across the backs of her eyes.

When they returned, Charlie Tanager was sprawled on his back on the cracked linoleum of the kitchen floor, his lifeless eyes open and staring, his body nothing more than skin-coated bones. A distant part of her, the murky animal motor that kept her heart beating and her breath going, took note that she was a girl who'd murdered her own father.

Fate and time worked desperately to craft a bubble where this didn't have to be the end of Ursula's self-love. If, in that moment, Velda had acted, had in any way stepped out of her own misery to comfort her daughter, to take responsibility, to explain, Ursula could have worked her way back to herself.

Instead, Velda turned away from her husband's death stare to call the police from the wall phone, wailing into the mouthpiece, throwing herself into the role of unexpected widow as completely as she had any other character in her life, as only Velda could do. She left Ursula to soak in the iciness of her father's lifeless gaze, and just like that, any intimacy mother and daughter had developed that day was severed. That golden thread that joined Ursula to her mother was the same strand that connected Ursula's heart to her body.

Snip.

I'll be back.

◆ ◆ ◆

Ursula'd need more than a plumber to quiet her mind tonight.

That's when she remembered a man, someone who'd been able to hold most of the shadows at bay, someone she hadn't visited in decades. She grabbed her coat and slipped into the night.

She watched Michael Baum outside his bay window. He reclined in his easy chair, sipping a beer and paging through the newspaper. The TV flickered across his face. His wife, Dagmar Baum, née Gottfridsen, sat stiffly on the couch, a book opened on her lap.

It appeared to be a Bible.

The scene hypnotized Ursula for several minutes. Dagmar was a woman with breath like a two-stroke engine and eyebrows that appeared as though they'd been pasted on backward. One glance at her and you knew she'd been a sour baby. She was a Gottfridsen to her core, from her crown of copper hair to her stubby pinkies.

Ursula should never have slept with the woman's husband.

Dagmar led Faith Falls' Daughters of the Mill, a group started decades before to fill the vacuum left by Eva and Ennis's absence, though none of them dared admit that truth. They met the third Saturday of every month to talk about volunteer opportunities, the town's needs, and more often than not—according to the grapevine—the problem that was "the Blackthorn Women and Their Looseness."

Dagmar's desperation to get pregnant combined with the test results showing Michael had lazy sperm had goaded her—even though, according to Michael, it pained her deep in her soul—into sending her husband to Ursula's cottage all those years ago. Ursula suspected Dagmar wanted the potions to work just a hair more than she wanted Blackthorn magic to be nothing but rumor.

Dagmar became pregnant with Heidi, now all grown and editor at the town newspaper, two months after Michael's visit to Ursula's cottage. Michael and Ursula's affair began the night he bought the potion. Rumors of Michael's unfaithfulness had raced through town like gasoline fire. Ursula released Michael shortly after Heidi's birth, but she'd always missed him.

Still, she hadn't visited him since. She suspected it was self-preservation keeping her away. If Dagmar wanted to, she could make Ursula's life very difficult. Yet Ursula needed a peace she'd only ever felt with Michael. She made up her mind when Dagmar disappeared into the next room. She hurried to the front stoop and rang the bell. If Michael didn't want her, he could send her away.

His bland face slipped into white shock when he answered the door. "Ursula?" He glanced over his shoulder. "Is everything all right?"

"I want you, Michael." Her voice was measured. "I want what we used to have." It had been glorious, their time together. The sex had been good, but it was the way he'd made her feel precious that had kept her seeking him out. Standing this close to him pulled all the memories into sharp focus.

He stepped outside and shut the door behind him. His eyes were sad. "What we used to have?"

She kept her cool gaze trained on him.

"Ursula, it was an affair. It's over. We can't go back."

Still, she didn't move.

"Go home," he said, as if she were a stray animal. He opened his mouth to say more, thought better of it, and retreated into the house.

She stood for a heartbeat, wishing she had the power to strike him down, to hurt him. Then she returned to her car to seek out the plumber.

The Blackthorn Book of Secrets: Poison

There is a story whispered of a woman who was so frightened for her daughter's future that she poisoned her husband. This wasn't unusual in a time when women were considered property and men treated them worse than animals. It also wasn't unheard of for a woman to choose poison over divorce; the former was accessible and looked like natural death, whereas the latter could be difficult to acquire.

The most common form of "home" poison is castor oil beans boiled in the same pot as brown beans, combined with a dash of oleander and mandrake root. Add salt and bacon, and the poison will be undetectable. If the poison needs to be administered in liquid form, mix ¼ teaspoon hemlock with the same amount of honey. If it is then mixed in a bitter liquid, like coffee or beer, neither the recipient nor the law will have a reason to suspect.

Chapter 15

Katrine

They'd enjoyed a spicy but delicious pre-movie dinner at Perfume River and now stood in the lobby of the Hobbes, which buzzed with patrons scrambling to buy candy and oversize sodas, smiling in anticipation of the evening's escape. The smell of popcorn and butter was overwhelming and as welcome to Katrine as laughter. She followed her aunts to the counter but demurred when asked if she wanted anything.

"You don't like popcorn," Tara said. It was a statement rather than a question.

Katrine glanced at her niece. In the short time she'd known her, she'd already observed that the girl possessed her grandma's habit of mirroring those around her. Now she wondered if Tara was a people-reader, too. "Not the taste, but I love the smell. Reminds me of working here when I was a teenager."

Tara took a cautious step closer. She'd been traveling nearer and farther from Katrine all night, like a tentative star on an orbit path. "Did you like it? Working here, I mean."

Katrine felt a tickle at the rim of her heart. Her niece was beautiful, with her big liquid eyes and pointy chin. Katrine wanted to simultaneously protect her from the world and take her shopping for clothes that didn't look like Cold War hand-me-downs. "Yeah, I really think I did. Do you have a job?"

Tara blew frustrated air out her nose. "I wish. I'm only fourteen."

"Don't wish your life away." On impulse, Katrine clasped her niece's hand. The smile she received was radiant.

Audish, the man Velda had brought to the party the other night, emerged from her peripheral vision. He was wearing a newsboy cap and an ironed button-up shirt in chocolate brown. His hands were shoved into his pockets. He nodded as if he'd planned to meet them all along. "Thought it would be a nice night to catch a movie. Care if I sit with you ladies?"

"Not at all," Xenia said, leading the way.

Katrine wondered if Audish was simply a friend of Velda's and not a lover after all, because he seemed to be taking an interest in Helena. He hung back to help Helena with her two brimming buckets of popcorn, one glistening golden and the other naked except for salt, and he appeared to be drinking in her every word. Katrine and Tara trailed behind. They managed to find the last five seats together three rows back from the screen and strained their necks watching a modern rom-com where they were supposed to laugh at the woman tripping in her high heels and the man being emotionally distant.

Halfway through, Katrine found herself growing sad and then, worse, detached. She'd felt that way last night, lying in her childhood bed. Hollowed out and rootless, the very feelings she'd hoped to escape by returning home to Faith Falls. The nightmare that'd woken her—her third in as many nights—hadn't helped. One minute, she was awake, staring at the white walls of her bedroom, certain she'd never fall asleep. Next thing she knew, she was in a smoky bar, a place she'd never been before yet was as familiar as the tops of her knees. It smelled like cigarettes and sour whiskey.

A man beckoned to her through the crowd, a tall figure wearing a cowboy hat. She elbowed her way toward him, desperate to see his face as she wove around people who were clinking beer bottles and twirling the ice in their sweating glasses. But no matter how fast she moved, she never seemed to get any closer to seeing his face.

Suddenly, a door slammed open in front of her.

That's where the cowboy'd gone.

She strode through the doorway and gasped. Instead of discovering the man she'd been following, she found her husband, Adam, between the thighs of a familiar woman.

She'd awoken with a start, so anxious that she'd gone straight to the Queen Anne's basement, selected a half-used can of mulberry paint that someone must have bought to touch up the porch trim, and returned to her childhood bedroom in the dead of night. She'd pulled all the posters off the wall, dragged the furniture toward the center, lined the floor with newspaper, and painted right over the creamy walls.

Each stroke made her feel safer. The rich, dark color kept her inside the house, at least while she worked, and the acrid smell reminded her she was grounded in her body. But once the walls were done, she found she was still unmoored. It was terrifying, a mixture of claustrophobia in her skin and agoraphobia in the world.

And so, she'd done what she swore she'd never do, but the only move that promised relief: She texted Adam.

It was the first contact she'd attempted since she'd left London. She told herself it was to let him know she forgave him so she wouldn't have to carry the burden of his betrayal anymore. Her hands shook, making it difficult to type.

Hey. It's me. I moved home. Thinking of you. Wishing you peace.

She hit send. Her heart raced into her mouth and pulsed there. All the images of him that she'd been keeping at bay flooded her. No facial hair, a smile that made her thighs buzz, sandalwood-scented skin. They'd talk for hours, holding hands, whispering, giggling. She waited three months to sleep with him, sure this one would be different. *Oh yes, it will be different.* She knew this looking up at him the first night they made love, gazing at his glorious naked chest, his eyes closed in concentration, caressing her, whispering her name, telling her she felt so good, she was the most beautiful woman in the world.

They'd met at a photo shoot; she was covering it as a freelancer for *Vogue* and he was in charge of lighting. He'd come to her wounded, his heart sliced by a critical mother, two ex-wives, and an Iraq tour of duty with the British Army. She would fix him, love him, decorate his life with her toothbrush and an overnight T-shirt. She helped him enroll in university, encouraged him to begin talking with his mom, tracked down a volunteer job for him working with veterans at the Royal Hospital Chelsea. They'd be everything for each other, no matter what. Most importantly, he'd never leave her.

He couldn't, not after all the help she'd given him.

Sometimes she worried about his quick temper and lack of interest in her ambitions, but when his head was between her legs, it sure felt like the real thing. *Make love to me,* she'd cry, when she couldn't stand it any longer. He'd laugh, and his hot breath would send her over the edge, shivering, quaking. He'd crawl up beside her.

I was, he'd murmur in her ear.

Three years into the relationship, she was offered the full-time position at *Vogue* and took it as a sign that it was time to go full adult and get married. She'd wanted to be a writer since her first journalism class in college. She'd assumed she'd be covering politics rather than fashion, but the money was good until something better came along. So she proposed. He said yes, his face bursting into the most tender grin. They married, a small ceremony, only close friends in attendance, before renting a West Hampstead flat together.

The first two years of marriage had been blissful, with the extreme highs and crashing lows she'd come to associate with love.

Then, four weeks ago came a low with no high to follow.

Adam had started screwing her intern, a pretty Welsh girl named Patsy.

At least, Katrine had *discovered* the affair four weeks ago; it could've been going on for months. It was only chance that she'd found out. Patsy had called in sick for work, had only lived in London for eight months and didn't know anyone, was stuck in her flat.

Or so she told Katrine.

When Katrine dropped by with soup and tea, walked right in when the unlocked door opened beneath her knock, Adam and Patsy were on the couch. Her husband was on top of and inside her assistant.

Guess she does *know someone in town* had been Katrine's first thought.

She went home and boxed up all his possessions, setting them out front of their apartment. He'd picked everything up without so much as a knock on the door to apologize. After, she'd alternated between walking past his workplace, hoping to run into him, and sobbing on her floor, praying she'd never see him again. She'd sustained that for a month before breaking their lease—which cost her the last of her savings; she'd been in charge of bills until he could "get on his feet"—and giving away everything she owned except for her favorite clothes, her laptop, toiletries, and a box of records and notes that included a framed copy of a newspaper article she'd written in college. The frame was bulky but she loved that story, an investigative piece she'd written on unfair housing practices. It had resulted in a family trapped in the local homeless shelter being finally approved for a rent-stabilized apartment.

The true horror of it was that Adam wasn't a bad person. Or maybe it was that she could make herself believe that. That, and the fact she still wanted him back, couldn't stop dreaming about him, smelling him, thinking about what could have been.

He wasn't the first romantic mistake she'd made.

Oh no.

Her past was littered with the retreating backs of emotionally stunted men who told her how beautiful and smart she was, who sucked her in, who cheated on her and then left. There was Quint, the eighteen-year-old farmer's son and her first sexual partner. He'd taught her the ropes in tenth grade, then educated her best friend, Samantha, a week later. She took him back afterward, felt like a queen in his arms, loved the way he loved her, wept for days when he skipped town with the substitute English teacher with big boobs.

Next came Jerry, ten years older and driving a Harley, all snaggle-toothed with a too-quick laugh. He'd hunted her like a deer, charmed her with his crazy jokes and obsessive attention, and had her spending nights at his place most of her senior year. Jasmine had missed her, she knew that, but Ursula didn't seem to mind. As soon as she'd merged her life with his so thoroughly that all his interests were now hers, Jerry began prowling for someone else.

Craig, her economics professor, had been different, reserved at first, which she took as a sign of maturity. They made it as far as engaged before she discovered the hundreds of porn sites on his computer, the secret emails from women looking for an anonymous tryst while their husbands were away.

She waited five years to commit to a serious relationship again.

That relationship was Adam.

In her childhood bedroom, now painted deep purple and smelling of bitter, creamy paint, she couldn't lie to herself. She'd messed up again. She'd believed that she needed to sacrifice to be loved, and then she'd chosen another unfaithful man. It was a fool's dance, one step removed from Laura Ackerdan, nicknamed "Get-Lucky Laura" in high school, a girl who'd give a blowjob to any guy who asked—even the ones who must have giggled with nerves while she went down—in the desperate hope that one of them would love her. Probably each one of those boys could better describe the part in Laura's hair than her face, and why would any girl let that happen to her?

Katrine knew why, of course: Humans needed love like oxygen. A lucky few were born into families that taught them healthy ways to get it. Everyone else was left to grab in the dark. *Shit.* She hadn't thought of Get-Lucky Laura—what a horrible nickname to have given a child—in over a decade. That's what coming home did to you. Roiled up your brain like a river in spring, unearthing liquid muck that you thought you'd built a bridge over, turning everything into a wet, flooded mess.

The deal was, it was one thing to recognize a pattern, a whole other to own it, and as likely as learning to fly to change it. She was just thinking how much it hurt, what she'd let Adam do to her, when her phone buzzed. Her pulse thundered. She'd removed Adam's contact information in a fit of rage the day she'd discovered the affair, and then written his phone number in ink in her journal, her address book, her calendar, overcome by fear that she'd forget it.

As if she could. She recognized it immediately.

He'd replied to her text with a single word: thanks

She heard something like the raw, wet pop of gristle releasing from bone, and the truth of what she'd done dawned on her, sending shame prickles along her scalp. She hadn't texted Adam to forgive him. She'd reached out to make him feel better, hoping that he'd do the same for her, that he'd save her from herself, from this mulberry room, from this haunted house, from her suffocating hometown.

He hadn't. He wouldn't.

He was an emotional hamster that she'd convinced herself was a bear.

Thinking back on it made the weeping start again, only now she sat in a theater watching a ridiculous romance with her family, three women who knew nothing about her, wearing a Chanel dress that cost more than the car they'd driven here in.

She felt Tara's eyes on her. Her niece was watching her like *she* was the movie.

"Stop it," she hissed, suddenly furious. Tara jerked her head back as if slapped. Katrine knew she was being unfair, that her niece didn't deserve her anger, but she couldn't rein it in. She stood, turned toward the audience, and repeated, "Just stop it!" in a louder voice. Shocked faces flashed at her in the dark theater, but she ignored them and stomped out, unable to tolerate the awful movie a moment longer.

She hurried into the humid August air, hoping the night would free her, but the pressure in her chest only grew tighter. One hand shot out to grab on to the brick of the Hobbes while the other tried to loosen an invisible scarf from her neck.

That's when a man approached. She recognized him, but couldn't place from where.

"Are you okay?" he asked.

Katrine knew her eyes were rolling like a panicked cow's. She glanced up and down streets both familiar and strange, the storefronts dark and the brass beavers gleaming in the lights, feeling like the world was swallowing her whole. She forced herself to focus on the tall, worried-looking man. He seemed like the only solid thing around. She drew a breath, and that's when she realized where she knew him from. "I bumped into you outside of Seven Daughters the other day."

He nodded. He'd followed her out of the movie theater, but now that they were standing on the sidewalk, he appeared uncertain what to do. He flexed a strong hand and then scrubbed the back of his neck.

"Robin?" she asked. His hands were mesmerizing, so beautiful they belonged on a Michelangelo sculpture. Come to think of it, all of him reminded her of a clothed, big-eared *David*. Her cheeks grew warm, and she was able to draw another deep breath.

"Ren," he said, the shadow of a smile on his lips. "But close."

She indicated the theater behind her. "Did you witness that star performance? The one where I made an ass of myself in front of a theater full of strangers?"

His eyes held hers. He repeated his question, his voice lower, softer. "Are you okay?"

She hugged herself. What was her life? "As good as can be expected. You don't have to miss the movie for me."

He tilted his head. "It wasn't that good."

Her brain was still careening. She couldn't shake the trapped sensation. She didn't know anything about this man with his curly hair and kind smile, but she was certain she couldn't stand here another second. "Can you give me a ride home?"

He glanced at his watch. "My daughters are inside. Let me go tell them where I am, and then I can. The Blackthorn mansion, right?"

She nodded. *Where else?*

Chapter 16

Tara

Tara stared after Katrine, jaw slack.

Helena patted the seat Katrine had vacated and motioned for her great-niece to move into it before stage-whispering to Xenia, "Should we follow her?"

"Let her go," Xenia muttered back. "We'll PINC her later."

Audish kept eating popcorn, his eyes trained on the screen.

"What's pinking?" Tara asked, forgetting to whisper. She was shushed from behind.

Tell you after, Helena mouthed.

Tara nodded and returned her attention to the movie, but her mind was racing. She'd witnessed something horrible inside Katrine, a barbed fishhook that rested just below her aunt's heart. It was bone-white, sharp, and deeply embedded. The flesh around it was brackish and bruised, stretched tight from infection. Tara'd always been able to see people's wounds, but never one so vivid, and never one that the owner actually *moved.* She'd seen her aunt tugging at the fishhook, but she'd been pulling at the wrong end, causing the trauma to swell even more.

Tara shook her head. She'd wanted to tell Katrine that she could pull it loose if she yanked on the barbed end and suffered through a bit of pain, but she was intimidated by Katrine's beauty. She was so mysterious, and exotic, and smart.

Forty-five minutes and a happy ending later, the four of them were out on the street, enjoying the pleasant bustle of being in a group of people all heading home.

"So what's pinking?" Tara asked again.

"It's an acronym, not a color. P-I-N-C," Xenia said, unbuttoning the sweater she'd closed to ward off the theater's chill.

Helena smiled absently. "It stands for 'Pretend It's Not Crazy.' Like, when the Queen Anne's outside faucet broke? It was the hottest summer in years and no place to hook up the hose. The garden was shriveling up. The easiest thing would have been to attach a hose to the kitchen sink and run it out the window, but your grandma decided she didn't want an old hose in her kitchen."

Xenia and Helena exchanged a glance, and Xenia picked up where her twin left off. "So instead, Ursula had us truck in and out of the kitchen with bucket after bucket, banging and dripping and tracking in about a hundred pounds more dirt than we would have if we'd simply attached the hose to the faucet. It was irrational, but Helena and I pretended like it made sense." She shrugged. "Women PINC each other all the time. It's an unspoken rule."

Tara rolled the concept around, tasting it from all angles. "Why wouldn't you just convince Grandma that there was a better way?"

Audish had been standing to the side, seeming not to pay attention until he spoke. "It's not often you can convince someone who's made up their mind that your way is the better way. You can just love them and hope to lead by example."

Xenia gifted him one of her elusive smiles, slow and cool like a cat's stretch. Audish seemed to be one of the rare men she tolerated. "Exactly. And here's the thing about being a woman in this world: You grow so accustomed to pushing up against everything just for a little space of your own that sometimes you see a fight where there isn't one.

PINCing is a way we women help each other conserve energy for the battles that matter."

Tara didn't understand what Audish or Xenia meant, but she liked Xenia's smile and so she stored their comments away. "What happened to Aunt Katrine to make her so sad? Mom won't tell."

Xenia sighed and glanced at her twin, who appeared to be leaning toward Audish for strength. "She left her husband. After she found out he was cheating on her with a friend."

Tara nodded. That's what she'd thought.

Chapter 17

Katrine

They sat in his small Honda parked in the Queen Anne's driveway. Not for the first time, Katrine was struck by how the mansion's windows were arranged to look like a smiling face. She'd always felt like the house watched her. Sometimes she liked it, other times she didn't. "You ever been inside?"

Ren kept the car running, his hands on the wheel. He shook his head. "I didn't grow up in Faith Falls. I moved here with my wife and daughters seven years ago."

"Oh." Katrine was disgusted by the disappointment she felt. Of course he was married, and what'd it matter anyhow? She was in no position to date. She put her hand on the door handle. "Thanks for the ride."

"You're welcome."

She stopped halfway out of her seat. "I'm not always . . . I'm actually a pretty stable person." She laughed, but it sounded too high, artificial. "Anyhow, I don't usually throw fits in a movie theater. It's been . . . a challenging month."

He glanced over at her for the first time since they'd entered his car. She felt the tug of his blue eyes again, the invitation of the great wide ocean to come swim in its waves. She couldn't look away.

"My wife took her own life two years ago."

Her cheeks grew hot. "I'm sorry. Jesus, I'm being so selfish." Tears pushed at her eyelids. The man had lost a wife, probably an amazing one. All she was out was a shitbag of a husband, a big ol' Should've Known Better.

He shook his head, tossing a curl into one of his eyes. "I didn't say that to make you feel bad. I understand challenging times, is all. Go easy on yourself."

She didn't know what to say to this stranger, and the suffocation was back, its hot fingers circling her neck. She fled, closing the car door behind her.

Chapter 18

Ursula

The sharp yellow scent of a match being lit dominated the space around Ursula. She'd been smelling it on and off in her cottage since Katrine had returned, and none of her potions could eliminate the sulfurous odor. She knew what it meant, what fire always meant: change.

Was it more of Charlie Tanager toying with her, or was it simply the flow of life? She wasn't afraid of change. She knew better than to store her heart in anything or anyone. So why did her belly feel lined with ice? She envisioned her sisters, daughter, and granddaughter safely at the movies tonight and Jasmine dining with her husband. She didn't sense any particular alarm when concentrating on any of them.

She *had* seen a man she was certain was Charlie Tanager in the grocery store today, ran right up to him and shoved him from behind. When he turned, she realized it wasn't her father. She'd apologized profusely and run outside, only to spot another man who walked just like Charlie disappearing down an alley. That guy was wearing a cowboy hat. Ursula let him go, her heart beating unpleasantly against her ribs. How long could she last like this, seeing ghosts everywhere she looked?

Her workshop called to her. She went straight to *The Blackthorn Book of Secrets*, laying it on the rough wooden bench. It opened up to a page titled "Mind, Body, Spirit":

> *The connection between the holy trinity has been forgotten as humans camp in their own minds like a baby afraid to be born. Until the brain is forced to share with the heart and the two are reminded that they are children of the spirit, fear will dominate. It will be expressed in many ways: anger, anxiety, melancholy, a need to control or fix, exhaustion.*
>
> *To balance the holy trinity, you must bypass the mind and speak directly to the spirit. (Dancing and laughing are the best ways to communicate with your soul.) The more people involved in this communion, the better chance it will work. You'll know if you've succeeded because you will sleep deeper, forgive quickly, and smile easily.*

Ursula slammed the book shut. Entries like that—a mixture of basic knowledge and vague, hippie-dippie instructions—annoyed her, but this one felt particularly personal. She knew depression and anxiety and a whole host of other mental health disorders were as real as a broken arm and required medical intervention. She also knew there were other people who believed they were ill but who'd simply lost their way. They felt too much and so became lost in their minds. Once they were trapped, medication became the route of least resistance. A form of this had happened to her beautiful Jasmine, and because her daughter was an adult, all Ursula could do was watch and be present if Jasmine sought her help.

But this idea that one could overcome the mind's prison by dancing or sitting around and laughing? *That* she didn't have time for. Ursula possessed a chemist's sensibility. She preferred clear measures. She tightened the apron over the worn but still beautiful brown empire-waisted dress Xenia had sewn her ten years earlier. People told her it made her silver-shot hair shine and brought out golden flecks in her eyes.

She liked that it was comfortable.

She was returning to a tincture of hempseed oil and peppermint, checking the blend with a whiff and a light tap against the glass tube, when she heard the footsteps racing down her walk.

She recognized the gait.

Her only question was whether Katrine would knock.

She didn't. The door swung open, and her younger daughter stepped inside. She didn't wrinkle her nose, as she had when she was a child, to convey her distaste at the strong smells of her mother's lab. Instead, her eyes ran across the hundreds of tiny blue glass bottles lining the shelves.

"You've been busy," she said.

Ursula's heart tugged. She wondered how this moment would play out if she was a mother who embraced her children, asked them how the movie had been, how their marriage had gone wrong. Even if Ursula was that woman, Katrine's emotional barricades were as visible as the bundles of thyme hanging from the rafters.

"Always am," Ursula said. Then, before she could think better of it: "You should avoid meeting any new men while you're in town. It's an inauspicious time."

She meant while Charlie Tanager was hunting them, able to inhabit any body he wanted to serve his wicked purpose. Such was the power of a dying man's curse. She couldn't possibly say that, though.

Still, Katrine's snort caught her off guard.

"My *life* is an inauspicious time to meet new men." Katrine picked up an empty bottle and held it in front of the window. The moon shot through it, reflecting the blue in a pale cerulean circle over her right eye. "Don't suppose you have anything for a broken heart?"

Ursula studied her daughter. She was gorgeous, more beautiful even than Velda had been in her heyday. She could use some more meat on her, but her sharp cheekbones would only grow prettier as she aged, and her full lips and sea-glass eyes had bewitched many throughout her life. The gray dust over her skin somehow made her seem more precious, like a forgotten jewel. Ursula felt pride for her baby girl swell her throat.

Yet she knew Katrine didn't want a spell. Her daughters had always refused their mother's elixirs, initially out of childish spite, and then out of habit. She'd never forced her potions on them, vowing to always let them have the last word in that regard and all others.

It was key to being an entirely different mother to them than Velda had been to her.

"Adam wasn't the man you thought?" Ursula asked. The family had been informed of the wedding ceremony after the fact, the infidelity shared almost as an afterthought when Katrine came home.

Katrine snorted. "I didn't see it coming, if that's what you're asking. Remember, I wasn't born with a gift, like the rest of you. Just a particularly powerful connection with my sister. That's as close as I've ever gotten to my own magic."

Ursula wanted to cross her arms, but she was afraid any movement would chase her daughter away. "Maybe you simply didn't want to see it."

Katrine dropped her hand so the glass was no longer reflecting on her face. "You ever make a mistake with your potions?"

Every time the snakes rise, I'll be there to steal your power.
Your children will pay, and their children, forever down the line.

"Not in making them," Ursula responded, shaking off the pall of those terrible words, "though I don't always give them to the right person. I'm sorry about Adam."

Katrine turned her gaze on her mother. The green in her eyes was storming. "You never met him."

"That was your choice, not mine." That wasn't entirely true, was it? It'd been unbearable having Katrine move so far away, but also a relief. The farther her daughters were from her, the less danger they were in. "Besides, I can still be sorry you're hurt."

Katrine opened her mouth, then closed it. She set the blue bottle on the table. She seemed ready to say something when a knock at the door broke the mood. Katrine's face cleared. "Guess your real purpose has arrived." She slipped outside, barely glancing at the person waiting on the stoop.

Ursula considered running after Katrine but then remembered the weight of Velda's "advice" on her own shoulders. She instead turned her attention to the new arrival, a woman backlit by the moon. She was striking, her head heavy with black, gold, and copper locs laced with beads and metal rings. She had amber-brown eyes, but one stared off in another direction than the other. Her body arced like a cello, and she held herself with a dancer's poise. If her eyes treated each other like sisters, she'd be so stunning that she'd be difficult to look at.

Ursula leaned against the counter, her hand itching to reach for the *Book of Secrets*. "You want me to fix your eye?"

The woman stepped into the workshop and closed the door behind her. Her left eye, the one that Ursula had taken to be the weak one, swirled in its socket twice before landing on her.

The woman shook her head, and the metal in her hair tinkled like fairy bells. "No."

"Then what?"

She sighed. "I just realized that if I found out I had a year to live, I wouldn't change a thing. It's made me so sad that I don't know what to do."

Near Ursula's hand, the *Book of Secrets* laughed.

Chapter 19

Jasmine

Jasmine watched her precious Tara play the viola, unaware that the focused smile on her face was identical to her daughter's. When Tara missed a note, Jasmine stuck her fingers in her ears. "Is it supposed to sound like that?"

"Mom," Tara said, rolling her eyes. "I'm *learning*, remember?"

"You make it hard to forget," Jasmine teased. She longed to stroke her daughter's hair, but it'd been a few years since Tara had let her get away with that. She kept the smile on her face. She felt lighter since dinner with Dean last night. It'd been an uncomfortable meal at first, as if they were playing themselves onstage. They were just starting to relax into each other—she thought—when he dropped the hammer.

"Pass the salt?" she'd said.

"Of course." Their hands touched. He looked into her eyes, and she thought he was going to ask to move back home. Instead he said, "Will you see a counselor?"

She was surprised at how alien his words sounded. They were meant for someone else, someone who couldn't stop turning on and off light switches or who wanted to fall asleep in their garage with the car running. She was neither. She was content as long as she kept Tara close and there were no surprises.

"What for?" she asked.

His pained expression was more eloquent than his words, but he tried. "You're afraid of the world, Jasmine, and you're teaching the same to Tara. That's no way to live."

A thousand needles of surprise pushed through her skin, and her eyes grew wet. She didn't know he had that depth, though she'd suspected. He wasn't the most handsome man, or the smartest, but he was a wonderful dad, and steady.

Most importantly, he didn't keep secrets.

"Okay," she said. There was nothing a counselor could do for her, but if seeing one would bring Dean home, she'd go through the motions.

He squeezed her hand. They finished their meal. Before he left his own home for the evening, he'd kissed her forehead. "I love you."

She was still clinging to the life raft of those three words.

"Hey, can Brittany come over later?" Tara asked, setting down her bow. "To watch TV with me?"

Jasmine blinked. She'd been remembering the warmth of her husband's lips on her forehead. "Did you finish your homework?"

"Yeah, you already looked at it, remember?" The eye roll was implied in her tone. "The hydroponic tomato science project."

"I remember." She did. She just liked to hear Tara talk. It seemed like her daughter was growing up so fast.

"And maybe you could teach me to make spaghetti sauce with the tomatoes I grew?" Tara smiled hopefully. "Helena told me you used to make a marinara so delicious that it could heal a broken heart."

Jasmine felt a pang. She wasn't sure if it was guilt or fear. Tara had heard the Blackthorn witchcraft rumors. She couldn't live in Faith Falls and avoid them, but Jasmine had been careful to dispel them at home and to redirect any of her daughter's skills that seemed to verge on the supernatural. She intended to protect Tara from the pain she'd experienced at any cost.

"That'd be some pretty good sauce," Jasmine said lightly. "I can't promise anything like that, but I can show you how to mince onions and steam-peel fresh tomatoes. Add a little of both to store-bought sauce and it'll taste better than homemade."

"Thanks, Mom."

The trust in Tara's eyes was almost too much to bear. Jasmine leaned forward to turn the page on the sheet music. When a knock came at the front door, she told Tara to keep practicing and went to answer it herself.

A delivery person in a brown uniform stood on her doorstep. "Jasmine Moore?"

She nodded. Who would be sending her a package?

"Sign here."

She took the shoebox-size parcel with her to the living room.

Tara stopped playing. "What is it, Mom?"

"I don't know." She reached for a scissors and slit open the cardboard package. Inside was another box, and inside that, pink tissue paper. She pulled it gently aside to reveal a ceramic dancing pig with ruby lips wearing nothing but a white mesh tutu. Her front hooves joined together under her chin in a saucy gesture.

"Mom, it's so cute!"

Jasmine held it up to the light. "I love it," she said. She was referring to the life she'd built for herself, one where she could look forward rather than back, where there was no magic, where her husband was a good man.

Chapter 20

Katrine

Katrine was scheduled to meet with the bead store's owner a half an hour before the class, ask her some questions about her new business, and then take photos of the beaders at work. Heidi had told her the woman's name. It was something Midwestern that she'd quickly forgotten. She'd brought her laptop, the *Gazette*'s staff camera, a steno pad, and a thin black pen. She hadn't written a newspaper article since college, but how calcified could that muscle be?

Helena had agreed to let Katrine borrow her car until she could scrape together some money of her own. Fortunately, that looked like it'd be sooner rather than later. Her heart had thudded when she'd recognized the *Vogue* London office's email address, but she needn't have worried. The note was from HR, offering her severance pay despite her walkout. All she had to do was sign over the files she'd left behind. They could have all of them, every silly bit of research on Paris fashion and Ivory Coast silk and Peter Pan collars making a comeback.

When she pulled up to the old Stearns Bank building, it was all sharp edges and neoclassical columns, the rainbow-lettered Stacy's Beads sign incongruous against the solemn brick. Hobbes Theater had done all its banking here, and Katrine'd been inside often to make deposits. She stepped from the hot sun into the cool of the building, curious as to how much had changed since then.

Her eyes took a moment to adjust to the dim light, and so her first sensation was the smell: dust and money. She'd always thought of the bank as cramped, but with its interior gutted—the teller counters removed and replaced by tables of beads glittering like pirate's treasure—it felt much larger. A young woman behind the counter flashed a smile before returning to her work organizing a bead tray.

Katrine was delighted to spot a familiar object from the bank days to her right: a grandfather clock made of polished maple. Instead of ringing on the hour, a little rabbit wearing spectacles would pop out and chime. He used to ring a gong, legend had it, but no one had seen the gong for decades. The clock had been an anomaly in a bank but fit right into a bead shop, though it must have been under the weather because a man with his back to her had his head shoved inside the timepiece.

Katrine's heart skipped when she recognized him. "Ren?"

He stood too quickly, cracking his head on the inside of the clock. He rubbed the spot and turned around, his face breaking into a lopsided grin.

"Hey!" He pointed his screwdriver toward the nearest beads. "What's a nice girl like you doing in a seedy place like this?"

His grin grew at his own dorky joke, and she couldn't resist matching his smile. "You don't get out a lot, do you?" she asked.

He shrugged. "Work keeps me busy. It's nice to see you."

She wanted to believe he meant it. "I need to thank you for the ride home last night. You didn't have to do that."

"My pleasure. Really." His smile widened.

She felt her face grow hot. *What is wrong with me?* "Well, yeah. So, thank you. And hey, work is why I'm here, too. I got a job at the paper." She flapped her arms for reasons unknown. "I'm supposed to interview the owner. You know her?"

Ren glanced over her shoulder, toward the back of the store, and lowered his voice. "She's at the counter."

Katrine dropped her voice to match. "She's so young to own a business! The Faith Falls of yesteryear would have been gossiping about her to beat the band."

His mouth quirked at the edge. "You being back in town is definitely bigger news, if half the rumors I heard at church are true."

Her nose wrinkled. "You go to church?" He drew back a millimeter, and her hand flew to her mouth. "I'm sorry. That was judgy." She shook her head. "My friends back in London weren't churchgoers, and neither was I. I forget what it's like here."

He tipped his head, his expression thoughtful. "I do go to church. I bring my daughters. I wanted continuity in their lives after Laura died."

"I'm a donkey," Katrine said, shaking her head. "An absolute, horrible donkey. I don't know why I keep saying the wrong thing around you."

"Does this mean we're friends?"

She tried to follow his train of thought. "What?"

"You said your friends *in London* weren't churchgoers. The implication was that I'm different from your other friends."

She stuttered for an answer before realizing he was teasing. She offered her hand, fighting the smile that was tugging at her cheeks. "How about we start all the way over? Hello, my name is Katrine Blackthorn, and I'm a recovering donkey."

His face grew mock serious. "Pleased to meet you. I'm Ren Cunningham, chief greeter for Faith Falls' Donkey Rehabilitation Program."

Katrine was chuckling deeply for the first time in weeks, but when his hand grasped hers, she was struck with a sensation so powerful that it knocked the laughter right out of her. He moved forward to steady her, concern in his eyes.

"Katrine?"

She rubbed her face, her stomach fluttering. When they touched, she'd seen secrets falling from the sky, where they turned into fireflies, flickering in air so clean it smelled like water. She had absolutely no idea what it meant. The stress of the last month was doing a number on her.

"I'm fine," she said. "Must've felt a static shock. The air has been so dry lately. Um, I better let you get back to work. Talk to you later?"

He started to respond, but she turned away to hide her discomfiture and made her way to the counter. Goodbyes weren't her thing, but even so, the guy deserved better.

If I were Ren, I'd go out of my way to avoid someone as messed up as me.

The interview was straightforward, the only oddness when Stacy Reller, the bead store's young owner, invited Katrine to a séance later that same evening. Apparently, the Stearns Bank, combined with the Pappas neighborhood, had been enough to generate a local interest in the occult. "It's like a book group, only with Ouija boards and scrying stones," she'd said.

Katrine had politely declined.

By that time, Ren had finished his work and left.

Standing outside the bead store, she felt disoriented, so she grabbed for something certain: She owed her niece an apology for how she had treated her at the movie theater. She was also desperate to reconnect with her sister. No one had been closer than the two of them as girls. She understood she'd taken that for granted when she moved away, and she'd grown self-involved and lazy in maintaining their relationship.

She wanted to fix that, starting now. She could no longer wait and hope for Jasmine to come to her and smooth everything over the way she'd done when they were young.

Katrine was going to her.

Chapter 21

Katrine

Her stomach clutched and tumbled as she pulled into Jasmine's driveway, same as it had when she and her aunts had driven up the day before. There was something horrible about the normalcy of the little box house, with its brown grass, dingy paint, and plastic flowers in the window boxes. Everything about it said, "I've given up."

Katrine punched those thoughts down and turned off the car. She should have called first, but Tara was homeschooled, so where else would they be? When she rang the doorbell, it echoed inside before momentary quiet followed by a puppy rumble of footsteps tumbling downstairs.

Then the front door flew open.

Tara stood in the entryway, a cheap oak closet door on one side of her, a key rack on the other, and a carpeted living room decorated with matchy, scratchy Midwestern furniture in graying pastels behind. Her face lit up at the sight of her aunt, and that made Katrine feel even worse.

"Hey," Katrine said, trying on a tentative smile, "I wanted to stop by and say I'm sorry for how banana pants I acted at the theater last night."

Tara grinned like she'd just been handed a present wrapped in plum-colored paper. "It's okay. Helena and Xenia taught me how to PINC."

Katrine tipped her head. The term sounded familiar. Then she remembered where she'd first heard it. Back when she was in high school, Helena had caught the tail end of a documentary on orphaned red pandas. She'd decided on the spot to sponsor all seven that the San Diego Zoo had, sending them regular checks and even flying out to visit the pandas twice. Katrine had asked Xenia if Helena had gone loca, and Xenia told her about PINCing. Katrine smiled at the memory, and then at the thought of being on the receiving end of her first Blackthorn PINC. She'd sure earned it.

"I brought this for you." She handed her niece a plastic bag containing clear lip gloss and mascara the same brown shade as Tara's long lashes. Katrine had picked up both from the apothecary on her way over after the bead shop. She'd also brought along a book she'd purchased in Europe, a guide that contained color photos of London's best restaurants, museums, and nightclubs. She'd topped the bag off with a peach-colored silk camisole that she'd never worn but loved too much to leave behind. "You might want to hide all this. Is your mom home?"

Tara accepted the bag and peeked in, her large eyes growing wider. "Yeah!"

Katrine felt a sudden, uncharacteristic shyness. "She's probably busy, and I—"

Jasmine appeared at Tara's side, her eyebrows arched. For the briefest moment, Katrine thought she saw happy surprise in her sister's expression, but it might've been the lighting. Whatever it was, it'd been fleeting. Tara closed the bag and hid it on her opposite side, but Jasmine was too focused on Katrine to notice.

"We're just sitting down to eat," Jasmine said. "Why don't you join us?"

Katrine followed without question. There was no quicker way to connect with Jasmine than her cooking. She did her best to ignore the interior of the house, which was as bad as the outside. It felt empty and repetitive, like a sitcom stage set between takes—plain furniture, knickknack shelves, everything done in institutional colors. The dining room was painted beige, and the table at the center lacked any decoration save for the salt and pepper shakers shaped like the front (salt) and back (pepper) of a pig.

"We're having lasagna," Jasmine said.

"Great! Is Dean here?"

Did Jasmine stiffen? "He's on the road."

Katrine felt rather than heard the pain in her sister's voice. Was that why Jasmine was so distant, because she was having problems in her marriage? They'd kept in touch through letters and occasional phone calls, but Jasmine had never let on that there was trouble. Wait—when was the last time Katrine had called?

She took a seat at the dinner table across from Tara, landing hard in the stiff chair. "Did you two have a nice date night?" she asked.

"We did." Jasmine's lips were tight. "We had dinner, and then we saw the town orchestra play at the city park. You enjoyed the movie?"

Katrine glanced at Tara. The girl must not have mentioned Katrine's meltdown. Her heart warmed to her niece even more. "It was fine." She held out her plate for a square of lasagna and pointed at a pile of green-and-blue fuzziness, about the size of a loaf of bread, on a side table. "What's that?"

"Mom and I are learning to make felt," Tara said. "Those are supposed to be slippers." She hadn't taken her eyes off her aunt.

Katrine's lip quirked. "They look partially digested."

Tara giggled and then swallowed the noise as she glanced nervously at her mom.

Jasmine and Katrine stuttered through small talk about the weather and Katrine's new job at the *Gazette* as Katrine choked down her meal, moving bits around so it'd look like she'd eaten more than she had. It wasn't that it was bad. The gummy plainness of it, though, when compared to the majesty of the feasts Jasmine once created, was hard to bear.

"Dean on the road a lot?" Katrine asked.

"Six days a week," Jasmine said. "Sometimes more."

"You miss him?"

"Yes," Tara said, answering for her mom.

Katrine nodded. She cleared her throat and directed her attention back to Jasmine, reaching out again for a connection. "I visited Ursula."

Jasmine pursed her lips. "Aren't you living there?"

"You know what I mean. She's always out in her shop, just like back in the day. Taking care of the whole town unless they happen to live under her roof. I should be grateful. The last thing I want right now is to talk." An unexpected dizziness washed over her. It was the speed required to navigate between the closeness she used to share with her sister and the reality of the distance between them now. "I already feel like I'm losing it. Can you believe she told me to watch out for men while I'm home? As if I needed that advice."

Jasmine only shrugged.

Katrine's stomach twisted, and she wondered if they'd ever be on the same side of the river again. She studied Jasmine, worried by this new version of her, this angry, deflated shadow of her sister. How long had she been like this, and Katrine oblivious to it? Jasmine's best features were her wide eyes, and even they looked different. Katrine had teased her growing up that they were cow eyes, they were so big. Now, they were puffy and flat.

It was time to fix this. Katrine glanced at Tara. "Will you clear the table, honey?"

"Sure." Tara nodded and disappeared into the kitchen with a stack of plates covered in half-eaten lasagna.

Katrine glanced at Jasmine while Jasmine stared at the table. "What's up, Jazzy? Why're you so distant? I feel like I don't even know you. I've been gone for a while, but I'm back now. Let's make up for lost time."

Jasmine's face twisted painfully, but she didn't respond. Katrine wished for river agates but, lacking those, decided to coax her with a story to draw her out of her sad temper, just as she'd done when they were children. "Remember when I came down with the chicken pox in eighth grade?"

Jasmine patted her mouth with her napkin, still not making eye contact. "It was terrible."

Katrine nodded in agreement. "I was covered in the bumps, and they were all full of pus. Then they blistered and scabbed over and itched so bad I wanted to peel off my skin. You cooked me garlic chicken soup, dabbed me with calamine lotion, told me I'd be pretty again. I thought it'd last forever, but then I woke up one morning in a bed of scabs that I'd sloughed like snowflakes."

Jasmine smiled, but it was so raw that it hurt to look at.

Katrine felt the pain emanating from her sister, so sinister and complete that she found it difficult to breathe. She indicated the house, the felt slippers, the congealed pan of lasagna. She leaned forward to put her hand over Jasmine's, their first physical contact since Katrine had left fourteen years ago. "What's happened to you? What's happened to *us*?"

When their hands touched, she caught just a lick of a memory traveling down the sister line. Katrine recognized the Queen Anne decorated like it had been when they were young, the smell of burning soup, and a man staring at a barely teenage Jasmine, his words like knives: *Your children will pay, and their children, forever down the line.*

There were snakes, too, thousands of them streaming through the kitchen door. Katrine was falling into the horror of the vision, grabbing flesh, hoping not to sink too deeply, her stomach in her chest, when Jasmine slammed the door on her thoughts with such force that Katrine's chair almost tipped over. She had to wrench her hand from Jasmine's to catch her balance. Everything that had been in her head before—Adam, flirting, Faith Falls, apologies—fled.

"What was that?" Katrine's voice was a hoarse whisper.

Jasmine appeared startled before hooding her eyes. "What?"

"That memory!" Katrine couldn't catch her breath. "What happened? And why haven't you let me see it before?"

Jasmine blinked rapidly. "I don't know what you're talking about."

A dark thought, almost worse than the slip of terror she'd just witnessed, entered her mind. The lasagna pushed back against her throat, a bloody, gluey, meaty mess. She gagged. "We used to know everything about each other, Jasmine. *Everything.* Why don't I have this memory of yours? It was the last time the snakes came to Faith Falls, wasn't it? That means we were still living at home. *Together.*"

Tears slid down Jasmine's face, but she didn't answer. She didn't need to.

"You erased it," Katrine accused, the reality piercing like a knife. "You fed me something that took my memory, and then you pushed me away as soon as I was old enough to move out on my own, sent me halfway across the world. Away from my family. Away from *you.*" Katrine felt hot and cold at the same time. "How old were we?"

Jasmine shook her head, her hair falling in her face.

Katrine fought so hard to reclaim the horrible image she'd just seen that sweat broke out across her temple. Too-serious Jasmine, who'd entered the world ready to sacrifice for others, who loved her sister more than she loved herself, had been fourteen, Katrine twelve. But then the memory wriggled loose again. "Who was that man? Did he hurt you?"

Jasmine wiped at her face, her hands vibrating like hummingbird wings. Her voice sounded high and unnatural. "I don't know why you keep asking that. Nothing happened."

The blatant lie, the thought of Jasmine cooking food designed to banish her from her *home*, Jasmine's unwillingness to face the traumatic memory, share it, free herself from it, all of it squeezed Katrine's throat. "Someone attacked you, didn't they? And you cooked your magic so none of us would know what had happened to you, and you . . ."

"No," Jasmine mumbled. Her face was swimming in tears. "I didn't want you to get hurt. You don't understand."

"No, I don't, Jasmine, *because you didn't let me.*" Katrine was well past the point of hearing. "That meant I couldn't help you. Not only that, I missed your wedding, and my niece being born, and *my family* because of you."

Jasmine paled, her eyes suddenly so dark that her face looked like a skull. "You could have broken it whenever you wanted to," she spit.

"Because look. Here you are. You just never cared enough to come back until it was *you* who needed something."

Something deep and elemental rumbled underfoot. It felt like the shifting of a giant hibernating animal. Katrine ignored it, her words flying like darts. "If I'm here, it must be because you called me home. And now you're jerking me around."

Jasmine's horrible, lonely suffering and the years stolen from their family pressed against Katrine's throat. She scrambled toward the bathroom, but she didn't make it. She threw up the red lasagna all over the plain gray carpeting.

Jasmine rushed to her side, trying to hold her sister and stay apart from her all at the same time. "I'm sorry. I thought it was the best thing."

Katrine wiped her mouth. "You were wrong."

She couldn't stay in this box of a house one second longer. She raced out the door, feeling more alone than she had her entire life. *What meal was it that Jasmine cooked to make me forget, all these years?* she thought wretchedly. *It must have been quite a feast.* The shrapnel of the reclaimed memory left ash in her mouth, and she fought to keep her remaining bile down.

She didn't know where she was running to, only that she had to get away.

Chapter 22

Tara

When Tara heard that Xenia and Helen's usual assistant would be out of town during their first canning class, she jumped at the chance to help. Her great-aunts said they'd be glad to have her wash tomatoes and sterilize jars, as long as it was all right with Jasmine.

She had to fib to her mom, her first real lie, telling her that she'd be at Ursula's all afternoon. She was surprised she didn't feel bad about it. The air had changed since Katrine came home. It was looser somehow. Like rules were just suggestions now, and miracles felt not just possible but inevitable. So today was going to be her first real glimpse into the Blackthorn mysteries! Her hands already itched with anticipation.

She had to pass three picketers to get inside Seven Daughters. Her great-aunts had mentioned the protesters before—regular as rainfall—but she still didn't understand why anyone would bother harassing the shop.

Oh well. She had work to do. She greeted Helena and Xenia and headed straight to the kitchen, where she reviewed the necessary ingredients list for the class: three five-gallon buckets of plum tomatoes smelling like spice and earth, four dozen quart jars and lids, two five-gallon pots, a pressure cooker, and tongs and ladles. Because of the tomatoes' acidity, Xenia told her, they wouldn't need vinegar. They would, however, need onions, salt, and celery, which Xenia was just about to run out and purchase.

"Want to come with?" she asked Tara.

Tara thought of the trio of women perched outside the storefront holding signs. All three of them attended the same church as Tara. She knew that the Queen Anne Blackthorns were different, and saw how certain people around town were almost scared of them, but to her, they were family. She couldn't make sense of why everyone didn't love them, but neither was she in any hurry to find out.

"Can we go out the back door?" she asked her great-aunt.

"I'm too old to sneak," Xenia said. "Besides, I didn't do anything wrong. Come on."

It was a beautiful late-summer afternoon, and the sun was still high in the sky. Two of the women didn't make eye contact, but redheaded Dagmar Baum, mom to Jasmine's good friend Heidi Lewis, refused to look away. She stormed right up to Xenia.

"You're going against God's plan."

Tara recoiled. Her parents never argued. In fact, Tara had never heard her mother so much as raise her voice, let alone confront somebody. She tensed, waiting to see what Xenia would do.

Xenia smiled pleasantly. "Nice to see you, Dagmar. How's your husband doing?"

Dagmar looked like she wanted to spit. Instead, she pointed a shaking finger at Xenia. "Witch," she said, loud enough for the other two women to hear.

"No shit," Xenia said, and strolled forward as the two shocked witnesses parted to let her through.

Tara followed, a bitty smile settling into the corners of her mouth.

It lasted only a moment, only long enough for Dagmar to cry out, "What happened to Charlie Tanager, Xenia? We heard you witches killed him. Murdered your own father. I bet the Faith Falls police would love to hear more about that."

Chapter 23

Katrine

Katrine parked her borrowed car outside the newspaper office, feeling like a fool. Heidi probably wasn't even inside, and if she was, why would Katrine want to hang out with her? The woman probably ate kittens for breakfast. Yet who else could Katrine go to? Certainly not her family, when her own sister was the one who'd sent her away. She barely knew Ren. The closest thing she had to a friend in this town was her old tormentor.

She sighed and exited her car. *Behold the beauty of having nothing to lose.*

She greeted Stephanie. "Heidi in?"

"Of course! Fightin' the good fight." The receptionist motioned toward the hallway. "Go on back."

Katrine took off down the hall and paused just on the other side of the open doorway, pasted on a smile that she hoped wasn't too clownish, and popped in.

Heidi jumped, guiltily clicking something on her computer screen. "Katrine! Back already. How'd the bead store interview go?"

Katrine felt sixteen years old all over again, trying out for the cheerleading squad. "Fine, I guess. Hey, you want to go to the Rabbit Hole?" It'd been a dive bar back when she was in high school. She hoped it still was. "I'll buy you a drink."

A peculiar expression crossed Heidi's face, somewhere between confusion and gas. "You're asking *me* to go out?"

Katrine began to back away. "Forget it. It was stupid."

"Wait!"

Katrine stopped. Heidi still looked flustered. "I have a lot of work to do," she began, squaring her shoulders.

"Like I said, it was stupid. I—"

Heidi slumped forward. "I'm lying. I don't have any work to do. I was online searching for photos of John Stamos." She had the good grace to blush. "You remember that actor? I had the biggest crush on him." She shook her head. "This is what my life has come to, by the way."

The unexpected honesty threw off Katrine's guard, surprising her into tears. *You wanna talk about stupid lives? My own sister kicked me out of Faith Falls, and I think she was right that I could have come home earlier if I'd wanted to badly enough, and what sort of person does that make me?*

Heidi made her way around the desk, grabbing a handful of tissues.

"Don't cry, please. By the way, I have this effect on people. I'm a load of fun at parties." She handed Katrine the Kleenex and leaned back, pausing with her head tilted. "It must be quite an adjustment. Faith Falls after London, that is. Probably you have reverse culture shock. As in, you left culture, and now you're stuck here."

"You ever have problems with your family?" Katrine asked, her breath hitched. This close, Heidi's floral perfume enveloped her. "Problems so big that you don't think there's any starting over?"

"Oh, honey," Heidi said, her round cheeks split by a rueful grin. "Let me buy *you* a drink."

"Gawd, he's hot." Heidi took a swig of her third rum and diet cola, staring raptly at the lead singer of the 32-20 Blues Band as he belted out honey-smooth promises in his deep, husky voice. His incongruous cowboy hat only added to his sexiness. "And there's something wicked about him."

"Too wicked," Katrine said. The guy had been making eyes at her since they'd arrived. He was attractive, certainly, like a fuller-lipped, dark-eyed, swaggering Matthew McConaughey. But the more she watched him, the more Katrine sensed something alarming. It felt like he was looking *through* her. Plus, his eyes made her shorthairs stand at attention. They seemed almost jeweled. Anyhow, she was having too good a time with Heidi to think about men. The woman knew everyone in town and was not afraid to gossip. The only off-limits topic seemed to be her divorce.

"*Too* wicked? Is there such a thing?" Heidi held her nearly empty drink up to the waitress, signaling for another. "You want a refill?" she asked Katrine.

She glanced at her glass of red wine, her first and only. It was still half full. "Sure. Why not?"

She spotted a familiar face at the bar, the owner of Perfume River. She didn't know the woman's name but had talked with her plenty of times back when she was in high school. It was the best food in town. But that's not why she was staring at her. She squinted . . . yep. The woman had that glow, the marker indicating she'd visited Ursula in the recent past. She was also staring at the singer with a naked yearning that was hard to witness, which surprised Katrine. She'd always thought the restaurant owner was happily married. Guess you never knew. She returned her attention to Heidi, who was swaying in her seat as the band started playing a sexy, sultry song with a drumbeat that thumped pleasantly in Katrine's lower stomach.

"You know why my mom hates your mom so much?" Heidi asked around her straw.

Katrine raised an eyebrow. "Yeah, you told me. My mom seduced your dad."

Heidi snorted. "It wasn't just that. Apparently, they did it in your mom's car in the ValuCo parking lot. Her head was bopping up and down like she was riding a pogo stick." Katrine winced, but Heidi kept talking. "I think that's what got to Dagmar more than anything. The position. I suspect she's purely a missionary-style woman."

Katrine was trying to decide how to respond when Heidi caught her off guard. "It was around that time that she became convinced your mom killed your grandpa, you know. Probably easier to get mad at that than at my dad."

Katrine had heard the rumor. Everyone in Faith Falls had. Only problem was Ursula had been thirteen years old when her father ran off, too young to kill him *or* chase him away. Besides, Katrine could say a lot of bad things about her mom, but she was no killer.

Heidi covered a burp. "Is there anyone in this town your mom hasn't slept with, by the way?"

Katrine sighed. She'd been mortified by her mom's behavior when she was growing up. Now it just annoyed her. Rather than crawl in those weeds, she tried to change the subject. "What about your mom? What's she like?" Katrine reached for her glass. "Other than her favorite sexual position, that is."

Heidi leaned forward. "Imagine if Imelda Marcos, Hitler, and Tammy Faye Bakker had a threesome." She sat back, nodding. "Dagmar Baum is the love child of that unholy union."

Katrine spit a mouthful of wine back into the glass. "She can't be that bad!"

"Worse," Heidi said emphatically. "So maybe you should think before you whine. Someone always has it crappier than you do."

Katrine thought of Ren, and the perspective he'd given her on her heartbreak without even planning to. "You're right. Want to dance?"

"Love to." Heidi's hands floated in the air, waving to the music. "Just don't block my view of that hot singer."

Katrine glanced at the guy again and shivered. His cowboy hat was now pushed low over his eyes, and despite her trepidation, the way he smiled when he caught her stare made her tingle in body parts that she thought she'd put into storage. She couldn't tell if it was because his attention made her feel appreciated or hunted, but in either case, she was beginning to fantasize about what sort of lover he'd be—rough, she bet—when the restaurant owner suddenly moved in front of her. She was dancing with a woman with gorgeous locs who also emanated the Ursula glow.

Katrine was used to seeing the shine of her mother's gift around town but had never seen it so focused. It was almost like the two women were intentionally trying to come between her and the band. Now that she was looking for it, Katrine saw that the man in the cowboy hat had a glow, too, only it was purple, like someone had thrown a cup of blood into the blue shine of her mother's gift.

Katrine danced to the side so she could see the singer better. She found herself being drawn to him despite her better instincts. He was just so damn good-looking, with that cocky grin. She was familiar with his type and assumed she was done with it. Still, she felt her hips grow looser and was considering moving nearer the stage when she was jostled so hard that she spilled part of her drink. She glanced over to see the Perfume River owner dancing next to her yet again.

"So sorry," the woman said.

"That's okay," Katrine responded, shaking the wine off her hand. Her eyes were immediately drawn back to the lead singer, along with nearly every other woman's. He pushed his hat back with this thumb, and suddenly, Katrine felt herself locked into the tractor beam of his stare, his lips moving as he sang just for her. The band had transitioned from blues to something a little faster, the singer's growl dripping with sex, driven by a grinding, dirty guitar riff. A woman near the stage actually moaned.

"Did you hear that?" Heidi asked, dancing alongside her and lost in laughter. "See what happens in a small town as repressed as this one? A little music turns everything into an orgy."

But Katrine couldn't pull her attention away from the music being woven around her, coursing through her blood on a warm bass beat, pulsing with the sultry, sensuous pound of the drums, circling, circling with guitar, and driven home hot on the lead singer's voice. He was crooning about the best woman he ever met, his eyes locked on Katrine's, and for a moment, irrationally, she wanted to *be* that woman. She began dancing toward the stage, a fish on a line, moving her hips to match the beat that was building toward climax, feeling every lick of the guitar on her flesh.

"Katrine?" Heidi grabbed her wrist, her face puzzled. "Where are you going?"

Katrine yanked her wrist loose, the thick, hot music filling her ears and guiding her forward. The singer's wolfish smile grew wider, and he tipped his hat low again and began to thrust with the beat. Another woman moaned, but he had eyes only for Katrine, hungry, glittering.

She would have made it to the stage except the restaurant owner was back, this time colliding with such force that she knocked the glass fully out of Katrine's hands, spilling red wine down the front of her dress. Had her mother spelled these women to cockblock her?

"Oh! I'm so clumsy!" The woman appeared upset enough to cry. "I wrecked your dress!"

The music immediately grew quieter, flatter, now just notes and words, the spell broken. Katrine shook her head, dazed. The woman with locs rushed over to Katrine's side. "Shoot, I hate it when that happens! Wine, right? Let me help you get it off. I used to work at a dry cleaner."

She led Katrine toward the bathroom. Heidi followed, dancing the whole way.

"He's all yours," Katrine said, nodding over her shoulder toward the lead singer. She'd need to find out what kind of red wine they served here. It must be powerful stuff. "I'm done with trouble."

Chapter 24

Tara

Tara had caught only snippets of the post-lasagna conversation between Katrine and her mom, but she didn't need to know the details to see how it'd affected the pain in both women. Their wounds had flared up, but then, the strangest thing happened.

They each healed an infinitesimal amount.

Not the wound itself, but the infection around it. As painful as the conversation had sounded, they'd both released a little poison as a result of it. That left more room for good stuff in Jasmine. Not a lot, but enough for her to make scratch pizza, the first time ever in Tara's memory.

"This is delicious, Mom!"

Jasmine smiled, and it had a new flavor. There was sadness in it, but also relief.

Tara jumped up from the table and hugged her, the gesture spontaneous. "I'm glad Katrine is in town. She makes everything better."

Jasmine chose that moment to close up, so Tara couldn't read her. Still, something good was happening, Tara could almost taste it, which was why she was so disoriented when her own scream woke her from a deep sleep that night.

Her body shot upright before her eyes had a chance to snap open, blankets as tight as a noose around her, blood roaring in her ears, breath shallow and harsh. Blinking rapidly, she made out shapes: A chair holding her favorite childhood doll. Her dresser, found at a garage sale and redone by her mom. The window to their backyard tire swing, the one she'd played in since she was a toddler and only just recently grown too big for.

So why was she scared? She squeezed her eyes closed again, and she saw it.

Her grandma Ursula, her heart broken loose from her chest and squeezed inside a small jar, Tara's own mother holding the glass.

A black-eyed man in a cowboy hat.

And snakes. Dear Lord, there were so many snakes.

They were speaking, a slithering of wet tongues and dry skin scraping against one another.

Not one of you can stop me.

Part 2

The Echo

The Blackthorn Book of Secrets: Digging

Pain makes a convincing treasure if you cradle it long enough, tucking away shame like silver, grief like gemstones, secrets like gold coins. But no matter how carefully you bury sorrow, it rots. And rot spreads.

If you find yourself returning to the same patch of earth—whether in your garden or your memory—don't plant more pain there. Dig. Unearth what you've hidden. Hold it to the light, ugly and trembling.

Then release it. The only thing worse than a buried secret is what it grows into if left in the dark.

Chapter 25

Ursula

Winter landed like a fist.

Today was 34 degrees below zero, a temperature that either crushed your spirit or turned it to steel. A local joke had it that if you whistled in air this cold, your music would freeze on your lips and drop to the ground as note-shaped ice cubes, which would pop and thaw in a chorus come spring.

Ursula was undeterred.

She stepped into the predawn darkness bundled in scarves, a thick pair of mittens, and layers of fleece and down. Three minutes' exposure would kill bare flesh, turn it as black as the plague, yet temperatures this cold also produced an enchanted snow globe world, if you knew where to look.

But Ursula didn't have time for wonder. She had to hurry to reach the end of the sidewalk in time. Hard-packed snow squeaked beneath her boots, the piercing sound of the earth crying out. Overhead, prismatic icicles dangled from the streetlamps and refracted light in kaleidoscopic patterns of yellow and white. The air smelled bleach clean. She barely made it to her post before the sun began to rise. At first, it was a rich orange-gold, followed by otherworldly purples and magentas and then tangerines the higher it rose, until it rested in the sky as if it'd always been there.

Ursula hadn't missed a sunrise since the day she'd poisoned her father. She'd made the dawn her confessor, then sought absolution in actual church. She'd kept up the ritual even after Katrine came home. She was surprised at how quickly they'd all merged into a comfortable pattern, Katrine working for the paper and spending more and more time with Jasmine; Xenia and Helena running their store; Tara preparing for her Christmas recital.

And dare Ursula believe that she'd managed to send the curse on its way? She'd worked every spell she could since that snake had shown up on her doorstep last August. Could things finally be peaceful for the Blackthorns?

She crunched and squeaked her way to Our Lady of the Lakes Catholic Church, entering through the unadorned side door. It'd never been locked in all the years she'd been visiting.

The interior was heavy with the scent of frankincense and the clack-thump of her boots across marble. She unwound layers of winter gear as she walked to the vestibule, lighting a votive candle from the flickering wick of another one. She whispered a prayer for her mother, sisters, two daughters, and granddaughter. None of them knew where she went in the mornings, nor would they understand why. She wasn't sure even she knew, except that she'd found herself wandering around after that last night with Charlie Tanager, and going inside Our Lady of the Lakes had offered comfort.

Velda had always warned her off religion, made her believe churches were a terrifying place, but Ursula's jaw had dropped when she first saw how beautiful this one was inside. It had a stunning bronze baldachin over the main altar, supported by six columns of black-and-gold marble. The sapphire, ruby, and emerald stained glass flooded the sanctuary with a divine light, and the statue of Mary looked like she was reaching out to sustain whoever entered. When Ursula first slid into one of the polished wooden pews, she'd felt held.

She'd returned every morning since—to this house of worship or another, if she was traveling—always attending in secret. It didn't matter so much to her what denomination it was. Lutheran, Jewish, Catholic, Baptist, Islamic. She was after not the sermon but the hush. In addition to praying for her family, she begged for help in erasing the memory of Charlie Tanager's curse and forgiving herself. The forgiveness never came, so she always moved quickly to a mother's plea, the only one that mattered: *Please don't make my children pay for my mistakes.*

She made her way to the front pew, dipping her knee and crossing herself before entering. The wood was warm and worn. She pulled out the kneeling bench and leaned forward. Bowing her head, she slid a pink quartz rosary from her pocket. The cross hung over the back of her hand, a flaccid thing. She'd bought it at the apothecary, having no idea why she desired it. She never entered a church without it, though, massaging each bead in turn, releasing the secret scent of lavender, emptying her mind as she moved from one cool stone to the next.

She finished her meditation and stood, feeling oddly, pleasantly weightless. She walked the two miles home, entering her car rather than her house when she arrived. The Toyota was parked in the garage and had its core heater plugged in, but it still took some coaxing to turn over. She let it warm for ten minutes before unplugging it from the wall and backing out. She drove for forty miles, to the outskirts of Alexandria, and pulled into the motel lot. His car was in front of room 23. She parked alongside it.

The room door was unlocked. She stepped through, closing her eyes and taking in his scent. She stood like that, leaning against the door, until he spoke.

"I didn't know if you'd come," he said.

She opened her eyes, glancing toward the bed. He was stretched out on it, a book open on his lap. His expression was both pained and hopeful. There was none of the guilty excitement she'd gotten used to in other men. She sloughed off her layers as she walked toward him, mittens here, scarf there, parka falling to the ground like shed skin.

It had taken many private meetings to convince Michael Baum to meet her here this morning, promises of discretion, of anarchy, of orgasms that would crack his spine. She knew he didn't love her and that he never would. She was aware that he did love Dagmar, even if she didn't reciprocate.

Dagmar *would* love him again, once Ursula was done with him. She would make sure of it.

Out of her winter clothes, she tugged off her shirt. The move was practical, not sensuous. She unzipped her pants and dropped them to the floor. He watched her eyes as she advanced, not even looking away when she stepped out of her panties. She sat on the bed, putting her hand on his zipper and opening his trousers. She reached for him confidently and leaned forward to put him in her mouth. He groaned. The noise excited her, and she took him deeper. His hips bucked.

"Ursula," he whispered. He wound his hands through her hair, grabbing one of her full breasts. "Jesus, Ursula. I've needed you."

And that was why she'd come.

In the winter of her heart, it was the closest she'd ever come to feeling loved.

Chapter 26

Katrine

"You don't think it's too cold?" Jasmine asked.

"It's always too cold," Katrine responded. "It's Minnesota."

They stood on the edge of the rink. It'd taken every bit of Katrine's persuasive power to coax her sister to the ice. As children, they'd owned one set of skates between them, every year a new pair as their feet grew but only one because money was tight. They hadn't been deterred. They spent two or three days a week at the Faith Falls public rink. They'd finish their homework, grab the skates, and walk the mile downtown, then take turns gliding across the ice, cheering each other from the sidelines.

Katrine had been trying to get Jasmine out of the house weekly since she'd thrown up on her carpeting. The horror she'd witnessed that day—the vivid orange shame—haunted her. Jasmine wouldn't give up that secret, and Katrine needed her to. It was The Thing that stood between them, Katrine now knew it for a fact, and she missed her connection with Jasmine like a limb.

It was almost with a sense of desperation that Jasmine turned Katrine down every time. Today, however, she'd finally agreed. Velda had taken Tara shopping, giving Jasmine nothing to hide behind. Katrine had dragged her straight here.

The rink was packed with skaters. Ice shavings sparkled where blades bit deep, and bright laughter threaded through the cold, slipping under collars and into gloves.

"I don't remember how to skate," Jasmine said for the twentieth time.

"Like riding a bike." Katrine strode to the warming house, and Jasmine had no choice but to follow. "Hey, should we rent a single set, just like old times?"

Jasmine smiled, and the sun rose for Katrine. She took a chance. "Jasmine—"

"No," her sister said quietly.

Katrine stopped, her mouth open, but Jasmine's tone was clear: She would leave if they talked about the past. So Katrine entered the warming house, waited her turn, and handed the teenage boy behind the counter a ten-dollar bill when they reached the front of the line. "Two size 8s."

She waited until they were alone in the warming house to come at it from a different angle. "Just answer one thing: Is this . . . thing, this memory . . . is it why you started taking the antidepressants? And can you tell me why you sent me away rather than give me a chance to help?"

Jasmine sighed. It was an echo of a sound. "That's two questions. Let's skate."

Katrine followed her onto the ice. She started out wobbly, but soon muscle memory returned. It wasn't long before she was skating around the edges, relishing the sensation of flying on frozen water, air prickling her cheeks and reminding her she was alive, balanced on the exquisite equilibrium of a skate blade.

She glanced at her sister gliding alongside her and was surprised by the Christmas Day smile on Jasmine's face. Katrine almost cried for the beauty of it. She reached for Jasmine's mittened hand, and they skated like that, two sisters against the world, at least for the moment.

"Did you hear that Ursula is sleeping with Michael?" Jasmine asked once they'd taken a break to buy a couple hot chocolates. "Michael Baum?"

"Heidi's dad?" Katrine asked. "I knew they had forever ago. Are they at it again?"

"Yup. Dean saw their cars parked side by side at the 'L' Motel in Alexandria."

"Christ." Katrine was mortified. Why couldn't their mother be more discreet?

"If Dagmar finds out their affair has started back up," Jasmine said, "she's going to come after us."

"Us?" Katrine raised her eyebrows. She tried it on for size and found it fit. She *was* feeling like a Blackthorn again, bit by bit. She took a sip of her hot chocolate, remembering the creamy drink Jasmine used to make from cocoa powder, real vanilla syrup, sugar, whole milk, and fresh-ground cinnamon. Drinking it used to make Jasmine and Katrine giggle so hard that one time Katrine peed her pants. She missed Jasmine's magic with a pain like heartbreak, but she suspected that for Jasmine to reclaim that power would mean reclaiming the memory of what had happened to her.

"Yeah, us," Jasmine said, not picking up on the significance. "What bothers me most about Ursula is that she doesn't have any scruples. She'll sleep with anyone."

Katrine nodded, trying to distance herself from her mother, just as she'd always done. "Guess that hasn't changed. Want another spin around the rink?"

"You won't try to play crack the whip?"

Katrine made an X across her chest. "Cross my heart."

Chapter 27

Tara

"Your mom and dad are coming to Ursula's for Christmas?" Velda asked.

She'd taken her great-granddaughter Christmas shopping every year since Tara was old enough to use a toilet. It was ostensibly for Velda to help her pick out presents for the entire family, but given the number of questions she asked, Tara suspected it was more of an annual fishing trip.

Tara pretended to study a hangnail. "Yep."

Velda nodded. "Think you'll all stay around longer than usual this year?"

Tara dropped her hand and stared out her window. Because her great-grandma drove a '73 Mercury Cougar, there was enough space between them to strap in a Christmas tree. Today the distance felt emotional as well as physical. "I think so."

She didn't want to jinx it, but her mom had been steadily growing happier than Tara had ever seen her, the swollen, gory inner wound she'd erected a brick wall around shrinking in tiny increments, the bricks themselves growing less volatile. Her dad hadn't moved back in, but he'd started sharing meals with them. Everything really did seem better with Katrine in town. The sky was brighter, food was tastier, laughter healed more deeply. Tara not only loved Katrine, she wanted to *be* Katrine.

And she worried that if she let anyone know how happy she'd been since her aunt came back, it'd all be snatched away from her.

"What aren't you telling me?" Velda asked.

Tara shrugged. She knew her great-grandma wouldn't let up until she gave her something. "The wall around Mom's heart doesn't look as red as it used to, like it's not so hot to the touch. It's been cooling a little bit every day since Katrine and Mom had a fight at our house last August."

Velda nodded. When Tara had confessed to her that she could see into the center of each person's greatest pain, Velda had one request: *Don't tell me what you see inside me.* Tara knew Velda preferred to look outward rather than in, and that perspective seemed to have served her just fine.

"Maybe she's cooking up something new in there," Velda said, tapping her chest, "something that doesn't require as much heat."

Tara returned to studying her fingernails.

Velda flicked on her turn signal. "You know where we're going?"

"Christmas shopping."

"Yes," Velda said, smothering both lanes as she turned right. "To Seven Daughters. I imagine you're old enough now for one of Xenia's dresses."

Tara's eyes widened, and she tugged at her hand-me-down winter jacket. Underneath, she was wearing a too-large snap-button shirt over too-short Wrangler jeans. All the clothes she had disguised her body to the point that some people thought she was a boy. "Mom won't let me."

"Pfft. You let me handle Jasmine." Velda tossed her a sly smile. "I was thinking we should pick up a dress for her, too. Think Xenia does rush orders?"

Tara closed her eyes and saw a universe of chartreuse, gold, and cream where before there'd only been shades of gray. "At Christmastime?" She shook her head. "Besides, Mom would never buy a Xenia dress. Too expensive."

"She wouldn't be the one paying for it, would she?"

They circled Elm Street four times until they located two empty spots front to back, big enough for the Cougar. The air was too cold for snow today, and it was clear enough that Tara could see the blue of the air when walking through it. The downtown bustled with cheerful shoppers. No store looked busier than Seven Daughters.

As they made their way toward it, people stopped in their tracks when they spotted Velda, hoping to catch her eye and exchange a word with her. Tara watched her great-grandma's Blackthorn gift at work, blooming around her like warm light, making each person in its reach feel singular and treasured. Tara would never grow used to how much each interaction cost her great-grandma, how each time Velda encountered another person, she had to tuck her spirit in a cupboard so she could give all the space to them. She did it for everyone except Ursula.

"Hello, Linda! How's your granddaughter? Wonderful! Oh yes, Seven Daughters *is* the best-kept secret in town. You can bet I'm proud of all my girls." She kept up a steady stream of chatter as they entered the store, which was so packed that they had to gently touch people's backs to get them to make room.

"To the kitchen," Velda called over her shoulder.

Tara loved the clamor, the shoppers' festive chatter, the scents of gingerbread and honey. Turned out she hadn't been party to any great reveals the night she'd helped out with the canning class—other than learning how to process tomatoes—but she still loved coming here. She followed Velda to the kitchen, expecting to see a flurry of activity as Helena scrambled to keep up with her holiday orders. She couldn't hold back the gasp when they entered.

Velda also stopped in her tracks. "What in the name of Peace is going on back here?"

The kitchen where Helena crafted her artisanal candies was as packed as the store floor. Eight women and two men wore full-on aprons and chef's hats, holding tubes of frosting and pots of sugar sprinkles. Make that eight women, one man, and a teenage boy.

Helena separated herself from the cookie-decorating group. In her apron, she appeared as round and cheery as Betty Crocker. "Hi, Velda. And Tara!" She hurried over to hug her great-niece, gesturing behind her. "This is the second-to-the-last of our End Times classes, only we're taking a break from the conclusion of the world to bake Christmas cookies." She chucked Tara's chin.

Velda smiled toward the tall man with big ears who was speckling a pan of gingerbread stars with edible glitter. "Who's he?"

Helena glanced over. "Ren Cunningham. He owns the watch store next door."

"Easy on the eyes, right?" Velda nudged Tara, trying to get her to look at Ren.

Tara jerked and flushed. She cut her eyes to the floor, but it was too late. Both her great-aunt and her great-grandma had caught her staring not at the tall man but rather at the teenage boy. He was gangly and loose-jointed, his nose dusted with flour. Tara was sure he must smell like cookies up close, and the thought made her blush an even deeper scarlet.

"Tara, do you want to meet Leo?" Helena asked. "He's our helper. You two are about the same age, I think."

Tara shook her head, and her golden hair fell into her eyes. She mumbled something about wanting to look at dresses and ran toward the kitchen door so fast that she upset a tray of pfeffernüsse. The clattering drew the attention of the cookie makers, and Leo glanced up, locking eyes with Tara for just a moment before the door swung closed behind her.

Velda took Tara for cheeseburgers and hot fudge malts at the A&W before driving her back to Jasmine. "You know, it smells like love is in the air," Velda said when they were within minutes of Tara's house.

Tara scrunched lower in her seat. She'd managed to avoid any sort of meaningful conversation with her great-grandmother since she'd laid eyes on Leo. She was confused by the rush of emotions she felt, and she wanted to be alone in her room to sort it all out. Surrounded by her stuffed animals and journal, she would make sense of this. She knew she was small and bony for her age, her hair a frizz-fest. Her elfin ears poked out on each side. They were pointy, like her nose and chin beneath her too-big owl eyes. Yet something about the way that boy had looked at her had made her feel beautiful.

"I sure wouldn't want to miss out," Velda continued.

Tara sat up, her curiosity winning over her instincts. "Are you in love with someone?"

Velda laughed. "Not me, child. I took a vow many years ago never to fall for love again. But it is fun to *be* loved. After spending the better part of this afternoon watching you pretend not to moon-pie over that boy at Seven Daughters, I have a hankering for some romance. I believe I'll stop by your grandma's for a potion before I head home."

Tara would remember the snow crunching under the Cougar's tires as they pulled into her driveway. It sounded like rabbits screaming. "Do you get elixirs from Grandma very often?"

Velda put the car into park. "Nope. This'll only be the second time."

Chapter 28

Ursula

Ursula had been shocked when Velda marched through the cottage door, knocking snow off her boots. Her mother had never visited her here.

Velda said only two words. "It's me."

Ursula stood behind the table where she'd been distilling anise, her blood running cold as the setting sun outlined her mother's petite shape. The air suddenly smelled like metal. Velda had requested only one other concoction from Ursula in her life, the poison that killed Charlie Tanager. "What do you want?"

Her smile held teeth. "What everyone wants when they come here."

Ursula wanted to say no. She needed to finally stand up to Velda. She was old enough, after all, had been her own person since she'd begun raising herself decades ago, but almost immediately, she felt the soothing comfort of Velda's charm wash over her. Velda so rarely used it on her that she found she was unable to resist her mother's full power even while being cognizant of the self-hatred burning through her veins.

Like most businesses, Ursula's was busy over the holidays. Love potions in particular were in demand. No one wanted to be alone for Christmas. Because she knew the truth of the cliché that you can't love someone else until you love yourself, most tinctures she sold were for self-love, though she'd never reveal that to her clients. They wanted someone else to complete them. So she kept the truth hidden, but not so secreted that they couldn't find it if they looked hard enough.

A rare exception was the elixir she began brewing for Velda.

Her mother was well versed enough in herbs to recognize a true love potion.

She shrank as she stirred the wild pink rose petals, clover honey, and brandywine under Velda's watchful eyes, a little girl who wasn't and never would be good enough. Ursula concentrated the liquids, strained the clear amber liquid into a blue jar, and corked it.

"Why do you need this at all?" Her voice sounded petulant even to herself. "Can't you just use your regular charm?"

Velda licked her lips. "This is an especially tough nut to crack. I think he might actually have true grit."

Ursula swallowed, her jaw set. "If he does, this won't work. But if there's so much as a crack in his core, and he drinks this and you're the next woman he sees, he'll be overcome with desire for you."

Velda nodded. "Exactly what I want." She put out her hand.

Ursula dropped the still-warm bottle into it. She didn't want to know the name of the man it was intended for. She consoled herself with the knowledge that at least this time it wasn't poison.

When Velda left, Ursula felt wrong and ugly, so she opened the *Book of Secrets*. Despite her turning to the first page, the book fell open in the middle, the borders hand-painted with tiny lavender and pink petals threaded with finger-shaped leaves of dark emerald. The writing was elegant.

Blackthorn Book of Secrets: Rue

Rue is a natural remedy for negativity. Dried rue tied in a red bag and hung over your door will dispel bad luck and welcome powerful good.

Ursula said a word of thanks. Leaving the book open, she strode to her wall of drawers and opened the third from the left, seventh from the top. She pulled out a sprig of rue, wrapped it in a scrap of red velvet, and bound it with a golden cord. She dragged a chair to the cottage's entrance and opened the door. A frigid gust of air tried to enter, confronted the peppery, witchy wall of heat inside the cottage, and retreated.

Before Ursula could climb onto the chair, she spotted a woman picking her way down the snow-packed path to the workshop, moving like her skin was the only thing keeping her bones in place.

Ursula was still feeling unsettled from Velda's visit. "Yes?" she said impatiently.

The woman stopped, her eyes afraid but her posture resolute. Her face was bland, as if it were missing glasses, and her ears stuck out like teapot handles. "Ursula Blackthorn?"

"Yes?" Ursula repeated. She ran her hand over her hair, realizing that a stalk of rue had found its way behind her ear. She tugged it out.

"My husband and I are new to town. Name's Merry. We live over in the Havership Development?" She blinked rapidly, like she had something in her eyes. "I've heard about you but don't really need a spell. I was just driving and got lost, and your lights back here were the only ones on."

The Queen Anne was dark at the moment, but Ursula had no doubt the lights had been on before. Damned house. It'd conspired with the night to send this woman to her. Merry was clearly the worst kind of client, a person who needed help but wasn't willing to come out and ask for it.

"I'll get you," Ursula said to the house in a tired voice.

The woman glanced over her shoulder, confused but not frightened. "Who are you talking to?"

"No one. I was just making some tea. Would you care to join me?" You could only assist those who asked for it, but there were tricks for hurrying them to that point.

"I really should be going," the woman said without conviction. "I was on my way to a class. It starts in twenty minutes."

Ursula didn't move a muscle.

"But I suppose, if the water's hot . . ."

Ursula always had hot water ready. She pulled the chair out of the way so the woman could enter, closing the door behind her. A bit of winter caught in the space between jamb and door, making an angry squeak. She stepped over to grab peppermint leaves from their drawer, then two mugs from a high shelf.

"Are you also a chemist?" the woman asked, staring at the wall of bottles and the labeled drawers. Ursula's worktable was covered with three hot plates, knives, pots of oil and alcohol, and above all that towered intricate glass tubing leading to beakers shimmering with liquids.

Ursula poured steaming water from a beaker into each of the mugs, not answering the question. Her guest would see what she wanted to see. She handed her a mug, then reached for honey and squirted a dollop into her tea before offering it to Merry. "You and your husband enjoying Faith Falls?"

"Yes." Merry accepted the honey, eyes downcast. "But he wouldn't approve of me being here."

Ursula immediately understood from the woman's tone. "Here" was not a specific place; rather, it was anywhere he wasn't. "What do you need the most?"

The question worked as a lancet, piercing the woman's protection and letting the words flow hot. "I was bedbound for a whole year when I was sixteen. I'll never get that year back. I think it would have been my favorite. They say your wedding is the best day of your life, but I wished I'd been sick for mine instead of back when I was sixteen, sick and young with my mom to feed me soup. It's not that my husband is *bad*. He likes to keep me close, sure, but he's got this energy. He's the red in my gray." She shivered. "He's always been that way, grabbing life and letting it know who's boss. But he lost his job, and we had to move, and I don't know anyone here, and I thought, just maybe, that I could do something for myself." She squeezed her mug so hard Ursula worried it might crack. "I lied to him and told him I was going to check out an evening service at the Catholic church so I could escape to this class I really want to take."

Ursula realized what it was about the woman's face that seemed off. It wasn't that she was bland, not exactly. Rather, there was an asymmetrical, unnatural smoothness to her, as if someone had broken every bone in her face and reset it from memory. "You want to make some red of your own?" Ursula asked.

Merry nodded into her tea. Her hands were shaking. "Can you help me?" Her voice was a husk, a tender slip of dried paper offered to a world that had burned her.

Ursula couldn't take her eyes off the pudding of the woman's face. "Yes."

In the end, she gave the woman a placebo. She needed permission, not a spell. That's all she gave most of her clients: permission to use their own magic.

The Blackthorn Book of Secrets: The Law of Helping Others

Only enter a house through an open door. There are always windows, or locks to be broken, but if the door isn't open, it's not time to enter. This is the same when helping others. You can provide help only when it's asked for. The rest of the time, all you can give is love.

Chapter 29

TARA

Tara was delighted to spend the first part of Christmas Eve helping her aunts arrange the nativity scene on the front porch. Xenia had received the half-scale set in exchange for a shimmering periwinkle dress she'd crafted by sewing strips of beads onto a simple jersey pattern. According to Xenia, the customer who gave her the nativity scene had been staring at the dress through Seven Daughters' front window for weeks, until Xenia invited her in. After much cajoling, the woman confessed that her beloved daughter was getting married, but she was a single mother who'd spent all her limited income on the wedding and had nothing left over for herself.

Xenia had been waiting for the owner of the dress to show up since she'd sewn it three years earlier. It would be a relief to get it off her hands. She'd have been just as happy to give it away, but the woman insisted on some form of payment. When she revealed that she was an artist who specialized in carving, painting, and clothing realistic sculptures, they'd agreed upon the nativity scene exchange.

"While not Christian," Xenia told Tara as she pulled the cradle out of a box, "I enjoy a good diorama as much as the next person." She glanced over at Helena, who was leaning over one of the wooden donkeys, gray faux fur glued to its body. "What are you doing, anyhow?"

"I'm brushing it," Helena said.

"You aren't supposed to brush donkeys," Xenia scoffed.

Helena poohed her. "You don't know that. Have you ever owned a donkey?"

"Of course. I'm a wise woman." Xenia indicated the robes she'd worn in case any carolers stopped by. She and Helena had brewed mulled cider and had insulated cups ready to distribute. "I know all there is to know about donkeys."

"Well, then you know they need to be brushed. A lot."

Tara smiled. So did the Queen Anne, and it sounded like an ice snap on a winter lake. The three of them would have jumped if they weren't used to the house's peccadilloes.

Tara loved the Queen Anne, always had. It managed to be big but cozy, lush, sentient. When she was inside it, her powers expanded, and she thought that must be true of all the Blackthorns. For Tara's part, she was able to share the Queen Anne's perspective when she was inside the house, seeing and hearing what everyone on the property was doing. If the other people weren't on guard, she could also read their hopes and fears, taste the sweet-salt of their memories. It was glorious.

She decided her aunts had all the hands they needed, so she made her way into the kitchen. Ursula was peeking inside the double oven and releasing a perfume of baking bread and roasting turkey.

"Hey, Tara," Katrine said, appearing in the kitchen from the opposite door. "You sure you don't need help with the turkey, Mom?"

Ursula had invited Jasmine to cook with her this year, as she did every Christmas. When she turned her down, as she always did, Ursula had said she wanted to prepare the feast on her own. She wouldn't even allow Helena to help. She'd stuffed the turkey with pearl onions, lemons, and sage. She'd already baked a ham drizzled in honey and spiked with cloves, its glaze crackling into a golden crust as it rested on the counter. Her cornbread dressing was bursting with slivered sweetbreads and almonds, velvety, crunchy, and comforting. The center island was lined with three different kinds of salads, cream for peas, candied yams glazed with browned butter, and six kinds of pie: pumpkin, cherry, mincemeat, apple, lemon meringue, and French silk. Tara knew that none of her grandma's magic aided her in cooking, but she poured all the love she had for her family into the meal, hoping they'd recognize it.

Ursula wasn't aware of this, of course. She simply cooked.

"I'm fine," Ursula replied, her face shiny. The kitchen was 10 degrees warmer than any room in the house. "You can relax."

Tara could tell that Katrine *was* relaxing. In fact, she was happy. It didn't mean she was healed, or that she'd gotten Jasmine to share the details of the event so horrible that she'd cast a spell to push Katrine away, but it did mean she was building something in Faith Falls. Not a life, exactly, but a safe resting spot. On top of slowly reconnecting with Jasmine, Katrine had grown close to Tara—it delighted Tara to hear her aunt think this—taking her out for day trips to window-shop, or grab lunch at Perfume River or Mort's Diner, or sneak a makeover at the Herberger's counter that they'd scrub off their faces before returning home. It felt like stolen time to Katrine, a way she could rescue Tara if not Jasmine.

She was also grudgingly enjoying working for the newspaper. She'd been out with Heidi a handful of times and believed they were building a friendship. There wasn't a morning she didn't wake up thinking of Adam, didn't wish he'd show up and whisk her away to the life they'd once shared, but reaching out to Jasmine made that ache less. In fact, every minute she spent in her sister's company felt like balm.

There was a commotion at the front door, and Tara and Katrine left the kitchen to see what it was.

"I'm here!" Velda called, a Santa hat perched atop her head. "Merry Christmas!"

Audish followed, pausing to tap the snow off his boots before removing Velda's coat.

"We'll eat as soon as Jasmine and Dean arrive," Ursula said, appearing through the swinging kitchen door holding a bowl of bacon vinegar salad. The tangy, salty scent curled into the corners of the room. "They let Tara come early to help and said they'd be here by seven."

"I'm going to grab something out of my room," Katrine said.

Tara was charmed as the Queen Anne pictured Katrine's calliope giggles as a girl, her knees always covered in bandages, the risks she took. The house had also borne witness to Jasmine's tragedy, Jasmine with her serious ways and magnificent heart, though it kept those details close to its chest. It wasn't the first time something had been stolen under its roof. Over the years, the house had witnessed how this world wounded girls and then stared down its nose at them as they shopped for clothes big enough to cover their scars, or looked away in distaste as they danced the jerky scarecrow dance of survival.

The house didn't judge, it observed.

"Do we have to wait?" Velda asked, bringing Tara's attention back into the room.

The doorbell answered her. The room tensed for a moment.

Jasmine had arrived.

Chapter 30

Tara

"Mom!" Tara exclaimed, looking at the dish her mother carried. "You made green bean casserole."

Jasmine's smile was tentative. Dean had his hand at the small of her back and urged her forward, Helena and Xenia on his heels. He'd agreed to join them for Christmas even though he was still living in his apartment. "Thank you for inviting us," he said.

"It'll only take ten minutes to crisp the french-fried onions in the oven," Jasmine said. She was beaming, her cheeks rosy with joy, but Tara could tell her mom was nervous. "Where should we put the presents?"

Ursula's heart was so full it echoed in Tara's ears. She'd have her whole family under her roof for Christmas. She'd known it, but until Jasmine had appeared, she hadn't trusted it. She accepted the green bean casserole and turned so no one could see her naked expression. "Make yourselves comfortable," she called over her shoulder. "Dinner in ten."

Helena asked Audish to help her run around the back of the house to gather a last bale of hay for the nativity scene. Tara was delighted to see the two of them were spending more time together.

After hugging the new arrivals, Xenia took off her boots and coat and went to put in a Christmas CD. Frank Sinatra singing "O Little

Town of Bethlehem" followed her back into the dining room, where everyone stood around in quiet awkwardness.

That's when Katrine returned from her room.

Tara could feel how enthralled Katrine was with the idea of being with her sister at Christmas. The thought was a kernel, budding green energy taking root just below her stomach, igniting a memory of the Christmas of 1976. Katrine had received a Lifelike Baby and Jasmine had gotten a Sears Holiday II typewriter. It was funny because Katrine had grown up to be the writer and Jasmine the mom. Katrine wondered whether it was those gifts, or their lives, that were switched.

"Come and eat!" Velda hollered.

Helena and Audish hurried inside, everyone performing a clumsy shuffle until they'd all found their seats.

"Dean would like to say grace," Jasmine said once everyone was settled.

Dean appeared surprised to hear this, but he moved ahead. Tara kept one eye open so she could watch how everyone responded. Velda didn't stop scooping creamed peas over her mashed potatoes, but the rest of the guests crossed their hands and dipped their heads until Dean finished.

"Amen," he said.

"Thank you for coming," Ursula said in a quiet voice at the end of the blessing, her eyes on Jasmine. "Tara mentioned you might be staying later than usual."

Tara held her breath.

"Maybe," Jasmine said. "We have our own family tradition, usually."

Ursula flexed as if warding off a blow. "I'm sorry to intrude on your tradition."

Velda snorted. "Those words were meant to be a door, not a shield, Ursula. You can be gracious, can't you? Now pass the rolls."

Tara saw her mother tense in response to the spark of tension, ready to bolt. Their "tradition" had been to come to Ursula's, have an uncomfortable Christmas dinner, and then return home to her mother moping as they sat around their own small tree, a sad relative to the magnificent fir in the Queen Anne's den.

She'd held out hope that her mom would continue to heal, the bricks around her trauma continuing to cool and crumble. It was going that direction, but Tara was hyperaware that it could all be robbed from her at any minute. She was desperate to change the feel of the room.

"Aunt Katrine, Mom said that one Christmas you two stayed up late to see Santa Claus," Tara began, the words tumbling out in a worried heap. "She said you rigged up a Polaroid camera so in case you fell asleep, he'd trip the wire and it would snap a picture of him." She looked to her mom for support, but her eyes were trained on her plate. Tara continued, her voice less sure. "Said you both crashed out before eleven, and the next morning, the Polaroid had taken a picture, but you couldn't find the snapshot anywhere."

The house remembered that night. Both girls had fallen asleep by ten thirty, sooty at the edges from crawling into the cool fireplace to set up the trip wire. If they'd been awake when the photo was taken, they would have witnessed a frozen moment of Ursula setting out presents and covering her girls with a handsewn quilt before retiring to bed.

"I think that was your idea," Katrine said to Jasmine, knowing it wasn't. She held her breath. Teasing Jasmine when she was so obviously fragile could go either way.

Jasmine tensed, then snorted. "Anything trouble was always your idea."

Katrine's relief was palpable, as was Tara's. Katrine moved the ball forward. "What about the time one of us wanted to sleep on the roof during a full moon?"

Jasmine's eyes grew wide, despite herself. She flashed a worried glance at Dean. "I forgot about that. Can you believe how stupid that was?"

"I don't know," Katrine said. "I thought it was pretty cool."

Tara followed her aunt through the memory. The frogs had roused Katrine that summer night, singing an urgent song outside her window.

She'd slipped out of bed, intending to crawl next to Jasmine like she did whenever she awoke out of sorts. When she couldn't find her, she searched the whole third floor before spotting the sheet tucked into the rooftop window. She'd peeked down at the ground seventy feet below. She knew if she hesitated that she'd never go, so she held her breath and curled her toes onto the edges of the dormer and inched out, not daring to glance down.

On the other side of the sloped roof, she'd swung a leg and arm over, trusting there'd be something to grab on to. There was. She found herself on the widow's walk, Jasmine wide awake and staring at stars that seemed close enough to pluck. Katrine lay next to her, and they'd passed the night there, neither saying a word.

The corners of Jasmine's mouth curled unpleasantly, and Tara went statue still. "Speaking of cool," Jasmine said, "remember high school? You were so popular. Heidi still talks about it."

Katrine dropped her fork with such force that it took a chip out of her plate. She barked a laugh. "Heidi hated me back then. And except for a couple of girls who hung around because I could get them into the theater for free, I was as popular as crabs in school."

"Really, Katrine," Jasmine said. Her voice was dismissive.

"*Really*, Jasmine."

"You know, I think I'll have some of that wine," Jasmine said.

This drew Dean's attention, though only for a moment. He handed Jasmine the bottle of white nearest him before digging back into his mashed potatoes.

Tara's stomach bubbled uneasily. They'd been doing so well. Why were Katrine and Jasmine fighting tonight?

Helena, bless her peace-loving heart, clapped her hands. "I remember the two of you being as pretty as pictures in school. I'm sure you were both popular."

Katrine's cheeks were pulled tight. She wasn't done. "You were the amazing one, Jasmine. You earned the good grades, kept this house running. You're the reason I had a lunch to bring to school and my hair combed before I walked out the door."

"Katrine," Xenia snapped, "that's an exaggeration."

Jasmine took a deep pull from her wine. "Is it?"

Ursula cleared her throat, and the house couldn't help but lean forward. The pressure caused a carved wooden bird to fall off a nearby shelf, and everyone at the table except for Tara jumped. Would Ursula finally speak her truth? Would she tell her daughters how after a full day working twelve and sometimes thirteen hours, seven days a week, she would check on them in bed, not missing visiting them a single night of their lives that they spent under her roof, brushing aside their hair and kissing their warm cheeks? Would she explain that she had gutted and remodeled this house to give them a safe shelter to grow up in, knowing even before they were born that they would be the most precious things in her life? Would she admit that she'd never had a long-term relationship, never even introduced her girls to one of her paramours, because she wanted them always confident that they were the most important people in her world?

"Your aunts were in the house for you, and I was always nearby," Ursula said.

The houselights flickered. *No. She would not tell the truth.*

"But no father around, *also* because of you," Jasmine said in triumph, refilling her glass. This confrontation had been a long time brewing. The air in the room began to sing like water in a teakettle.

Ursula blinked rapidly and continued to eat.

"Plenty of good men around, though, even if they weren't your father." Helena's voice was strained. "Ursula, do you remember that Connor fellow you dated back in the '70s, the one who always brought you flower seeds? I liked him. Whatever happened to him?"

Ursula was ever-so-slowly curling the tablecloth into a clenched hand, the gesture unconscious, the dishes moving toward her. She brought a morsel of ham to her mouth.

"I know!" Xenia said, glad for the change of subject. "He ended up opening a nursery in Iowa. A friend of a friend saw him when she went home to visit family."

Katrine, who'd been gearing up to jump in the ring, was startled out of the fight. "You dated, Mom? I thought you only slept around."

Dean clenched his jaw and glanced at Jasmine and Tara. Audish sat straighter in his chair.

"I'm sorry if my lifestyle bothered you." Ursula's voice was icy.

The air smelled of ozone, then crackled, and then as quickly as it'd begun, the tension released. Ursula had refused to claim the fight.

Jasmine wasn't yet done with it, however. She stood, ready to say something to the entire table, swaying from the two glasses of wine she'd slammed.

What words she would have chosen, not even Tara knew, for at that moment, the doorbell rang.

Chapter 31

Tara

The carolers crowded the sidewalk in front of the Queen Anne. They all appeared red-cheeked and happy except for Dagmar Baum, who scowled inside her winter bonnet. One of her eyes was milky, a skin of cotton over moist flesh. Ursula seemed to notice it at the same time as Tara because she gasped. Tara studied her grandma, saw the shock written on her features. Her best guess was that her grandma had set some sort of protection spell that had landed wrong. If so, that was completely unlike Ursula. What would have shaken her enough to miscast like that?

Tara ran her eyes over the carolers. They were all women except for one man, the kind-eyed guy she'd seen making cookies in Seven Daughters' kitchen. Tara guessed he was the reason all the women were standing so straight, tummies in and chests out as if their winter coats didn't turn each of them into a potato. Katrine seemed most interested in him out of everyone, and he was returning her gaze.

Dagmar stepped to the front of the group. You didn't need to be a mind reader to know that she didn't want to be at the Blackthorn house, but she went where God-via-her-pastor directed her to go. The carolers huddled inside a held breath. Tara caught a thought as clear as day. *Everyone knows Ursula is sleeping with Dagmar's husband.* Was *that* the cause of her milky eye? Tara couldn't imagine her grandma would deliberately curse a woman she was already hurting.

Helena broke the tension, as usual. "Carolers!" she called out, stating the obvious. "Let me get you all some hot cider."

She bustled into the house, leaving room for Jasmine and Dean to squeeze out. Jasmine blanched when she spotted Dagmar—an elder at their church—but it was too late to hide. It made Tara sad that her mom wanted to.

"Visiting family for Christmas?" Dagmar asked, her brows arched imperiously despite her cloudy eye.

Jasmine nodded and stared at her hands.

Katrine glanced at her sister, then back to Dagmar. "You're Heidi's mother?" she asked, stepping forward to hold out her hand.

Instinct drove Tara to jump between them, taking Dagmar's hand so Katrine didn't have to. She wasn't surprised when they touched and the images came to her: brown-yellow constipation, fear, anger toward how the man and Katrine were making eyes at each other. But there was something else there, too, a pregnant seed in the mix. Suddenly, Dagmar's thought came to her as vividly as if it had been whispered in her ear.

Send her to prison. Make her pay.

Tara recoiled, startled by the direction and vehemence of Dagmar's rage. It'd been aimed at Ursula, who grimaced and returned inside.

"What are you going to sing?" Tara asked, breathless as she reclaimed her hand.

"'Silent Night'?" Dagmar asked her fellow carolers. She didn't wait for an answer.

Overhead, stars salted the sky, brighter even than the twinkle lights reflecting off the diamond-eye snow crystals. The man strummed his guitar. Tara felt Katrine grow breathless and realized her aunt felt the same thing every time she saw the man, whose name was Ren. *Time.* Waterfalls of moments cascading into clear streams of flowing, beautiful possibility. It made Tara both happy and sad for Katrine.

The carolers hit their notes with such precision, and the air was so clear and cold, that their music became a magnificent science. Helena stepped out with a tray full of steaming mugs of cider, and Audish brought coats, scarves, and mittens for Dean, Jasmine, Tara, and Katrine. While the carolers sang in pure voices, a soft snow began to fall one perfect flake at a time.

Dean held Jasmine, who wrapped her arms around Tara. Helena rested her head on Xenia's shoulder. Audish smiled and sipped hot chocolate with a splash of peppermint schnapps, standing among the family as if he were one of them. Katrine closed her eyes so she wouldn't feel vertigo as the music Ren made blended with the music that he was.

The house noted all of this with the deep appreciation that could only be felt under the clear, starry sky of a Christmas Eve.

Chapter 32

Katrine

Katrine was *seeing* Ren for the first time, the whole of him, as he strummed his guitar between his two singing daughters. The man was golden chords with sapphire eyes, the laughter of someone you love, a warm fire on a snowy day. She felt something tugging just below her heart, a pain so exquisite that it could only be healing.

Next to her, Tara gasped. Katrine looked toward her. The girl's eyes were as wide as wheels and glued on Katrine's chest. She looked down. Could her niece see what Katrine was feeling?

A deep voice interrupted the singing. "What's this? Carolers!"

Katrine recognized the lead singer of the 32-20 Blues Band, a snow shovel over his shoulder, his breath coming in mighty plumes. Katrine felt a blend of excitement and shock at seeing him here, at the steps of her home. He was just as hot in his winter coat and cap as he had been in his cowboy hat, hot in a way that reminded her of sex and knives. It was incongruous on Christmas Eve. She hadn't laid eyes on the guy since that night at the Rabbit Hole with Heidi, hadn't even known he lived in Faith Falls.

Most of the singers stopped at the new arrival, but Ren and his girls continued to the end of "Joy to the World."

"Decided I'd shovel sidewalks for Christmas but didn't know I'd get music with it," the man said.

Dagmar stepped forward. "I don't believe we've met. Dagmar Baum."

"Baler Trempeleau, humble musician, trying to make up for past sins by doing a good deed on Christmas." He glanced up at the falling snowflakes, caught one in his hand, and offered it to Dagmar. "I figure that's the message this snow was sending me."

"Would you like some cider?" Helena asked from the porch.

Baler turned toward her, but his eyes hooked on Katrine. A broad, perfect smile transformed his face. "I know you. You came to one of my shows. I'd never forget a face like that."

Katrine felt the sudden tension, Ren putting his arms around his daughters and moving them behind him, the caroler with locs—the same woman who'd cockblocked Katrine when she saw Baler play—glaring, the Queen Anne creaking and snapping. Above all that, she sensed Jasmine trembling next to her. Did her sister know Baler? Was she simply cold? "How many sidewalks have you shoveled so far?"

His smile seemed to slip for a moment. "This is the first. I was going to start at the end of the block and work my way down when I heard the music. I thought there must be angels here." He winked at the carolers. Two of the women blushed. Velda, however, watched him with a rare intensity.

"Don't let me stop you," he said, dropping his shovel to the snow. "I have a lot of houses to get to tonight."

"You're a musician, you said?" Dagmar was leaning toward Baler. "Maybe you'd like to sing a song with us before you shovel. We could use another tenor to balance us."

He held up his free hand. "I wouldn't want to disrupt your style."

"Please," one of the carolers begged. He was that handsome.

"Well, if you insist." Baler pretended his shovel handle was a microphone and swiveled his hips like Elvis. Dagmar jumped back, and a few carolers squealed in delight. "A-one, a-two, a-one-two-three-four," he sang in his gravelly voice, fingers in the air counting off, head tipped forward over his shovel-microphone, hips cocked suggestively. He launched into "Santa Claus Is Back in Town," infusing it with such sexual rawness that the snow at his feet began to melt. Katrine couldn't help the tug she felt toward him. He was magnetic. She found herself wondering what he was doing later that night when the house shifted and a load of snow slipped over the side and onto Baler's head.

"Whoa!" He laughed and jumped back, brushing off the snow. Several of the carolers, Dagmar included, hurried forward to help. He let them, smiling into the eyes of each. "Guess that's just what happens in the winter," he said.

"We should probably get moving," Ren suggested, avoiding Katrine's eyes. "We have a lot of other folks to visit tonight."

Dagmar yanked her hands off Baler's coat and blinked. "Of course!" She clapped her mittens. "On to the next house!" The carolers followed her down the sidewalk, dazed ducklings, many of whom glanced longingly over their shoulders at Baler.

"I'll probably follow the music," he said to the Blackthorns left on the porch. "As soon as I finish your sidewalk."

Chapter 33

Ursula

Ursula had gone inside to get away from poor Dagmar. She knew the woman despised her and suspected the hatred had grown so intense that it was stealing her natural sight. A self-curse. She watched the carolers from behind the curtain, was trying to think of what potion she could make for Dagmar, when Charlie Tanager walked up to her house with a shovel in his hand.

She swallowed a scream.

Her father had finally shown himself.

She recognized him immediately. He'd chosen the body of a man in his thirties, but his eyes were all Charlie Tanager, the eyes and the dark-purple hate pulsing around him. She barely made it to the bathroom, where she lay hunched over the toilet, vomiting all her Christmas dinner.

You'll pay for this, he had said.

For once in his life, Charlie Tanager had been true to his word. Her hopes, all the protection spells she'd set out into the world, none of it mattered. He was back, maybe had been back for a while, toying with them. How like Charlie that would be, never making you suffer for a day when he could torment you for months.

As soon as Ursula could stand, her stomach and heart empty, she stumbled out back to her workshop. She could still hear caroling as she made her way through her yard.

The moon lit her path, turning the falling snowflakes into fairy lamps. She was too deep in her own fear to notice. Surely the *Book of Secrets* would have some magic for her, some way she could protect them all from Charlie Tanager, something that she'd missed. A wild, desperate part of her still hoped it wouldn't be necessary. The snakes had already come once, back when her girls were teenagers, and no Blackthorn had been hurt then, had they? Maybe he wasn't as powerful as she thought and would have to settle for taunting them. In any case, the snakes couldn't rise in the winter. That meant they were safe from the worst of it, at least for a couple more months.

"Mm-hmm."

The polite throat-clearing startled her, but she wouldn't show it. She tipped her head at the man standing in front of her workshop door, the shadows disguising him until she was nearly on top of him. He wore a hunter's cap, which covered most of his face. It wasn't until she was almost nose to nose that she saw he wasn't a man at all, but a boy whose bones were growing faster than his muscles. He stepped to the side, and she unlocked the door and flicked on the lights. She neither invited him in nor shut the door behind her.

She heard him step inside and waited for him to speak as she bustled around her herbs, checking quantities in the apothecary drawers, rearranging beakers, sweeping clippings into a pile, brushing off loose seeds that clung to the velvet of her dress, striving to calm herself. After several minutes passed and he hadn't said a word, she finally turned, impressed by his patience. "Yes?"

The teenager had removed his hat and held it in his hand. His coat was draped over his arm. He wore brown corduroys and a green sweater, bringing to mind a plant. It wasn't just his appearance—hair curling like tender artichoke leaves over his collar, eyes blue and bright like bachelor's buttons, a strong, craggy branch of a nose, rose-colored lips—but also his presence. He was calm, and he made the air around him easier to breathe.

He was a good man, or would be, if nothing got to him first.

"My name's Leo." He held out his hand. "I've only seen your granddaughter once, but that's all it took to know I love her."

Chapter 34

KATRINE

"He had eyes for you."

"Who?" Katrine asked. She and Jasmine were sitting on the couch in front of the roaring fireplace, their legs twined together just as they'd done when they were children. The table and kitchen were cleaned up. Everyone had long since gone to bed, including Dean, who'd taken Tara home. Katrine had talked Jasmine into spending the night at the house for old time's sake, and it was the greatest gift she'd ever received.

"The shoveler," Jasmine said. "What was his name?"

"Baler Trempeleau, he said. Heidi and I saw him play at the Rabbit Hole last fall."

Jasmine mock shuddered. "He made me feel funny."

Katrine patted Jasmine's leg. "Those tickly feelings are perfectly normal, honey," she said, doing her best imitation of Mrs. Diego, their high school health teacher.

Jasmine swatted her hand away. "Not like that, dummy. There was something off about him. And he looked familiar, though I'm sure we've never met. It was creepy. And did you see how Velda was staring at him? Like she'd rather see him dead than happy."

"Um, I believe you're exaggerating, but yeah. I think he's trouble, too. I wouldn't touch him with a ten-foot pole." Katrine rubbed her own arms. "You gotta admit that he's cute, though."

Jasmine reeled back. "Cute? Did you look at Ren Cunningham? *That's* cute."

Katrine sighed. "He is dreamy. And far too good for me. I only date losers, remember? Besides, I'm not even officially divorced yet."

"Hey, Katrine?" Jasmine asked, setting her head on her sister's shoulder.

Katrine caressed her soft hair. "Yeah?"

"What happened between you and your husband?"

Katrine thought of their childhood, her lack of a specific Blackthorn gift, the series of troubled men she'd dated, Adam cheating on her, her attraction to both Baler and Ren even though she knew better, the spell Jasmine had cast to banish her before she'd forsaken her beautiful cooking powers, their mother fleeing to her workshop on Christmas Eve, this house that felt like a living skin around them.

"Who the hell knows, Jazzy? At least we found our way back to each other."

Part 3

The Awakening

The Blackthorn Book of Secrets: Accepting Gifts

A gift freely given creates a vacuum which moves the recipient to new levels if they accept it.

Always accept the gift that is offered to you, even if you don't like the wrapping.

Always.

Chapter 35

Jasmine

Spring weather exploded in March—prematurely, for Minnesota—arriving as yellow as daffodils and lightning. Jasmine's backyard was thick with gangs of robins pecking at the thawing lawn, drunk on winter-fermented berries, chattering and chirping. The air was swollen with the scent of thaw, dirt, and possibility. Yet something sinister was on its way, and you didn't need to be a witch to sense it. People jumped at memories. Dogs growled for no reason, and all creatures smaller than a cat had disappeared, gone into hiding.

Jasmine was aware of an impending threat, but distantly. She was too busy being excited by the fact that she and Dean had grown even closer. He still hadn't given up his apartment, but he'd spent some nights. Nothing could stand in their way, she was sure of it, and the weather only backed up her mood. The sun was a trembling lemon, fighting to ship its heat to the town below. By noon, it would be at least 60 degrees, and the bright buds on Faith Falls' oaks and maples were paying attention. They shivered and stretched, waiting for the perfect moment to unfurl in a symphony of green.

Beneath it all, the earth continued to rumble.

Locals were saying another snakening was on the way. Even that couldn't dim Jasmine's happiness. She'd never tied what had happened to her to any specific weather pattern or event. It had simply been terrible luck.

She'd stopped by ValuCo to pick up toilet paper and other groceries—even small chores made her happy, because she was doing them for her family—and was trying to balance it all on one hip and open the car door with her free hand. She almost had her key in the lock when it slipped free and fell to the ground.

"Need help?"

She spun around. She didn't immediately recognize the man wearing the cowboy hat. She just knew he made her feel unsafe, all her happy thoughts fleeing. She glanced around the parking lot. No one else was out.

He laughed and raised his hands in the air. "I'm not going to steal your toilet paper, ma'am." He squinted and leaned closer. "Hey, I saw you at that big ol' house on Christmas. When I came by and shoveled? You were next to the beauty who'd come to one of my shows. The two of you must be sisters."

Jasmine nodded, the memory of him clicking into place. He looked different in his Stetson. She grew ashamed that she'd judged him so quickly, or was it a different emotion she was feeling? It was hard to tell with her blood pumping fast enough to make her queasy. "Yes. I remember."

"Name's Baler. Baler Trempeleau. Can't recall if I introduced myself that night." He held out his hand. She reached for it. When they touched, her panic returned, this time so thick that it blinded her.

She swayed, started to fall, but he propped her up and kept holding on. "You okay?"

She yanked her arm back as soon as she was able. The nausea cleared almost immediately. "Fine," she said, blinking rapidly.

"That's good, because you're a little pale." He pushed his hat back to get a better look. "Probably this weather. It isn't right for it to be so warm in March, you know? Say, speaking of your sister, can I ask if she's single?"

Jasmine forced her stomach back down her throat. Her life had gotten so good since Katrine had returned. Why did it feel like this man was going to wrest that away? She shook her head. She was being ridiculous. It was a beautiful sunny day. She was in a public parking lot. This was *not* the man who'd hurt her, couldn't be. That guy would be in his fifties. "I don't want to talk about her personal life."

Baler laughed in a way that made her feel like she'd overreacted. "I didn't mean to pry. I just wanted to ask her out, that's all. Can you blame a guy?" He looped his thumbs into his jeans and rocked on his heels. "How about this? How about you let me know if she works at the paper, like the bartender at the Rabbit Hole said. You can do that, right? In fact, I imagine that's public information."

Jasmine didn't want to answer him. "She does."

"And what's her favorite flower? Lilies, I bet."

"Exactly. She loves lilies." Jasmine didn't know what had provoked the lie. Katrine hated lilies. Said they reminded her of funerals.

He chuckled. "See? That wasn't so bad. You sure you don't need help with your groceries?"

She managed a smile. "I'm okay. Thanks."

"All right, then. Have a good day, and don't get too warm! It's supposed to top 60 today."

Jasmine watched his retreating back, suddenly very much wanting to check on Katrine. Car loaded, she made her way to the Queen Anne. Except the entire town seemed intent on keeping her from her destination—every car in front of her drove ten miles under the speed limit, a rabbit darted across the road, construction rerouted her five miles and across the river—but it only made her more desperate.

Chapter 36

Ursula

Ursula was in her cottage, nose deep in an ancient botany book the library had tracked down for her, a musty treasure with gold flaking off the edges of the page, when something outside the cottage door drew her attention.

She'd been hyper-tuned into the scratchy feeling in the air, particularly as the anniversary of her father's murder neared. He'd begun haunting her dreams as soon as the early spring thaw arrived, laughing at her, changing shape, promising he was on his way. It was clear none of her protection spells had worked, and Ursula had waited too long to tell her family what she'd done to their patriarch. She saw no other choice except to wait for him to strike and hope that, when he did, she was strong enough to fight back.

Was this him at her door?

She searched the air for a threat and felt none.

Michael Baum was supposed to visit her—they'd set the date at the end of their last one—but this was too early to be him. Must be a client. Would he stand her up if he arrived and found her busy? She hoped not. She needed his touch more than ever these days. She yanked open the cottage door, planning to make short work of whoever stood on the other side. A small sound of shock slipped from her lips at the sight that greeted her.

Dean, Jasmine's husband, stood on her workshop doorstep, his posture slightly stooped as if burdened by an unseen weight. His wavy hair peeked out from beneath a weathered baseball cap. His eyes, a deep brown, were framed by crow's-feet that hinted at years of squinting against the sun.

Lightning forked through Ursula's nervous system. Dean had never come here on his own and certainly never set foot into the cottage. "What's wrong?" she demanded.

His hands hung at his sides almost like a child's, and his expression was uncertain. "Can I come in?"

Ursula stepped aside, allowing in the man and the clean scent of spring. Her relationship with her son-in-law had always been superficial. That's how Jasmine wanted it, and Ursula supported every one of Jasmine's decisions, whether or not she agreed with them. She found Dean to be dull but stable. She desperately hoped she wouldn't discover anything else on this visit.

He glanced around the cottage's interior, his face registering mild surprise. "This place looks smaller from the outside. And not so warm." He unzipped his parka to reveal a white button-down shirt and navy tie. Ursula didn't know whether to be charmed or worried that he'd dressed up.

"Can I make you some tea?"

He shook his head. "I came for a spell."

Ursula's throat tightened. She'd heard appeals over the years that had defied logic and morality equally—requests for leprotic poisons to drip on the genitals of exes, potions to turn enemies into bugs. She'd thought nothing could shock her anymore. She'd been wrong.

"I can see what you're thinking," Dean said. "But everyone in town has heard about your magic, even if we don't talk about it at my house. I don't know whether to believe in it or not, but I figure the worst that can come of this is that I get your blessing."

Ursula's mouth was almost too dry to speak. "What spell do you want?"

He closed his eyes as if he were gathering nerve. "I want Jasmine to stay happy. I want Tara to be safe. Things have been so good since Katrine came back to town, and I want to keep them that way." His eyes opened, his gaze pleading. "Can you give me something that'll do that?"

Ursula hadn't been aware that she'd been holding her breath. "I can't stop time."

"No, I'm not asking for that." He clenched his hands, maybe in frustration. "I just want to protect them both. It's foolish, but I feel something bad coming. Almost like an itch you can't scratch, you know? But one that hurts."

Ursula's green eyes shone. She'd underestimated this man. She wouldn't make things worse by interfering. "I can't help you."

He lifted his cap and ran his hands through his hair, a frustrated gesture. "Yeah, it was stupid to come. I drive a truck. I don't believe in magic." He turned so quickly that he upended a burning candle, spilling wax all over the front of his dress shirt. "Dangit!"

"Take it off," Ursula commanded. "If I get some hyssop on it right away, it won't be ruined."

He sighed, scratching at the hardening wax. "This is my best shirt. I got some on my pants, too." Reluctantly, he stripped off his parka and then the button-down. The hot wax had left a red streak near his heart. Ursula automatically whispered a protection spell and went about mixing the tincture needed to bleed the wax from his shirt and the front of his trousers. Then she started to scrub.

She was so intent on her task that she didn't see Michael glance in her window, witness her bent at the waist in front of a half-naked man, and leave.

The Blackthorn Book of Secrets: Protection Spell

Use this spell if someone is introducing dark energy into your life. First, step inside a circle. You can create this circle with anything handy: towels, string, scarves, salt, etc. Once inside, envision white light surrounding you.

Next, picture the person intending harm as being trapped inside a clear, soapy bubble. Hold this image in your head and chant the following three times:

Any bad you do will return to you.
All words of hate become your own fate.
Likewise, all good you do will reflect back true.
Any kindness you create will heal this strait.

Chapter 37

JASMINE

Her husband's car was parked in Ursula's driveway.

Jasmine was surprised, and then relieved. Dean was supposed to pick up Tara from a friend's later today. He must have gotten her early and was inside with her, which meant her whole family was here, and she could make sure they were *all* safe. She suddenly, desperately craved a protection spell. She'd never before asked Ursula for a potion, but now was the time. She raced to the back of the house, took the corner at the gate, and ran straight into Michael Baum with such force that she fell on her butt on the sidewalk.

He was so flustered that he almost didn't offer her a hand. "I wouldn't go back there," he said. He seemed to be weighing his emotions and landed on resentment. "Your mom's with a new lover. Some things never change, eh? I don't know why I thought they would."

Once he'd helped Jasmine to her feet, he strode off. The slam of his car door and the squeal of his tires still rang in her ears as she stood rooted on the sidewalk, staring toward the front door of her mother's workshop. *Where is Dean?* Her insides felt plunged into ice, every instinct screaming to retreat to the Queen Anne, yet her feet carried her toward the little cottage. The air crackled with warning as she moved, each step heavier than the last. She reached for the doorknob, the hair on her neck pricking like pins, then hesitated and stepped back, only to find herself drawn to the cottage window. She peered inside.

Dean's back was to her. His shirt was off.

She couldn't see her mother's face, only that she was crouched forward, on her knees in front of Dean, her hands working furiously.

Jasmine reeled back, her mouth a perfect circle of horror.

Your mom's with a new lover.

The ground rumbled underfoot, and the terrible recollection tried to surface. She fought back. She'd given up her power so she'd never have to fully remember it again. She'd distanced herself from her family as much as she could, and she'd raised her own daughter without magic to protect her. She'd swallowed the antidepressants.

She would not allow in that memory.

But she already had, hadn't she? A little bit, all because Katrine was back in town. Her sister's return had tipped the balance, and look what that had wrought. Her mother had seduced Jasmine's very own husband. Fire pushed against her throat, a hot acid that released a slip of the awful day that she'd worked so hard to suppress.

Tart, creamy avgolemono simmers on the stove. It's Xenia's favorite. Jasmine's also got bread rising and plans to make a salad. The snakes are slithering outside on the ground, have been all day, rasping like sandpaper in the too-hot spring air. She doesn't know how Katrine can be outside amid the horror of their invasion, but once she'd learned Jasmine needed saffron to make her favorite flourless orange cake, she'd gone straight to the store.

There's a honeybee in the kitchen that tries to whisper to Jasmine when she turns to knead the bread dough. She fans it away. She's complete in the kitchen, happy, her true self, in the right place at the right time.

Her soup smells so good, Velda once said, that it could raise the dead from their graves. She doesn't know about that, but she likes the scent of the chicken bubbling in the rich, velvet broth. She is up to her elbows kneading the bread when her neck prickles. She turns.

ssssssssssssss

She was launched out of the memory, the hissing inside her brain, the keening that had begun on the other side of her ornamental pig shelves.

She turned her back on her cheating husband and her traitorous mother and drove away.

Chapter 38

Katrine

Katrine was worried. Jasmine hadn't returned her calls for days. It was like she'd dropped off the earth. Katrine would have known what to do with old Jasmine. New, tender Jasmine was different. She cracked easily. Better to give her some space. In the meanwhile, she'd turned to something that'd calmed her back when she was growing up.

Gardening.

Which was why she was on her knees in the dirt of her secret childhood garden, perched between the woods and the river behind the Queen Anne. A trowel, a spade, and a compost bag rested on one side of her, and the Rum River ran on the other. The silver water sluiced and whistled through ornate ice patterns, reveling in the freedom of an early spring. When the ground cracked and moaned, Katrine wrote the sound off to the unusual warm-up.

"You've taken over completely, haven't you?" she said to the sprawling fern that'd claimed her childhood sanctuary. She worked her hands around its base, tugging until the roots gave way with a satisfying pop. This hidden corner behind the Queen Anne had been hers once, a patch of earth she'd cleared without asking permission. She didn't want to let Ursula know they shared an interest.

She'd been careful to keep it hidden back then, this small rebellion. The watermelons had thrived here by the river's edge, fat and sweet. The peas and beans had been stubborn, the tomatoes hopeless, but the melons—*those* had been her triumph. She'd brought them to Jasmine like gifts, sometimes green and hard, sometimes perfectly ripe, watching her sister's face light up as she planned what to do with each offering.

Katrine liked that she had to sneak to her garden, that she was the only one who knew about it. The secret made her feel strong when she was young, and maybe it would do the same now. It was too early for any sort of planting, but something about yanking at the weeds and creating order scratched at that same deep itch. Her brain began to empty, leaving a peaceful rhythm in its wake. Pull horsetail. Turn over dirt. Get at the root of the crabgrass. Turn over dirt.

Thoughts of Jasmine and why she hadn't returned her calls would enter, or the question of what she was doing in Faith Falls and how long she'd stay would flit through, but the harmony of working the soil gently shooed them away. She was encased in the comfort of practical action.

"Ursula would crap her pants if she knew I liked gardening. Best to not get her hopes up," she said out loud in response to a breeze riffling the dried leaves still clinging to the oaks above. She heard her voice and laughed.

"Whatcha doin'?"

Katrine jumped. She turned to see Tara standing behind her wearing an oversize yellow parka and a matching cap. She got to her feet, brushed dirt off her knees, and glanced behind the girl. "Are you alone?"

"Yup." Tara tugged her cap tighter on her blond hair. Though it was warm for March, patches of half-melted snow still littered the ground like brittle glass. "Are you gardening? Ursula'd probably let you use some of hers, you know."

"How'd you find me?"

Tara rubbed her nose. "I stopped by the house, and no one was there, so I came to the river."

"Your mom with you?"

"She's sleeping." Tara blinked rapidly, like she was holding back tears.

Katrine's stomach dropped. "What? It's past noon. Is she okay?"

Tara shrugged. Her face was pinched.

"Tara?" The child's quiet made Katrine uneasy. The soil that moments before had felt warm and welcoming now sucked at her shoes, the cold seeping into her body.

Tara shook her head, opened her mouth, closed it, and then opened it again. "She went grocery shopping five days ago. She hasn't been the same since."

"How do you mean?"

"She stays in bed all day." Tara squeezed herself. "She says she hears hissing, like a leaking pipe. I got her aspirin and said she should go to the doctor. She made me promise not to tell Dad. He doesn't live with us anymore, so it's just me and Mom."

Katrine knew this, though Jasmine had never told her. She'd seen Dean and Jasmine growing closer, though, and had hoped husband and wife would be living under the same roof before the summer. "Hissing?"

Tara ignored the question. "She won't shower. She won't eat the food I bring her. I don't even know if she drinks water." She bit her lip, looking anywhere but at Katrine's face.

Katrine strode forward and pulled her niece into a hug, not caring if she got her dirty. "Let's go into the house, make some hot chocolate, and figure out what to do, okay?"

She felt Tara nod, but barely.

She'd gotten herself cleaned up and fed Tara some hot cocoa and cookies before driving her to the grocery store to pick up food for her and her mom. From what Katrine could gather, Jasmine and Dean had a terrible fight, and it'd knocked Jasmine for a loop, though Tara made Katrine swear she wouldn't tell anyone.

When Katrine drove Tara home, her niece had insisted she not come in, had made her promise not to tell anyone else about how weird Jasmine was behaving. She said she didn't want to betray her mom. Katrine had agreed on one condition: If Jasmine wasn't up and around in forty-eight hours, she would come in and drag her back into the world. This compromise seemed to relieve Tara, though it left Katrine unsettled.

After dropping off her niece, she headed into the newspaper office, where Heidi handed over her latest assignment. Covering the spring Sadie Hawkins dance at the high school—a tradition where the girls asked the boys to the dance—wasn't the worst way to spend an evening, she figured. As much as she was confused about living in Faith Falls, there was comfort in the familiar.

"Can you spare a photographer, or do you want me to snap pics, too?"

"Kevin's covering a baseball game," Heidi said, barely glancing up from her computer. "It's all on you. Now, get going. The dance starts in an hour, and I want shots of the decorations before the gym fills up."

Katrine reached for the digital camera. She still couldn't believe she was rekindling her love of writing through the Faith Falls newspaper, of all places. And she hadn't texted Adam since her slip-up last fall and was only thinking about him every *other* day rather than every day. The door was opening. Cracks of sunlight were streaming in.

On her way to the dance, tooling through the streets of Faith Falls in her new-to-her raspberry-red Honda Civic with over two hundred thousand miles on it, strangers waved at her, surprised smiles on their faces. She figured it was difficult to fight the promise of spring in the air, the vibrating hum of buds preparing to pop.

She found herself smiling when what she imagined to be the townspeople's unprotected squirrel thoughts reached her, sweet morsels of *time to put in the garden I think I love her opportunity finally passion new business green.* Of course, she wasn't really reading minds—that was just a game she'd played since childhood, pretending she could glimpse the bright flutter of other people's inner worlds. She shut off the old habit and pulled into the high school parking lot. Since the dance wasn't set to start until seven, she nabbed a spot close to the back entrance, near where she'd snuck outside to kiss Kyle Hansen all those years ago.

When she slipped through the gym's propped-open double doors, the musky-tart smell of contact sports and industrial cleaners brought her back to the first wrestling match she'd attended. Heidi had been there as well, head of the cheerleading squad. Katrine had tried to look cool, slipping out to inhale a Virginia Slims that Heddy Nistler had pinched from her mom, then prancing back in lightheaded and reeking of smoke. She'd thought life was so difficult back then. It almost made her laugh. If teenage Katrine could see herself now, working for her worst-enemy-cum-newest-friend and scarred by battles of her own making, she'd be humbled.

The pep squad had done a passable job decorating the gym with blue and gold streamers, the school colors. The wooden bleachers had been pushed back. Folding tables lined half of the far wall, full of iced tubs of canned pop and bottles of water, each available for one dollar as a 4-H fundraiser. A DJ was setting up his booth near the drinks, and a janitor was stringing up a single disco ball, a glittering uvula dangling in the warm mouth of the gym.

"Are you here to dance?"

Katrine was surprised to find Ren standing next to her, and even more startled to discover she was thrilled to see him. She'd fantasized about him more than she'd cared to admit since he'd caroled at the Queen Anne, hoping against hope that he'd felt the same zing as she had when their eyes met, that he would maybe track her down and ask her out. He hadn't, and she'd accepted that as her fate, even had the wisdom to be grateful. She needed to figure out how to be herself before she could even try being in a couple.

But here he was, in his tall, sturdy glory, his blue eyes crinkling at the edges, his hands stuffed into his jeans pockets. Part of her was screaming to hide, to protect herself from any potential pain. Instead, she held up her camera. "I'm here as an official representative of the *Faith Falls Gazette*."

He scanned the gym. It was the picture of small-town Midwest, with hopes and dreams writ large in crepe paper and hand-penned banners decorated with sayings like WE'VE GOT SPIRIT, YES WE DO. He cocked an eyebrow. "I presume this isn't investigative reporting?"

She smiled. It was his words combined with the easiness about him. When he brushed his curly hair back from his forehead, her eyes were drawn to his fantastic hands. "Pretty straightforward human-interest piece," she said, "though I've heard talk about a student strike if the cafeteria doesn't stop microwaving the hamburgers. Some things never change. You didn't go to high school here, did you?"

He shook his head. The same lock of hair fell into his eyes, and he brushed it away absentmindedly. "Born and raised in Duluth. Met my late wife in college, and we moved here when I got a chance to buy the store downtown."

She felt a twinge at the mention of his wife. She didn't want to pry. "So, what brings you to the dance?"

He pointed at the name tag on his chest. "Chaperone. Both my daughters are attending, and I want to make sure they stay a ruler's width from any boys. Don't tell 'em I said that."

She drew an X across her chest with her pointer finger. "I wouldn't dare."

A woman on the other side of the gym waved at Ren. Katrine recognized her as Mrs. Tappe, the same English teacher who'd been here during Katrine's tenure. Dagmar Baum was standing next to her, the top of her face completely covered by dark sunglasses. Katrine wondered if she'd gotten cataracts surgery.

"Oops," Ren said. "Guess I better get to work."

Katrine watched him amble away, her skin tingling pleasantly.

◆ ◆ ◆

Soon, bright, chattering teenagers began filing in, and the lights were dimmed and the disco ball lit. Pop songs as empty and smooth as soap bubbles filled the gym. Katrine snapped occasional photos and gathered quotes from teenagers, but her attention kept being drawn to Ren. She was asking a young woman with the most darling freckles about her college plans next fall when someone tapped her shoulder. She turned to see Ren holding out a hand, and her heart bongoed behind her ribs.

"May I have this dance?" he asked.

A mercifully slow song was playing. Most of the teen boys had gravitated to one side of the gym, the girls to the other, leaving the long-term couples in the middle, swinging and clinging.

She felt flustered. He recognized it and held up his hands. "This is purely a fact-finding mission." He nodded over his shoulder toward the dance floor. "See the blond with the boy in the orange T-shirt? She's my oldest."

"Hold my camera and notebook?" she asked the girl she'd been interviewing.

When Ren whisked her onto the dance floor, a wave of anxiety washed over her. She didn't want to be in his arms. Would he know that she'd been cheated on? Would she sense darkness in him? But the fear soon passed. He held her, but not so close that their bodies touched, a firm hand on the small of her back, the other clasping her right hand. He led, but gently.

It was over too soon, the romantic song replaced by an upbeat Paul McCartney tune from her youth.

She began to walk off the floor—after all, their slow dance was over—and was surprised when Ren didn't follow. She turned to see him still dancing, in a way. Everything sort of came loose on him. His body vibrated with the music, full of silliness and innocence, his hands in the air. Katrine covered her mouth to swallow her laugh, then returned to wiggle her hips by his side, reclaiming some of the rebelliousness she'd honed to a fine point in this very school but had somehow lost. She was aware of teenagers rolling their eyes and Ren's daughter appearing mortified, but the attention only made the moment sweeter.

Eyes closed, Ren rotated his upper body, his hips gyrating and his thumbs up, swaying and smiling.

It was the most honest thing she'd ever witnessed.

She felt herself begin to fall, and for once, she didn't fight it. She let herself believe that finally, maybe, just this once . . . she'd found a good man.

Chapter 39

Jasmine

The hissing that she'd first heard on the other side of her basement wall after Katrine came home to Faith Falls had returned with a vengeance. The sound scratched itself into every cell in her body, a distant scream that Jasmine could not escape no matter where she went or what she thought. Its pitch was somewhere between a baby's wail and the cry of the wet yarns of a cheap sweater rubbing against one another. She couldn't sleep for it, could barely eat. It was pushing her to the brink of insanity, a place where her mind vibrated so fast it was as if it stood still.

She'd been drinking steadily since she'd seen what Dean and her mother had been doing, barely left her bed, but even in those rare snatches where her body quit from exhaustion, she still dreamed of the snake song on the other side of the wall.

Dean had left on a long haul after she'd confronted him about Ursula. He'd denied he was having an affair with her mother, but what else could he say? She knew what she'd seen. Tara was worried for her, she recognized that. Her child walked on the edges of the room, scared to speak to her own mom. This morning, Jasmine had caught a glimpse of herself in a hallway mirror and understood Tara's fear. Her eyes were sunken, her lips a tight gash across the lower half of her face.

Her solution had been to throw the mirror away.

Through it all, the hissing continued, an itch that couldn't be scratched, a dream destroyed, a lover killed. She believed if she could put a name to it, like the lyrics of a distant song, she might be free, but just when she thought she recognized a string of notes or a clear word, the hideous sound switched tenor. In her lowest moments, it was enough to make her consider slicing off her ears and, if that didn't work, shoving the sharp silver point of the blade into each ear canal and scouring until only black silence existed.

Tara's presence kept her from this drastic act. She didn't want her daughter to find her in that state. But her tenuous grasp to even Tara was fading. Jasmine, the woman who'd protected her daughter from every harm, sewn her clothes, cooked her meals, tucked her in at night, homeschooled her so the world couldn't damage her beautiful spirit as it had clipped Jasmine's own wings, could no longer care for her child for the hissing in her head.

On the sixth day, she knew she was at the point of no return. "Tara, we're going to Ursula's."

Tara twitched, but she followed her mom out the door.

Jasmine didn't have a plan, just a sense that her mother was to blame for everything bad that'd ever happened to her. The ground rumbled underfoot, and so she ran to the car, Tara hustling to keep up. A heavy rain had begun. The air smelled like crushed worms.

Jasmine drove without saying a word. The noise faded the farther from the tunnels that she got, but it never disappeared. When they arrived at the Queen Anne, Jasmine ordered Tara to wait in the car. She slammed her door and ran up the porch. Whipping open the heavy oak door, she continued to the kitchen, where she discovered the other Blackthorn women seated around the breakfast nook in some sort of uneasy silence.

She looked at their shocked faces. Helena and Xenia had jumped to their feet, but they seemed frozen at the precipice of movement, unsure whether to cross the terrible distance between them. The secret lodged in Jasmine's throat felt like a stone, sharp-edged and heavy. She understood that this was her moment—tell the others what had happened to her in high school or shatter completely—yet she'd carried the poison for so long that releasing it felt like tearing away a piece of her soul. If she held on to it, she would explode into a million quivering pieces. But speaking it aloud might kill her just the same, the exquisite death of exposure, of finally letting the terrible truth breathe in the world where others could see it, judge it, recoil from it.

Tara. Tara Tara Tara.

Her daughter's name became a lifeline. For Tara, she would endure this tearing open. The words gathered like a storm in her chest, and she finally released her secret. "Something terrible happened to me when I was fourteen. I was attacked by a man. Not one of you bothered to notice how different I was afterward. You didn't even know."

She hadn't meant to say any of that, was in fact shocked to hear that it was the betrayal of her own mother, aunts, and most of all her *sister* not knowing, not intuiting, that she'd clung to harder than anything else all these years. She recognized the unfairness of this thought, but that didn't change her feelings. Suddenly, a brick fell out of the structure guarding her wound. A cooling air rushed in, but it didn't stand a chance against the blazing fire of Jasmine's pain.

"I wanted to protect Katrine, and save all of you from the guilt of thinking you'd failed me, but I guess . . ." Her voice caught, the next words rising like breath through water. "I thought you'd figure it out. I thought if you loved me enough, you would know my secret." She pulled her sharp eyes to Ursula. "And I saw you seduce Dean in your workshop." She swayed where she was standing. She'd thought she had fight in her, but it was only desperation. Her voice broke. "Please don't take my husband from me."

"Oh, baby," Helena said, stepping forward, her arms out. Xenia and Katrine followed right behind. Ursula, wearing an expression of pure horror, stayed put, Velda by her side.

Jasmine heard a shuffle behind her and craned her neck, embraced by her sister and aunts. The hissing in her head was growing louder, each hissing beat accompanying her slow swivel until she was staring into the spooked eyes of her daughter. "Tara!"

The girl's face was an exclamation point of shock.

"How long have you been standing there?" Jasmine asked.

The answer was obvious. It was written on Tara's face. She'd heard everything. She turned and ran, leaving melting, boot-shaped puddles of water.

"Tara!" Jasmine ran after her, her aunts, mother, and grandmother close behind. But they were too slow. Tara was gone.

Chapter 40

Ursula

Ursula felt Xenia watching her. "I'm fine."

Xenia shined her flashlight on Ursula's face. "You look pale."

It was after eight o'clock, dark. Tara had run off two hours earlier. The rain had stopped but the air smelled gloomy, like thaw and fish. They walked the slippery banks of the Rum River, hollering Tara's name. Audish and Helena were on the far side. Velda and Katrine were driving up and down streets, and Jasmine was in the Queen Anne, phoning any person Tara might have run to.

But Ursula knew it wouldn't matter, and the thought split her clean through. The earth had been whispering warnings for days. The snakes were rising, called forth by blood and broken promises. Charlie Tanager's reckoning was nearly here. She'd failed them all, and the shame of it suffocated her. But there was still a chance for her to absorb all the pain of the curse herself. There had to be.

"I'm not pale," Ursula said. "It's the reflection of the moon."

"It's more than that," Xenia said. "You look nervous. Like a conservative in a think tank."

Ursula recognized Xenia's attempt at humor but didn't have it in her to respond. "Worried, more like it. How far could that girl have gone?"

Xenia made a sad noise. "How far would you run if you recognized that your mother was losing her mind, had heard that she'd been abused as a child, and realized there was nothing you could do to save her? Oh, and by the way, you'd also just found out your grandma might be screwing your dad?"

Ursula rubbed her face. "So far that I don't know if I'd ever come back."

Xenia's voice dropped. "Do you think Tara guessed what we were talking about before she and Jasmine showed up?"

Ursula shuddered. She'd gathered the other Blackthorn women in the Queen Anne's kitchen because she'd sensed that Jasmine had tipped over an edge earlier in the week, though she hadn't known what had driven her. When Katrine shared that, according to Tara, it was even worse than they thought, Ursula excused herself and went straight to the *Book of Secrets*.

It'd opened to this page:

The Blackthorn Book of Secrets: Revoking Power

Every person enters the world with a gift at exactly the strength they need it, though occasionally families pass on extra magic like they pass on eye color or allergies. Some are born knowing their gift, others need to discover it.

In any case, an unused gift can grow feral and turn against its owner. When this happens, it may be necessary to revoke their power. This dangerous operation is irreversible and will leave the person half alive. It should be done only when no other option remains.

To strip a person of their gift requires all living female relatives to be present in a single room along with the person whose power will be expunged. The female relatives need only to cross four of their fingers and mutter a single word in unison: SEVER.

Horrified understanding had squeezed Ursula's heart. Jasmine's buried power had rotted inside her and was driving her mad.

Ursula had run back into the house to tell the others what they must do. That's when Jasmine showed up, her eyes spinning, her mouth twitching, confirming that they had no choice but to strip her latent power if they were going to save her. Learning that she'd been molested and thought that her own mother had slept with her husband didn't change that.

"Tara has a gift, probably more than one," Ursula told Xenia as they walked the bank, bathing the sloping earth with their flashlights. It wasn't unheard of for a Blackthorn to be blessed with multiple powers. Jasmine had made them promise not to speak to Tara about it, but it was clear the girl had a heavy dose. "I hope those powers protect her tonight."

And to herself: *So many damned secrets in this family. So many. They rip us apart.*

But hers was different. She had to hang on to hers. It was the only way to protect the others.

Chapter 41

Tara

Tara had known the moment was coming.

The moment she'd need to run.

That was why she'd sought out Katrine in the quiet green of her secret garden, to speak the truth about her mother so that Katrine could go to Jasmine when Tara had to leave. Jasmine was trapped inside her own sorrow, thrashing against it with everything she had, like a moth pinned to a board. What her mother didn't know, what would kill her to discover, was that Tara absorbed every flutter of panic, every surge of despair. They were two hearts sharing the same bloodstream, and her mother's poison was becoming her own.

If she didn't escape in time, she wouldn't just lose Jasmine. She'd lose herself, too.

But still, she couldn't bring herself to leave. The best she could do was hide a packed bag in the trunk of her mom's car under the emergency kit: twenty-two dollars she'd saved from odd jobs she'd done for her grandma, an empty blue glass jar, a change of clothes including a silk jacket Katrine had given her that was too beautiful to wear, string, cans of ravioli plus an opener, her diary, and an old sleeping bag.

And she waited, praying she'd recognize the moment before the point of no return.

It had arrived tonight.

She hadn't known that her mom had been molested, but neither had it surprised her to learn it. She'd observed the resulting trauma from the inside while incubating in the warm red of her mother's womb. Jasmine's particular wound back then was an absence where there should have been something, like a face without a nose, but what had been stolen from her was more essential. When Jasmine started taking medication, the absence just grew lonelier and larger, until last week, when it became a pulsing vacuum that occupied more space inside Jasmine than her own spirit.

The same way she knew about her mom's pain, Tara knew that Ursula had a hand in helping Velda kill Charlie Tanager. Tara couldn't ever remember not knowing that because unlike most people, Ursula didn't hide her sickness. It was there, in plain sight, shaped like what it was: the potion that'd killed her own father. She lived inside that blue bottle at her center, separated from all the joy she could possess.

Tara had noticed tonight, when all the Blackthorns were together in the kitchen, that the bottle that kept Ursula captive had an impressive crack in it—what could have done that?—but it was too soon to tell if it was a shattering or a healing. Katrine had stopped tugging at the fishhook through her heart—with the exception of Christmas Eve, when she'd pulled the correct end while watching Ren sing—but she still hadn't realized she could remove it altogether.

And then, the man with the cowboy hat had shown up with a snow shovel, and Tara immediately recognized her great-grandfather curled inside him like a rotten seed. She'd wanted to say something, to Katrine, to her mom, to anyone, but she'd been born and raised on the understanding that you held secrets close. So when the man with the cowboy hat began following her, showing up in the corner of her vision whenever she left the house, she kept it to herself. But even the earth was beginning to rumble like an animal with a bellyache. It was all wrong. Everything good around Tara had been slipping away for a while.

So why tonight? What had set her racing to the trunk of the car to grab her backpack and flee into the shadows of a warm spring evening? It wasn't because of her mom's confession. Rather, Tara understood her grandma, great-grandma, aunt, and great-aunts were up to something that could not be reversed: They were going to extinguish her mom's power. It was one thing to medicate it, a different animal entirely to amputate it. Tara couldn't protect her mom from the mutilation, but she could distract her relatives until she thought of a better plan.

It was her friend Brittany who'd told her where in Constantine Pappas's abandoned sanitorium you could access the underground tunnels. Brittany had heard from a friend who heard it from a friend that if you went into the third door from the left when you were facing the east side of the asylum and took the first set of stairs on your right down to the weedy, mucky basement, there you were.

Tara ran straight to it from the Queen Anne.

It'd been terrifying to enter. She'd had to push aside vines that grabbed at her hair like corpse fingers. The air inside was thick with dust. When her eyes adjusted to the darkness, she saw she stood inside a lobby that gaped like a hollow mouth, its floor littered with glass and fallen plaster. Wheelchairs and rusted gurneys slumped in the shadows. Every doorway yawned black. She forced herself to walk toward the basement stairs, but each step she took seemed to amplify the silence, interrupted only by the distant creaking of the old building settling. The temperature dropped the lower she went, and the smell of damp earth and decay grew stronger. The sound of dripping water echoed ominously, almost as loud as her heartbeat thundering in her ears. Every nerve in her body screamed for her to turn back, but she pushed onward, each step heavier than the last until she reached the tunnel entrance.

It was exactly as Bethany had described. Dark, haunted, eternal.

It would do.

Flashlight in hand, she'd dropped into Pappas's subterranean network, prepared to stay until the world above returned to normal.

Chapter 42

Ursula

Tara'd been missing for forty-eight hours when the boy who'd claimed to love her showed up at the front door of the Queen Anne. Ursula answered.

"Hi. My name is Leo. I stopped at your workshop last Christmas. I work at Seven Daughters?"

She was quiet. She'd given him the love potion he'd asked for, as she gave everyone what they came for. She was not responsible for how they used it.

"It's closed," he continued, pointing vaguely toward the downtown, "and I'm wondering what's up. Are Helena or Xenia here?"

"They're out looking for Tara."

He clenched his hands. "She's gone?"

Ursula regarded him with sharp eyes. "Ran away."

"I'm a friend of hers."

Ursula could see he was lying, knew he hadn't taken the love potion. It didn't take magic to intuit either. First, the boy was a terrible liar, all twitches and pinballing eye contact. Second, if he'd taken the potion, he would have known Tara had run away because the two of them would be joined at the hip. Ursula found herself liking him even more. Still, a lie couldn't be tolerated. She let her eyes speak for her.

It didn't take Leo long to break. "That's not true. We're not friends. I haven't even talked to her yet. But I'd like to help. When did she run away?"

Ursula felt her mouth twitch. A good man, at least a young one, was as predictable as a puppy. "Two nights ago."

"Did you call the police?"

She sighed, any temporary lightness erased. "Yes. There's not much they can do that we haven't."

"Leo!" Xenia slipped past her sister. "What're you doing here?"

"I went to work. It's closed."

"Of course," Xenia said. "It was closed yesterday, too, but you didn't work, so you wouldn't have known that. We have much more important concerns now. We need to find Tara."

"Let me help."

Ursula and Xenia guided him to the kitchen. Ursula saw his eyes widen as he took it all in: copper-bottom pans hanging from a rack in the center of the giant room, perched over an island scattered with sandwich fixings: a mustard pot, tomatoes, ham and cheese. Glass-front cupboards. Spices, dishware, and exotic cooking tools. The massive cookstove with the curving porcelain look of an antique. The smell of the space that shifted depending on where one stood—blueberry muffins here, roast pork there.

The rest of the family was taking the shortest of breaks to scarf down a quick meal before they left to search again. Ursula watched his gaze travel over all of them—Helena, Katrine, Xenia—and then stop on Jasmine. She was bony, crazed-looking, an eyeless creature unearthed. The sight of her condition stopped Ursula's heart anew every time she saw it, and she could see it was the same for Leo.

His glance returned to Katrine, likely looking for a safer place to land.

She stared back.

Ursula was impressed to see Leo stand tall despite quavering in his fingers. Katrine's full gaze could strip a man to his core.

"Where have you all looked?" he asked.

Helena glanced up. "Leo!" She rushed over to put her arms around the boy. "We've searched along the river. At all her friends'. Up and down every street. The library, the grocery, the bus station. We've searched everywhere."

"Everywhere an adult would," Leo said, out the door before Helena's words had cooled.

Chapter 43

Katrine

Betrayal.

That's what Katrine had felt when her mother told them two days earlier that they had to strip Jasmine of her power. Ursula's betrayal of Jasmine and her own betrayal of her sister for even thinking of maiming her like that, because she *was* considering it.

Sever.

Jasmine would be dust afterward, flat and light and transparent.

Tara must have realized what they were about to do. Katrine was certain the girl had run to save her mom, and something that felt like steel girded Katrine's heart. There was no denying her niece had courage, but in the end, Ursula was right. If Jasmine was being poisoned by her own unused magic, drastic means were required to save her.

But first, they had to find Tara. Katrine went back out to search right after Xenia and Helena's assistant ran out of the Queen Anne. As she drove up and down the streets of the Pappas neighborhood for what felt like the millionth time, hoping against hope that Tara had stayed close to her home, she found herself wishing Ren were by her side. It was such an unexpected thought, but so natural. Her instincts told her he was someone she could lean on. The awareness was dominating her brain when her cell phone rang.

"Katrine?"

"Who's this?"

"Dagmar Baum." A pause. "Heidi's mom?"

Katrine was suddenly on edge. How had Dagmar gotten her phone number, and why was she calling?

"We think we found Tara."

Katrine's heart soared. Of course. Dean or Jasmine must have informed their circle that the girl was missing so everyone could search. "Where?"

"The Catholic church, of all places. Our Lady of the Lakes?"

Katrine was so happy that she barely registered Dagmar's odd tone of voice—flat, disaffected—before hanging up to carve an illegal U-turn and race the three miles to the church. She hadn't allowed herself to feel the full worry for her niece until this moment.

The evening was unseasonably warm. Her car bumped a little as she drove, as if she were hitting tiny potholes. It wasn't until she pulled into the church parking lot that she saw she'd been driving over snakes. She shuddered.

The snakening was upon them.

She parked next to Heidi's car—Dagmar must have called her daughter to help, too—and ran inside. Her feet barely touched the ground as she flew up the steps, her breath coming sharp.

Inside the hushed apse, she saw immediately that Dagmar had never meant for her to find Tara.

She'd sent her to get her heart broken.

Heidi and Ren stood at the front of the church, Heidi in Ren's arms.

Katrine backed out silently, carrying a ball of lead in her gut. She stumbled down the stone steps. The air was scented with moldering leaves and splinters of bright green. The snakes that'd been a trickle moments before were now running thick, slithering and tripping her. Twice she almost fell before she made it to her car.

Once inside, she locked the Honda's door, her chest filled with hardening cement, her blood slugging through her veins. The crescent moon shone on her like a Cheshire cat grin, and below, the reptiles flowed, hissing, rubbing against each other, squirming, making her see what she didn't want to see. In that moment, the weight of her family struggles and the loss of her silly schoolgirl hope that Ren would sweep her off her feet crushed her. She put her head in her hands.

A knock at her driver's side window startled her.

She glanced up.

Baler Trempeleau stood there, his jeweled eyes glowing like answers, his cowboy hat tipped low. She fell into his wicked smile.

Chapter 44

Katrine

Baler told her he'd been out walking when the snakes started bubbling up from the ground. He asked for a ride home, and she said yes. She drove him back to his apartment, veering to miss the bump and pop of reptiles under her wheels before realizing such a thing was impossible.

She shouldn't be with the man. He was dangerous. Yet, when he told her she should come up for a drink, she found herself agreeing. She crawled out through her driver's side window and was balanced on her hood, looking for a way to get inside without wading through the snakes, when he tossed her over his shoulder and carried her up to his second-floor apartment.

The force of him was exciting, but a warning was scraping at her. Before she could nail down the thought, he kicked open his door and hauled her inside, dropping her onto a leather couch before closing the door behind.

A plug-in room freshener emanated the cloying smell of funeral lilies.

He removed his cowboy hat when he turned to face her. He looked vulnerable without it, painfully handsome, his sandy hair tousled, his face chiseled. A charming smile played on his full lips.

Katrine felt like she was acting in a play she couldn't step outside of. "I guess they've come before, but I don't remember very much about it," she blurted.

"Huh?" He leaned over to rest his hat on the back of the couch.

"The snakes." She felt like she was hyperventilating. She wasn't supposed to be here. She didn't know this man, and she should be out looking for Tara. It'd been silly to come, so why couldn't she escape this web? The living room was small, the only furniture a stereo, a coffee table, and the leather couch, a guitar leaning against it. A single dim lamp cast weak light, deepening the shadows. The apartment walls were white and bare.

Katrine glanced at the door but couldn't bring herself to move toward it. The air felt heavy, pressing down on her.

Baler strode to the window and pushed back a curtain. "There sure are a lot of 'em." His chuckle was low. "I've heard stories of blackbirds raining down, but nothing about so many snakes coming out at once." He turned, his eyes piercing her. "You say they've been here before?"

"Yeah." She shook her head. "I think it has something to do with the unseasonably warm weather. You're not from here originally?"

The question seemed to amuse him, but he didn't answer. Instead, he stepped away from the window. She felt like she was falling. Even though she was already sitting, she put out her hand to steady herself. "I should go," she said.

He glanced at her sideways. "You scared of me?"

He was just a man, a beautiful one, but only human. Yet . . .

"No," she lied.

A grin lit up his face. "Then let me get you that drink."

She didn't trust her voice, so she nodded, lowering her head toward her knees to restore her balance once he was out of sight. From the kitchen came the hiss of two beers opening. She removed, folded, and then refolded her coat. A hunting magazine lay open and face up on the table in front of her. He must have been reading it before his walk.

He reappeared, flicking on his stereo as he passed it. In the background, Dusty Springfield sang about spooky boys. Katrine accepted the cool brown bottle he offered her.

"Thanks." She swallowed half of it. Outside, the wind rose up, whipping against the apartment windows, enlisting branches in hopes of waking her up from the hypnotist's spell.

Even the snakes seemed to increase their song, desperate for Katrine's attention.

But she couldn't remember how to listen.

Baler watched her, his jeweled eyes hooded. "I've got more beer if you need it."

She forced herself to focus on him fully, scanning him from top to bottom. He was vibrating with a sexual energy too strong to read anything beneath. She considered it. Wouldn't it be nice to feel good, if only for a little while? And weren't they safe up here, away from the snakes?

It all felt so inevitable, and she wanted to get it done and over with, so she put the half-drunk beer on the table, stood, and strode to the bedroom, her breath sharp and beer scented. He was suddenly behind her, his corded arm wrapped around her waist. He shoved her hair away and kissed her neck. She moved into it, turning until his hot mouth was on hers.

He laid her on the floor and climbed on top. His weight was good. It made her feel like someone else was in charge. She bucked her hips, and he made a noise in the back of his throat, a growl more than a word. He unbuttoned her shirt, yanked it off, and pulled her bra down to her waist. She'd have an abrasion circling her rib cage from the force of it, but for now, she welcomed the pain, just as she welcomed his mouth on her breasts, his bites, his hand thrusting into her jeans.

She hadn't had sex with anyone since Adam, the man who'd followed her their entire relationship with an eraser, trying to remove her, everything she'd done, so all her energy was spent trying to redraw herself. It'd made it so easy for him to move on, yet she hadn't been able to. She was desperate to feel another man's mark on her, to do her own erasing, to heave every thought away so she could just *be*. She shoved Baler's hands away and wiggled out of her jeans. She tried to stand, wearing only underwear and her bra around her waist, intending to move them to the bed. He yanked her back down.

"We're going to do it here."

He used enough force to throw her off-balance, and she landed next to him on the carpet, cracking her elbow on the edge of the bed frame. "Stop it," she said.

Those words inflamed something in him. She saw it flare up for a moment. His eyes went shark-black, and something crawled behind them like beetles in a hole. He recovered himself, but it was too late. She'd witnessed it. She suddenly felt sick that she was in Baler's apartment. So what if Ren and Heidi were dating? Good for them. It didn't mean she needed to be here.

Her vision had cleared, and it felt like a death row pardon.

"I have to go." She pulled her bra up, adjusting it before sliding the straps over her shoulders.

"What?" Baler sat on his haunches, his voice incredulous. His erection pushed against his pants like a ridiculous spear. Outside, the wind picked up, screaming its warning. *Listen. Please listen. You're not safe here.*

But she already knew that. This was her body, and she was going to take it outside now. "You heard me."

"Hold on." He started to reach for her shoulder, noted her expression, and instead held up both hands. "We were just having fun."

She grabbed her shirt and buttoned it up as best she could, not arguing. He could think what he wanted.

"I can make you feel good," he pleaded.

She felt his eyes on her blue silk panties, still wet from the earlier passion. "I don't want to—"

"We'll just have fun," he promised, his voice hypnotic. He put a hand on her ankle and gripped. "This is just about you. I don't need anything out of it, baby."

She tried to break free, but he pulled her toward him. As he did, movement caught her eye. A sidewinding shadow glided over the carpet and vanished beneath the bed. Beneath her ragged breathing, she heard the whisper of scales against carpet.

A snake had reached the second level.

She had to get out of there. She kicked at Baler, but it was too late, she saw it in his eyes. He was not going to let her go. She felt the backdraft that precedes horror. He grabbed her wrists, pinning her. She fought, but he was too strong.

If not for the snakes, she would have been lost.

They poured through the walls, a sea of reptiles, benign in thought but sheer in number. His face screwed up in anger. He tried to keep hold of Katrine, but she broke free, flowing with the snakes. Her brain couldn't piece it together, couldn't understand what was happening. It was her substantial, tenacious heart that commanded her. *Get out of here. Don't let him take anything more from you.*

She flew to her feet and grabbed her pants just before the snakes covered the floor. She had to wade through them, their cool bodies rasping across her calves, their smell overwhelming. She'd almost reached the door when she heard him roar behind her. She couldn't help it. She turned.

He stood like a scarecrow, arms out, covered in snakes, only his face his own. "You leaving so quick?" he demanded. His expression was terrifying, a mockery of innocence. "Like I said, I've got more beer."

She lunged for the door.

He began reciting a litany, his words ugly, ridiculous: *"Every time the snakes rise, I'll be there to steal your power. Your children will pay, and their children, forever down the line. Not one of you Blackthorn witches will find a better man than me. Not one of you can stop me."*

"Looks like the snakes are on my side tonight, you son of a bitch," she yelled, and stumbled away.

Chapter 45

Katrine

Her bravado lasted only until she pulled on her pants and reached the reptile-run streets below. Once away from Baler, she felt dirty and small. What had she been thinking, going up to his apartment in the first place? And *enjoying* it, at least at first? The self-respect that she'd been nurturing the past few months fled like a hunted thing. Unable to find her car keys, she ran until her breath was raw, slipping and sliding over the reptiles, sometimes falling to join them, always getting back up and running some more. Police sirens rang out on the other side of town, but no one was out in the Pappas neighborhood, or on any other street she crossed.

The snakes kept them inside.

When her breath began cutting her lungs, she slowed to a walk. That's when the tears came. She hadn't protected her sister from being molested, hadn't even known about it, had left town as soon as she'd graduated, and had blundered from one disastrous relationship to another since. The pungent scent of the snakes girded her ankles as she walked. She ignored it. She deserved everything bad that'd ever happened to her. She knew better, and yet she'd closed her eyes at every opportunity.

The tears intensified, and she felt herself drawn to the Rum River, water calling water. She could picture what Adam was likely doing at this moment. Sitting in front of a fire with a glass of wine, Patsy wrapped in his arms as Heidi had been in Ren's. Well, Ren was far better off with Heidi than he ever would be with Katrine. And most important of all, what about Tara? Was she safe? She'd spent enough time with her niece. She should have known the child planned to run away.

Katrine had failed everyone.

The tang of the spring-thawed river drew her forward, stumbling, her thoughts swirling. She was back in her neighborhood, the twenty blocks between here and Pappas traveled in a blur. She avoided the Queen Anne (*don't look at me, I'm so ugly*), instead treading through a neighbor's yard, the snakes thinning as she neared the water. The sly shard of moon shone on the rushing river. Katrine didn't slow.

She waded straight in, the cold stealing her breath.

She wasn't sure what she intended. A baptism to wash the feeling of Baler's hands and mouth on her? It didn't matter because the force of the water stripped her balance. She was suddenly being scraped along the river rocks, fierce whirlpools whipping her head around before shoving her back into the calmer edges, only to yank her toward the raging center again.

Panic overtook her as the world had become icy black.

Water penetrated her nose and mouth and pushed into her lungs. She fought it as long as she could, but her heart kept her down like an anchor, a red muscle cast in lead. She was soul-tired, wearier than she imagined a person could be, and nothing felt more natural than following the flow. She had nothing she could call her own to stand on, not for any length of time. She extended her arms and legs. A rock chewed her right ankle. Her mind's eye followed the blood from the gash as it churned into the current, diluting from salty red to formless pink to racing silver, becoming clear river water diving through waving weeds and fish gills. She felt the pull to follow her blood and opened her eyes to the confusing murkiness before taking a deep breath of river.

The water burned like fire. It felt good against the breathtaking cold.

When she'd taunted Jasmine as a girl, telling her sister she was a liverless chicken-licker for not joining her in the chicken drop, it was because she'd been terrified herself. She'd wanted Jasmine next to her. Even though Katrine would jump in again and again, her fear never lessened. She was always sure the next time would be the time the falls won. But she kept leaping in. Why? The question trailed out with her blood as her head scraped against a rock and the cold forced her deeper into herself.

It felt so good to stop fighting.

I'm doing the chicken drop, Jasmine, and I'm not chicken this time.

Chapter 46

TARA

Sleeping in an alcove in the dank tunnel hadn't been difficult the first night. She had her sleeping bag and the heat of risk to shelter her. The tunnels were quiet except for the sound of water dripping and the occasional skitter of rodent feet, and her dreams dug down like tree roots.

She spent the next day reading and crying. That night was much harder than the first, laced with nightmares and groaning sounds. She tossed and turned until she realized there'd be no sleeping. To distract herself from her fear, she decided to explore the tunnels, tying her string to a hook in the alcove so she could find her way back to her stuff.

The underground floors were musty, hard-packed dirt. The walls were cold poured concrete, and they shed copper-colored dust when she trailed her fingers along them. Old wiring lay exposed, and empty light sockets stared down like eyes. At one corner, someone had spray-painted SEX, HUGS, AND ROCK AND ROLL and surrounded it with a white heart. Her flashlight caught all of this in epileptic bursts, but mostly it lit the area exactly four feet in front of her in a yellow circle that she followed until she found herself standing in front of the door that led to the basement of her house.

She knew it was her place because the doors had numbers above them fashioned of pieces of blue and white tile. Her house number was

2227. All but the tail of the third 2 was intact. She reached out to the mildewed wood, once-powerful oak that'd grown spongy with time and moisture. She knew that on the other side was more wood, fresher, nailed there by her father on her mother's command, and on the other side of that, brick laid on brick and cemented in place to keep out the dark, a shelf full of porcelain pigs the final layer.

Tara put her ear to the wet wood. It tingled, like a snake's kiss, and smelled like the deep rot of a fall forest. Could she hear crying? Laughter? But that was a trick. The three layers of protection were too thick to let any noise through.

Loneliness descended, a smothering embrace that made her sleepy. What time was it? She'd lost track navigating the tunnels. She should rest. She was winding her string back up when she heard the scrape of a door opening, followed by the heavy breathing of a man.

She thought immediately of the demon in the cowboy hat, coming for her, coming for every last one of the Blackthorn women.

He was at his most powerful tonight, and he was done waiting.

Chapter 47

Ursula

Ursula sat up in bed, the scream echoing in her flesh. It took her several beats to realize the shriek was hers. Once she became oriented, she reacted without hesitation, not even slowing to grab her glasses. She shot from her first-floor bedroom, where she'd tried to steal a couple hours of sleep before resuming the search for Tara, and raced down to the river in her frayed pajamas, her hair whipping around her like bats. She was sobbing, yelling as she ran, screaming Katrine's name.

The night air smelled like freshly dug dirt.

Snakes curled around her ankles.

She stumbled to the river's edge, icy mud squishing between her toes, scanning the frigid water until she caught sight of a white flash of cloth. She dove in, stroking powerfully, gliding between rocks, and catching her daughter just before the falls, twenty descending feet of rocks and pools. Using the branches of a fallen tree that had spanned the river since she was a girl, she heaved them both to shore.

The mud made a sucking noise when she knelt next to Katrine, shivering with exertion and cold. She rolled her unconscious daughter to her side and slapped her between the shoulders as hard as she could, anguish powering the blow. She didn't stop when Katrine started gasping, either, not right away.

The coughs erupted into big wet burps chased by buckets of silvery vomit. The moonglow caught the chrome streaks as they fled down the bank, returning to their source. Katrine heaved, her muscles contracting with every tremor. The painful-looking spasms continued until she rolled over onto her stomach. "Leave me here."

Ursula pushed her daughter's matted hair from her face, her breath puffing out in cumulus clouds. The snakes were giving them space. "What the hell were you doing in the river?"

Katrine slowly dragged herself into a sitting position, her teeth chattering violently. "I had a right to make up my mind about him, but he didn't tell me the truth."

"Adam."

"Sure. Let's start with him." Katrine tried to laugh, but it morphed into juicy retching.

"You couldn't have known."

Katrine stilled temporarily. The house snapped as if it were moving closer to hear her response. Even the river seemed to be listening. She sighed, and when she spoke, it was with the gravitas of old wisdom. "I *could* have. I can see the truth of people. That's my gift. It's always been my gift, though I never wanted to believe it."

Ursula started wheezing. It grew until her whole body was vibrating with it. She was astonished to find she was laughing. "Is that what you thought your gift was, all these years?" she asked. "To see the truth in people?" She laughed even more, the sound full-throated.

Katrine appeared deeply offended. "I thought you'd be happy that I finally claimed it."

"Then you have a lot to learn." Ursula leaned forward to rub Katrine's cold arms. "Besides, being unfaithful wasn't the truth of Adam. That's why you didn't see it. Things like that are a part of a person, a part that they work hard to hide, but it isn't all of them.

Not by a long shot." Ursula needed to tread carefully. Her laughter had surprised even her, but she'd held on to it to spark the blaze of anger in Katrine. Her daughter needed the fire to burn away the fog of helplessness. She knew that if a person stared too long at the dark strands that made up a moment, they were lost. It was what was killing Jasmine, and she'd be damned if she'd let it finish off either of her girls.

Katrine hugged her knees, still trembling with cold. "I make terrible choices with men. I want a new story."

"You can't have the apples without the worms." Ursula studied her beautiful girl, all headstrong will and careening intuition. She squeezed Katrine's arm. "Let's go inside."

"I'm damaged," Katrine said. She hiccuped. "I let this singer . . ." She switched tacks, a yelp of hysterical laughter startling out of her mouth. "Forget the singer. You know what's even more pitiful? Adam's a selfish monster, but I miss him. I miss him most in the places I least expect it, like the grocery store when I see his favorite food and realize I have no one to cook for."

Ursula put her arms around her daughter for the first time in years. "You're going to be okay."

"I let him use me."

Ursula didn't know if she meant the singer or Adam, but it didn't matter. She took Katrine by the chin and turned her so they were nose to nose. "They can hurt you, but they can't break you. *Ever.* You're stronger than you know."

Ursula felt the sudden power of Katrine's complete attention, but her daughter's words caught her off guard. "Why'd you sleep with Dean, Mom? Of all the guys in town, why Jasmine's husband?"

What saddened Ursula the most was that she knew she deserved the question. "He came to me for a spell. When I turned him away, he knocked over a candle. What Jasmine saw was me trying to clean it off."

Katrine studied her mother and seemed satisfied by what she heard. Then she sighed. It sounded like a ship being retrieved from the bottom of the ocean. "Hey, next guy I date, I'm going to take him to a psychologist to get him checked out the way you take a used car you're considering buying to a mechanic."

Ursula smiled in the dark and helped Katrine up. As they walked toward the Queen Anne, shivering and leaning against each other for support, both were aware that they'd never communicated so much in a single sitting. They felt the bond laying up, something unshakable and essential.

"Hey, Mom?" Katrine asked tentatively. "Why the hell do snakes keep coming to Faith Falls?"

Ursula twitched, the memories connecting. "They called you home, baby. When the snakes come, it's time to face facts and clean house. That means something different for each of us, but I'm guessing you're doing it right now."

Katrine nodded, whispering what she could remember of the words Baler had called out to her. "Every time the snakes rise, I'll be there to steal your power. Not one of you can stop me."

"What?" Ursula asked, her heart locking. She was falling deep into the earth, a great whooshing in her ears, her eyes flooding with water and then dirt, ever deeper, into the grave she'd dug herself using secrets as the shovel. "What did you just say?"

Katrine shook her head. "The singer. The man who . . . lured me in tonight. His name's Baler, and he said those things to me. You know what it means?"

Ursula sank even lower. Velda had made her promise never to tell that they'd murdered Charlie Tanager, but it was Ursula who'd allowed her shame to seal that deal. She had to fight him before he took everything from her. "If he already came for you, he's going to get Jasmine next."

Katrine shook her head. "This guy doesn't even know Jazzy, except for when he stopped by last Christmas. With the carolers. You were in the house."

Ursula shook her head. "It's not the man," she said. "It's the curse inside him. It's coming for my children when the snakes surface."

Katrine's cheeks hollowed, her face a sudden mask of realization, like the sun rising over a crime scene. "Then I think he already got her, Mom. When she was attacked as a girl? It happened last time the snakes were here. I'm sure of it."

The words doubled Ursula over. It was all her fault. The secret she'd buried had grown roots in the dark, twisting through the years until it rose like a poisoned tree. She'd fed it, watered it with her denial, and now the harvest was upon them. "He said he'd come for every Blackthorn down the line," she whispered.

She and Katrine locked eyes, realizing at the same moment.

Tara.

They raced through the snakes to the Queen Anne, were nearly inside the house before they heard the noise. It sounded like a deep chant, everywhere all at once. The massive hum was followed by a booming knock on the front door. They hurried through the house, Ursula covering her daughter with a blanket on the way.

She opened the door with a feeling like dread, but she held her shoulders straight. She would face this as she'd faced all but one thing in her life: head-on. Still, she felt an electric shock when she realized what was making the noise: dozens of people, all of them talking at once, their flashlights punching holes into the night.

"Stop!" The woman's voice wasn't loud, but it had strength. The people surrounding her quieted, and the silence spread outward. Ursula recognized her as Cleo, the woman who'd come to her for a potion once she'd realized she wouldn't change a thing about her life if she found out she only had a year to live. Once the crowd was quiet, Cleo addressed Ursula. "We heard Tara is missing, and we're using the church's phone tree to get out the word. We'd all like to help search."

Katrine stepped past her mom and onto the porch, the nubby blanket tight around her shoulders, her eyes glistening. "She ran away two days ago," she said.

Cleo clucked her tongue. "You should have called us earlier. But don't worry, we'll find her. Can we use your house as a central communication point?"

Ursula stepped to the side, hot tears rivering to her chin.

Cleo marched past, accompanied by two off-duty police officers, three firefighters, and every parent who'd heard of Tara's absence, including Diane, the owner of the Vietnamese restaurant. The house made room for all of them. One of the off-duty officers unrolled a map on the kitchen island. The town was broken up into grids. Areas were assigned. Cell phone numbers were exchanged, checkpoints established. People stepped into the night.

No corner would go unsearched.

Ursula felt herself grow brighter. The hope and love surrounding her were beyond anything she'd ever felt. It wasn't pure, of course. Caramine, the mayor's wife, knew he'd cheated on her with Velda last month. While he was stepping out, for the first time in her life, Caramine had enough space to realize that she had less work and more fun when he wasn't around. She wasn't eager to run into Velda tonight, though she was prepared to pay that price to help find Tara.

Another woman, Isabel, had been picketing Seven Daughters for months alongside Dagmar and was wrestling with guilt for any part she'd played in this family's misery. Suzy, the Daughters of the Mill secretary, had been picketing Seven Daughters as well, and she couldn't stop thinking about an orange dress she'd spotted in the window. The A-line had since been sold, and she was hoping to run into Xenia tonight to ask her to sew another.

One of the policemen had a crush on Ursula and wanted to catch her eye, and a few people were worried whether they'd get home in time for a good night's sleep before work tomorrow, but every one of them was concerned, and they all had love to give.

Ursula watched Katrine take it all in. Her daughter must have recognized that the search for Tara was in the best possible hands, because she slipped upstairs, returning moments later in dry clothes. She grabbed a jacket and stole into the night.

Ursula prayed Katrine would have the courage to do what she herself should have all those years ago.

Chapter 48

Ursula

Ursula had been assigned a grid four blocks over. She'd already walked it many times, but she wouldn't stop until they found her granddaughter.

She followed the stream of slipping, hissing, urine-scented reptiles away from the Queen Anne. The crescent moon howled at her. People stared from their windows, horrified by the vision of Ursula stumbling across the reptiles, her gray-black hair tossed by the sharp breeze. But she didn't stop. She didn't even think, barely registered the siren going off across town. She needed to get to Tara before Charlie Tanager did.

"Ursula Blackthorn, come inside!"

She glanced over at the woman standing on her porch, her face panicked. Ursula shook her head and kept walking. The snakes were inside her ear, whispering to her, their melody hypnotizing.

It was dizzying. She would have kept walking, kept searching desperately, if the secret snake whispers hadn't abruptly stopped, leaving her both exhausted and energized. She blinked.

She stood outside Michael and Dagmar Baum's house.

Reptiles slithered across her feet, bumping against and past her, but she could no longer hear their voices, only the cold leather of their bodies rustling against the ground. And over that, another, smaller sound.

She cocked her ear. The noise was pure sadness. It seemed to be emanating from inside her head, but no, that wasn't right. The sound was coming from above. She had to squint through the shadows to spot the source: a woman, curled in the lowest branch of the magnificent maple tree in the Baums' front lawn. She wore a patch over her left eye.

"Dagmar?" Ursula asked.

The woman hugged her knees tighter to her body, but her weeping didn't stop.

Ursula stepped closer, wading through the snakes. It *was* Dagmar, and in addition to the patch over her left eye, her right eye appeared to be clouding over. "Are you all right?"

"Don't come any closer!" Dagmar's voice was ragged. She was staring frantically in every direction, as if searching for Ursula. Groceries were scattered on the ground below her, a gallon of milk and bag of chips peeking through the thickness of reptiles.

Ursula was overcome with pity. How had she possibly found her way home? She must be nearly blind by now.

"Dagmar, it's Ursula Blackthorn. The snakes are here. We need to get you inside."

"You." The word was so sharp that the snakes froze for a razor-moment. "You witch. You did this to me! And you brought this horror."

Ursula waded through the snakes and put her hand on Dagmar's ankle, the only part of her she could reach. Dagmar flinched. Her right shoulder ticked to a rhythm, a clock that counted pain rather than time, and her hands were rubbing circles into the bark of the tree. Left alone with her thoughts and her soul, with her only remaining window to the outside world clouding by the minute, Dagmar was going batty.

"I'll help you into your house, all right?" Ursula asked.

"I'm not letting those snakes touch me." The tic in Dagmar's shoulder increased its pace.

Ursula's gaze dropped. She couldn't see her feet for the river of reptiles. They should probably disgust her, but they didn't. "You can ride on my shoulders. Come on now. You can't stay out here all night. You'll be safe inside."

Dagmar's mask slipped, but she grabbed it and pasted it back on. "I'll let you help me into the house, *witch*, but that doesn't change anything. I'm going to take your house, your children's happiness, your *freedom*. I'm going to prove you killed Charlie Tanager, and you'll lose everything."

A surge of anger ignited in Ursula. For a moment, she considered walking away. Dagmar may not have created her own pain, but she'd nursed it like a child. If she hadn't looked so lonely, so absolutely lost, things may have ended differently.

As it was, like nearly every woman since the beginning of time, Ursula moved her own pain to the side to help someone in need carry theirs.

The Blackthorn Book of Secrets: Sight

When the world grows dim and fear clouds your vision, this spell will help you see what matters most. Place a clear piece of quartz in a bowl of water. Light a white candle so its flame reflects on the surface. Add three drops of lavender oil to the water, naming one thing you wish to see clearly with each drop. Blow out the candle and carry the quartz with you for seven days. Remember that the clearest sight requires seeing past anger to the pain beneath. This isn't to excuse harm others have done to you, but to free yourself from carrying their darkness.

Note: This spell works best when performed in quiet determination. Magic favors the steady heart over the desperate one.

Chapter 49

Tara

Every nerve in her body trembled, screaming at her to run, hide, protect herself, but she was trapped in the tunnels with that demon. Her terror grew shoots and then cords that wrapped around her ankles and held her to the earth as sure as cement. She waited, quivering, for the man in the cowboy hat to come into view, strip her, separate her from herself. Her hand went to the hem of her shirt, kneading it.

If you can move your hands, you can move your feet. Run!

But her body wouldn't listen. And so she stood, chilled to her marrow, awaiting the executioner's blade. Which was why, when the boy appeared, a dim flashlight wobbling in his hand, she couldn't make sense of it at first.

"Tara?" he asked.

She'd been panting. She tried to draw a breath but couldn't get her lungs around it.

He stepped forward, turning the circle of light on his own face so she could see him clearly. "Are you okay?"

The air wouldn't move past her mouth. She grew lightheaded.

He began to step closer, concern painting his face, but stopped himself. "I'll leave if you don't want me here. I'll go right now."

"No." The word released the iron cage around her chest. She drew air all the way to her belly, sucking desperately at it, grabbing for another breath before she was through with the first. She hoped he understood that she meant for him to stay.

"My name's Leo. I work for your great-aunts. At Seven Daughters?"

She recognized him as the boy she'd seen last Christmas. She could smell the pfeffernüsse and feel the magic of Christmas morning. She still couldn't find her tongue.

"Is someone else down here with you?"

The gentleness in his voice allowed her to breathe even more deeply. "No." She thought of the dark-eyed man, couldn't stop thinking of him. "At least, I don't think so."

He nodded, shifting his stance.

"What are you doing here?" she asked.

His smile was sheepish. "I came looking for you. I stopped by the Queen Anne, and they told me you'd run away."

She tensed, waiting for him to ask her why, or to tell her to go home. Instead, he glanced around, flashing the walls with his feeble light.

"This place is like I remembered."

"You've been here before?" she asked.

"Once." He glanced at his feet. "It was a party. I drank peach schnapps. I can still taste it anytime I'm sick." He smiled ruefully. "I don't think I'm much of a drinker. Anyways, if I am, I'd prefer to do it aboveground in the future."

A warmth radiated out from her chest. She was glad she was no longer alone down here. "I have a hiding spot near the entrance. Want to see it?"

"I think I passed it coming in." He paused. "It didn't look very safe. You've slept there the last two nights?"

She nodded, rolling up the ball of string to lead them back to her hidey-hole. They didn't talk. When they reached the alcove where she'd made camp, she stopped in her tracks, seeing it through his eyes. Her penlight caught a glimpse of purple—her sleeping bag. Her backpack was right behind it. She'd been foolish to think she was protected down here. Her cheeks burned. She felt incredibly naive. She didn't want to look at him.

"Wait here," he said. "I'll be back in an hour."

◆ ◆ ◆

When Leo returned, he carried a sheet of plywood, stainless steel nails, a cordless drill, and two dark blankets. He explained that he wasn't as good at carpentry as his father, but he'd picked up enough. He began constructing a wall in the front of the alcove. If someone was looking for it, they'd see it, but the wall would help to conceal it.

She watched him warily at first but found herself moving closer. The next time he went for a nail, she handed it to him, a smile blooming. "You're PINCing me," she said. "With wood and nails. I didn't know boys could PINC, too."

He glanced at her, and his mouth dropped.

She understood in that moment that he loved her smile and wanted to kiss her, that he'd have given up a million dollars to do it. Instead, he went back to work. That made her like him even more, then *that* thought made her giggle. Her laugh tickled his funny bone, and he started to laugh, too. She reached her hand out to feel his laughter in the air. It popped like citrus-scented bubbles.

"Are you hungry?" she asked, suddenly shy.

"No," he said as his stomach grumbled.

She laughed again, a calliope sound, and then wiped her smile away. "Your belly sounds like the walls down here. They've been grumbling since I came." She dug through her backpack and handed him a small box of raisins.

He seemed reluctant to take her food, but equally uncomfortable turning down her kindness. "Thanks," he finally said.

When he offered some to her, she held out her hand. She was about to pop the raisins in her mouth when a scraping sound stopped her. It was coming from the entrance. The noise chilled her blood.

The cowboy. He was finally here.

She knew it without seeing him, the same way she knew the sun would rise tomorrow and that water flows downhill. He'd already gone after Katrine, and now he'd sniffed Tara out like a mongoose, found her underground, was going to chew on her flesh.

"We have to run!" she screamed.

Leo didn't hesitate. He grabbed Tara's hand and pulled her away from the entrance. His flashlight beam danced wildly as they scrambled down the tunnels.

"This way," he whispered, finding a narrow passage she hadn't noticed before. The walls pressed close on either side, forcing them to move single file. Behind them, footsteps echoed—slow, confident, patient. The man in the cowboy hat wasn't rushing because he knew they had nowhere to go.

The passage split into three directions. Leo hesitated for a fraction of a second before pulling her left, deeper into the earth. The air grew thicker, mustier. Water dripped somewhere in the darkness ahead.

"Do you know where we're going?" Tara's voice was barely a breath.

"No," Leo admitted.

The confession terrified her.

They stumbled through the inky blackness, their footsteps impossibly loud despite their efforts to move quietly. The tunnel curved sharply right, then left, then split again. Each choice felt like a coin flip between safety and the end. A low chuckle rolled through the tunnels behind them, bouncing off the walls until it seemed to come from everywhere at once. Tara's skin crawled. He was playing with them, letting them think they could escape.

"Tara . . ." The cowboy's singsong voice drifted through the darkness. "You can't hide forever, little mouse."

They ran faster, abandoning stealth for speed. The tunnel opened into a wider chamber, and Leo's light caught glimpses of old medical equipment—a table, some gurneys—left to rot. Three more passages branched off from here.

"Which way?" he gasped.

Before Tara could answer, a sound made them both freeze. A rhythmic pounding, distant but steady. *Thump. Thump. Thump.* It was coming from the middle tunnel.

"What is that?" she asked.

Leo strained to listen. The pounding was irregular. "Maybe . . . machinery? A pump?" Hope crept into his voice. "If there's functioning equipment, there might be people. Workers. Help."

But the sound filled Tara with dread. It reminded her of a heartbeat. Like something waiting.

Behind them, footsteps scraped closer. A thin beam of light—much stronger than Leo's—began to probe the chamber they'd just entered.

"We have to choose now," Leo urged.

The pounding grew louder. *Thump. Thump. Thump.*

"Found your little love nest," the cowboy called from the passage behind them, his voice so close. "Cozy. But you forgot something, darlin'. Me."

His chuckle sounded like something popping. A bottle cap, a joint, a weapon. The noise turned Tara's bones to glass. She grabbed Leo's hand, and they plunged into the middle tunnel, toward the pounding sound, not knowing if they were racing to salvation or something worse than what pursued them. The tunnel seemed to stretch forever. Their breathing echoed harshly. Behind them, the cowboy's footsteps quickened, no longer patient.

"Almost got you now." His voice carried. "You're gonna love what I brought you."

The pounding was now loud. *THUMP. THUMP. THUMP.* And underneath it, another sound that made Tara's blood freeze—a low moaning, like wind through a graveyard.

Leo's flashlight flickered and dimmed. The batteries were dying.

A hand brushed against Tara's shoulder. She screamed and spun around, but it was only a root hanging from the tunnel ceiling. In her panic, she stumbled and fell, skinning her palms on the rocky ground.

"Got you—" The cowboy's voice was right behind them now.

Leo hauled Tara to her feet and they sprinted the last few yards toward the pounding. They nearly reached it.

And then the cowboy caught Tara's shirt.

Chapter 50

Jasmine

Dean drove straight back to Faith Falls once he learned Tara was missing and had been searching tirelessly ever since, pausing only to bring Jasmine home when he saw she was coming apart at her seams. That only served to leave her alone with her panic. The devil was at her daughter's door. Jasmine knew this. All her years devoted to protecting Tara, keeping her close, and on the night when it mattered most, she could do nothing. The terror set Jasmine outside herself, lending her a grotesque calm. She simply sat on her couch, legs crossed at the ankles, hands clutched in her lap, staring into darkness.

When someone knocked feverishly at her front door, she sleepwalked to it and found Katrine on the other side, looking like she'd been thrown out of a moving car.

"What happened to you?" Jasmine asked. Her question lacked any emotion. She'd employed the words because it somehow seemed an appropriate response to a bruised and bedraggled person showing up at her door.

Did Katrine, already in rough shape, grow even paler when she laid eyes on Jasmine? Did she put her hand to her mouth in horror? It didn't matter. Jasmine had the knives sharpened. She'd deal permanently with the hissing as soon as they located Tara.

"I'm not leaving you behind this time," Katrine said. "Where's Dean?"

"Driving around. Looking." The sibilance was so loud that she wondered if Katrine could hear her over it. *Sshhh.* Was the hissing really music? Bluegrass? It almost sounded like . . . no, the thought slipped away again, leaving a maddening buzz that never turned off. She knew in her mother's heart that the monster had found Tara, just like he'd found Jasmine, fifteen years earlier. He was going to clip her daughter's glorious wings. She could not reach her baby, could not save her.

She felt her shoulders being shaken.

"Jasmine, look at me. Ursula never seduced Dean, and she never would. You saw her cleaning candle wax off him. He was in her cottage to get a potion, probably one to keep you all together." Katrine's voice cracked. "I'm so sorry you were attacked, and that I wasn't there to stop it, and that I didn't fight the spell that sent me away. Please let me in. We can deal with this together."

Jasmine cocked her head. She didn't understand the words. And why were snakes coming in through her front door?

Katrine lunged forward and wrapped Jasmine in an embrace. Jasmine noticed that her sister's hair was matted and tangled. She smelled like the river.

"You have to face it, though," Katrine was saying. "Face it head-on and claim your gift, or it'll kill you."

She cupped her hands over Jasmine's ears and they stared into each other's eyes. Jasmine got lost in Katrine's for a moment. She'd felt the absence of her sister's gaze acutely when Katrine had first left Faith Falls, because Katrine's glance had always been a blessing. She'd been born with the ability to expand anyone she focused on. Her attention didn't just make people *feel* smarter, funnier, or kinder, as Velda's did. Katrine raised them up a level by locating and amplifying their best self.

She was the sun to each person's divine seeds.

She'd worked her powerful magic on Jasmine growing up. Jasmine's food tasted twice as delicious and healed those who ate it in half the time when Katrine helped her cook. She'd also unknowingly applied her magic on her high school friends, who were more popular and scored better on tests when Katrine was around. Jasmine even knew via letters that Katrine had worked her talent on Adam, nurturing him from an angry, underemployed graphic artist to a painter who'd discovered that he had a flair for poetry and didn't mind public speaking.

She'd opened up his world. That he ended up resenting her for it was the ultimate irony.

Of course, there were people who even at their best were not worth scraping off your boot, in Velda's words. Why had she thought of boots? Was the incessant hissing a marching song? Had it been military music all this time? Jasmine caught the tail end of the tune and then it slipped away.

"What?" Jasmine asked. She and Katrine were still standing in her entryway. The air had gone scratchy. Katrine's lips were moving. What was she saying? *Lever? Sever?* Was that more knocking at the door? Knocking, knocking, knocking, always the knocking of the bass drum, a backbeat to the rhythm guitar that took the trumpet and bleated fear and buried her alive. But—a change! The knocking suddenly seemed to be coming from her garage, which inspired her to run toward it to grab Dean's sledgehammer from his wall of implements. It was the hissing that was driving her mad, and it had originated on the tunnel side of the wall in her basement. She was going to tear down the wall—*why hadn't she thought of that before!*—and she was going to hiss back. If that didn't put an end to the sound, she was prepared to shove a knife in her ears and puncture that mighty, noisy itch.

She charged down the basement stairs, sledgehammer in hand, the air around her electric. She swung the hammer, taking out the knickknack shelves first. They clattered to the ground, a pile of useless pig-pink pieces landing on top of wood shrapnel. She swung harder, and for a moment, she matched the beat on the other side of the wall. The synchronicity was the closest thing to silence she'd felt in days. She almost wept. Fleeing up the stairs and back to the garage, she gathered more hammers and a crowbar and hurried back to the basement.

Katrine watched her, open-mouthed.

Jasmine raced to the basement wall, going at it with the strength of a mother, pounding, scraping, prying, pounding, scraping, prying, finding a harmony. She didn't notice Katrine had taken up a crowbar and had begun demolishing the wall alongside her. Swing, pound, pry, pound, swing, pound, pry, pound.

And then, finally, an opening.

It was no larger than an apple, a lucky strike on soft brick. Wood appeared on the other side, the first layer that Dean had constructed over the original tunnel door when they'd bought the house. Jasmine scrabbled to widen the hole, clawing until her fingers bled. Katrine shoved her aside and stuck the end of the crowbar into it. With a pop, she released a whole brick.

Jasmine's eyes widened. One brick gone, and the hissing had quieted one measure rather than grown louder. Ripping the crowbar from her sister's hands, she worked with a ferocious intensity. Katrine lent her strength, and together, they forced the tunnel opening to grow.

They were surrounded by dust and mess, shards of cement, and with every brick smashed, the hissing continued to lessen. When Katrine returned with Dean's chainsaw, Jasmine laughed and clapped. Together, they held it against the exposed wood. They let the saw scream, slicing through the wall that Dean had built. Sawdust filled the air along with a gassy smell. The original tunnel door on the other side of the fresh wood was so mildewed that Jasmine could push through it with her bare hand.

When she did, the earth exhaled a breath of underground air into the basement.

Jasmine jerked her hand back and shoved her eye against the hole like an animal trapped under river ice. It was bottomless black on the other side, the ultimate screen against which to play the hissing movie that had consumed her mind. She'd been burying it since the attack, rarely letting down her guard, slamming the door closed tight when bits managed to escape. But she didn't have the strength to keep it down any longer, and so the movie played, her eye serving as the projector displaying the image into the deep.

Young Jasmine, flushed and happy, leans over a simmering pot of avgolemono soup. Her hair is pulled back into a ponytail, her focus complete. A honeybee buzzes lazily into her line of sight. She waves it away, but it's drawn back to her sweet breath. Smiling, she lowers the burner under the soup and turns to usher the bumblebee out through the open window.

The rich, enticing smell of avgolemono—tender morsels of chicken bubbling in the rich, bright broth—wafts outside, but the bee stays. Jasmine doesn't mind. She's in the perfect spot at the perfect time, doing what she loves. She begins kneading bread dough, the floured ball giving way under her palms like warm flesh. She presses rhythmically, pouring her love into the dough. It's Katrine's favorite, and her face will light up when she smells it baking. Jasmine is filled with warm pleasure at the thought, and at the image of Katrine coming back proudly bearing the saffron from the store, but then her neck prickles.

She goes to the window. Snakes are slithering across the lawn, so many she can no longer see the grass! Before she can react, there's a noise behind her.

She turns.

He stands just inside the door, his face grim. At first, she thinks he's a ghost, so dark is his form, but then he darts forward, slapping one rough hand over her mouth and sliding the other around her waist. She struggles, and her arm goes out, knocking the pot of soup to the floor. It clatters loudly. She twists, but he's too strong. He drags her into the pantry. He tightens his grip on her mouth, pinning her against the wall. The pain burns through her, splits her in two.

The bee has followed them.

It buzzes, buzzes softly in her ear, begging her to forget before it's even over.

The man releases her. She slides to the floor. He laughs as he speaks the words that have introduced her nightmares ever since: Every time the snakes rise, I'll be there to steal your power. Your children will pay, and their children, forever down the line. Not one of you Blackthorn witches will find a better man than me. Not one of you can stop me.

He disappears. She lies there for minutes before straightening her clothes, pushing herself to a standing position, and limping back to the kitchen. She cleans up the soup and then she begins a fresh pot. It keeps the horror at bay.

Katrine must never know. Nobody must ever know. Because she believes it's the magic of her cooking that drew him to her, she will use it only two more times, first to hide her shame from her family and second to push her loving, curious sister away as soon as she's old enough to leave so that the man can't find her and do this to her.

And so she cooks the feast of a lifetime, soup and puddings and pies and meats and salads, stirring feverishly, desperately, until she has enough food to bewitch her mom, and her aunts, and most of all, her sister. Jasmine is cleaned up when they enter the kitchen, and they are enchanted by the smells of her magical food, and they walk past her without seeing her, just as she'd hoped, and they eat, turning blind to what has happened to their beloved girl.

Her later spell, the one she casts when Katrine is eighteen, is so strong that it begins to push her sister away even before she finishes eating it. Jasmine's heart feels like it's being carved from her chest, to watch Katrine go, but she knows that the only way to protect her is to send her halfway across the world.

But Tara was completely at his mercy.

How could she have failed so terribly?

"Help me get in there. Please," Jasmine rasped, her eye wide against the cold wood of the tunnel door. The movie was playing across the darkness on an endless loop. She was weeping but too numb to feel it.

Katrine pushed Jasmine aside and began to yank barehanded at the rotting wood of the tunnel-side door with a crazed intensity until she'd cleared a hole large enough for Jasmine to crawl through. Katrine hoisted Jasmine up. She went feetfirst and dropped to the ground on the other side into the dark recollection of it.

She was finally, completely, inside the memory.

The movie of it played all around her, again and again, the bumblebee, the snakes, the man, the spells. The bumblebee, the snakes, the man, the spells. Whatever it was going to do to her, it must do now. It might kill her, eradicate the last bit of *Jasmine* that was left, but she wasn't going to run anymore. She heard Katrine crawl through the hole and felt her presence behind her.

"Can you see it?" Jasmine's voice was a shell. "Can you see what happened to me?"

"Yes," Katrine choked out, embracing her sister. "I see it."

With her words and her touch, the film abruptly stopped.

It took Jasmine's eyes a minute to adjust.

When they did, her daughter and a boy were standing a few feet away, out of breath as if they'd been running, a shadow slinking deeper into the darkness behind them. They both appeared terrified. Cords of snakes slithered around their feet, kissing the air with their tongues. The boy held a dim flashlight pointed at the ground and kept glancing back toward the shadow.

"Tara," Jasmine heard herself say through a thundering quiet.

The hissing was gone. Her daughter was safe.

Jasmine fell to her knees and wept, Tara and Katrine holding her. The three of them were still clinging to each other when Ursula, Xenia, and Helena arrived moments later, pouring in through the wall. Dean, when he discovered them all in a heap on the other side of his basement, clung to his wife and child like a saved man.

The wickedly handsome man in the cowboy hat watched from the darkness. His face shifted, and he was Charlie Tanager cursing his wife, Julius Caesar betraying Cleopatra, Perseus murdering Medusa, Adam telling his God lies about Eve because he was jealous.

The snakes had another twenty-four hours in Faith Falls. He was patient.

Part 4

The Severing

The Blackthorn Book of Secrets: Scrying

The most commonly held principle of magic is that it must harm no one. Lesser known is the fact that love and magic derive from the same element. This knowledge is the key to scrying.

Pour a handful of any finely ground herb onto a mirror laid flat. The mind must be free from distraction in all acts of divination and so release any thoughts except for loving ones. Rest the tip of your pointer finger into the herbs. With your eyes closed and your body holding visions of love, allow the finger to move at will.

Open your eyes. The message you seek will be inscribed in the herb.

Chapter 51

Ursula

Xenia, Helena, Katrine, Dean, Jasmine, Tara, Leo—who seemed to be sticking close to Tara—and Audish, who'd been waiting for them on the front porch, had gathered around the island in the Queen Anne's kitchen. Velda was nowhere to be seen.

Ursula told those in attendance everything.

After all these years, it turned out it wasn't much of a story at all.

Charlie had beaten Velda, and she'd borne it, would have kept bearing it if he hadn't set his sights on Ursula. Because he wasn't a man you left, Velda had Ursula mix the hemlock. Her father had died gruesomely and by her own hand, his final words activating a curse against all Blackthorn women through eternity.

Xenia and Helena didn't seem surprised, though their faces twisted in pain to hear the truth of it spoken. Katrine and Jasmine took the news grimly, both of them visibly shuddering.

"This type of evil may sleep, but if you don't face it, it never dies," Ursula continued. "I was too young to know that then."

The unspoken message was that Velda had *not* been too young.

"So he's not done with us," Katrine said. She glanced at Tara, who appeared to be in shock but otherwise whole. She'd revealed that the cowboy had found them in the tunnels, had Tara in his grasp before Jasmine broke through the wall. "Right? He'll just keep coming back."

Ursula repeated the curse that had been tattooed on her heart. "Every time the snakes rise, I'll be there to steal your power. Your children will pay, and their children, forever down the line."

Jasmine and Katrine joined in at the same time, speaking the words that had been uttered to them. "Not one of you Blackthorn witches will find a better man than me. Not one of you can stop me." They wore identical expressions of despair.

The words had the opposite effect on Tara. Her face lit up. "Not *one* of us. That means all of us!"

Ursula didn't understand at first. It was Leo who had to explain. "All of the Blackthorn women together. If everything you said is true, the only way to stop him is to join forces."

Dawn rose across the women's faces, starting with Ursula and ending with Katrine. Even Dean nodded.

"We have to promise no more secrets between us, too," Jasmine said, grabbing her daughter's hand.

Ursula sighed from the depths of her soul. "Then I have one more thing to show you."

Chapter 52

Ursula

"It just opens to a page like that?" Katrine asked. She'd tried turning the book to different sections several times, but it kept returning to the scrying spell.

Ursula nodded, placing her hand over the tome. It suddenly flew open to a page she'd never seen before. She leaned forward, her chest tightening. She didn't know if it was excitement or fear.

The Blackthorn Book of Secrets:
Breaking the Line

Some curses are too old, too deep, too tangled to face alone. When the wound runs through generations, it takes the whole family—bound by blood or choice—to speak the truth that breaks it. Only together can they unmake this type of curse, uttering these words over the one who cast it:

With the power of my blood,
And the strength of my verse,
I reclaim my own path,
And I destroy your curse.

Air. Earth. Water. Fire.
As these words are spoken,
Your spell is forever broken.

Ursula swallowed. "Read this," she commanded the others.

The others crowded close. Together, they studied the page, their gaze fluttering as they moved from one word to the next.

It was Xenia who broke the silence, speaking matter-of-factly. "We need to call Velda."

Ursula's organs shrank. On some level, she'd known this confrontation with her mother was coming. She'd hoped it would not be tonight. She forced herself to stand tall. "We don't need her."

Tara pointed at the spell, her fingers dancing over the intricately inked instructions. "We need all of us. It says so right here. It takes the whole family, whether chosen family or blood relatives."

Katrine nodded. "She's right, Mom. We need Velda here."

Ursula shook her head, her lips drawn into a thin, colorless line. This was her cottage, her safe place, but she still couldn't find her voice. She'd broken her promise to Velda, shared the secret she swore to take to her grave. Despite knowing it'd been necessary, despite being a grown woman and then some, she didn't want to face the disappointment that would bleed into her mother's eyes, didn't want to experience that eternal feeling of death as Velda closed off her love forever.

Xenia grabbed one of Ursula's hands, Helena the other. They understood, as much as a person could, but they didn't know. They'd always had each other and so a steady diet of love. They'd never been starved for it.

"Mom." Jasmine and Katrine spoke as one. "We need to get Velda. Now."

Still, she hesitated.

"Grandma," Tara said, "he's coming for me."

Ursula finally crumbled. "Call her." She reached for a courage potion. It was time to finally stand up to her mother.

"What do you mean, Charlie's back?" Velda scowled, her hair in disarray, her face free of makeup. She'd been sleeping deeply when Xenia pulled her out of bed and drove her to the Queen Anne. While happy Tara had been found, she'd seemed irritated to be led to the cottage and on guard since Ursula had started talking.

Ursula continued bringing her up to speed, outwardly confident but trembling like jelly inside. She would do this for her daughters and for Tara, even though it was ripping at the festering wound she'd buried decades ago.

Velda's expression didn't shift as she listened to Ursula explain how Charlie had come back with the snakes, as he'd promised, first to attack Jasmine over a decade ago, and then to get Katrine and Tara with this most recent snakening.

Ursula wondered if the woman had ever loved anything but herself. The thought was oddly freeing. "And he'll keep coming back," she finished, "unless we deal with him tonight, before the snakes disappear."

"What kind of potion did you mix for him back then? A halfway one?" Velda's words were dipped in accusation. "I thought it was clear that I wanted him dead. *Forever.*"

A faint burning smell emanated from the apothecary drawers, the odor of a forest fire right before the spark hit the pine needles. Dean and Leo glanced around, alarm written on their faces.

"She was thirteen years old," Katrine said, her voice level. She ignored the scent to focus on her grandmother. "You shouldn't have asked her to do that."

Ursula hadn't realized how bent her posture was until she straightened it.

Jasmine brushed Tara's hair back. "She was only a child, Velda. Not even Tara's age."

A new crack appeared in the brittle jar surrounding Ursula's heart, meeting the other one that'd started when Katrine returned from her banishment. Ursula suddenly smelled a wash of scents she hadn't encountered since the day she'd mixed her father's poison: strawberries, lemon drops, mint. Her children were standing with her.

Helena and Xenia still held Ursula's hands, which were now glowing blue.

"What you did was wrong, Velda," Xenia said.

Helena finished her thought. "No one should ask their child to do something like that."

The glass around Ursula's heart began shivering, a thousand tiny cracks shooting like fevered lightning, making it sing.

"You should tell her you're sorry," Tara added.

A bundle of sage hanging from the wall spontaneously burst into flame, tossing orange sparks. Audish doused it with water. Velda watched it all, still scowling. Her liquid green eyes, usually piercing, darted around defensively, narrowing with a cold intensity. She held her chin high, but a flicker of uncertainty flashed across her face.

"We're wasting time," she finally said, ignoring Ursula's tender pain. "How do we kill him once and for all?"

The *Book of Secrets* sighed. It was a disappointed, papery sound.

Chapter 53

Tara

Her mom was out of her mind with worry at the plan they'd landed on, but they all agreed it was the only way: Tara would lure Baler Trempeleau, current host of Charlie Tanager's evil, to the Queen Anne.

Dean, Audish, and Leo would shadow her as she walked to Baler's apartment. She was to holler up to his window (*under no circumstances do you go inside,* Katrine kept repeating, her face drawn) and convince him to meet her outdoors. Once he came down, she was to feign interest in his music, asking him if he'd come back to the Queen Anne to give her singing lessons. She was to tell him her whole family was away for the weekend.

"How could that *possibly* work?" Helena asked. Tara could see her great-aunt didn't want her anywhere near the apartment.

"It'll work," Tara said. When she'd first laid eyes on Baler caroling, she'd recognized him for what he was: a puppet that would go where led. A black spirit held his strings, and that spirit wanted Tara, could only capture her while the snakes still ran. He'd been forced to melt into the shadows when Jasmine and Katrine burst through the wall into the tunnel, but that had only flamed his ravenous hunger.

Of course he'd follow her back to the Queen Anne.

Still, she couldn't stop her teeth from chattering as she waded through the snakes under the sliver of spring moon, humming to keep from thinking about what writhed underfoot and thereby losing her marbles. The smell was bad, the whole world reeking so powerfully of pee and worse that it was as if Faith Falls had been sealed in a jar with the snakes. The closer she drew to the Pappas neighborhood, the tighter her chest grew. The streets were deserted except for her and the snakes. She caught sight of Leo slipping behind some bushes once, and it calmed her, but only until she reached Baler's window.

"Hey," she yelled, or at least meant to. But it came out as a squeak, unintelligible, a noise so tender it was immediately swallowed by snakesong.

It didn't matter.

"Hey yourself," he drawled from behind her.

She spun around, her heart thudding. He was leaning against a streetlamp, his cowboy hat casting a shadow, the snakes making a wide berth around him. She couldn't suppress the shudder. She recognized that the skin suit he wore was handsome, but all she could see was the evil lurking inside him, the red raw demon that craved her. She recoiled and almost stumbled, but she didn't let herself fall. If she had, her dad and Leo would have been by her side in an instant, and this would all be over. The Blackthorn women would be forced to wait another decade or more, always looking over their shoulder until the next time the snakes ran.

"My family is away," she said. She didn't need any of the rest of the story. He pushed himself off the streetlamp, trembling with anticipation, his lips wet. He was old, this demon, far older than her great-grandfather would have been. Ursula and Velda had done the right thing by trying to kill it fifty years earlier. But Tara didn't care about its story. She wanted the curse broken and the demon sent back to whatever hell it'd come from.

She turned and threaded her way through the snakes. He caught up and took her hand. His was hot and dry, far warmer than human body heat. She allowed the contact, even though his energy wormed its way beneath her flesh, making it difficult to breathe.

She walked faster.

He tried to pull her into the bushes once. "Not here," she said, pulse lurching. "Someone could see us." He was milking her innocence with his hot fist, and she would never get that back. She made peace with it on the spot. She was fourteen, after all. She was gonna shed that soon anyhow. As long as he didn't go too deep . . .

When the Queen Anne finally came into view, the snakes that'd been avoiding Baler also moved aside for Tara, allowing quick passage to the house. He hesitated on the steps, the puppet master inside him dropping a thread, allowing the man's fear to leak through. "You sure no one's home?"

Tara nodded and skipped up the stairs ahead of him, onto the wide wraparound porch. The second their hands were no longer touching, her heart bloomed again, careening off her rib cage. "Come on."

He remained on the bottom stair. She licked her lips like she'd seen the lead in that romantic comedy do the other night. When that didn't lure him up, she tossed her hair over her shoulder. The clumsy seduction turned her stomach, but it got him moving. She opened the door and danced ahead, just beyond his reach.

For this to work, she had to lead him all the way into the kitchen.

Chapter 54

Ursula

A single bottle of beer rested on the kitchen island next to a steaming apple pie that Jasmine had worked furiously to bake, using rusted muscles she hadn't flexed since she was fourteen years old, Katrine by her side. The smell was heavenly, caramelized apples bubbling in a delicate golden-brown crust dusted with cinnamon.

Two chairs rested alongside the island. The whole setup was ringed with a nearly invisible circle of salt. When the kitchen door swung open and Tara strode in, her eyes wild, Ursula whispered a prayer for her beautiful granddaughter and shrank deeper into the shadows behind the basement door.

She witnessed the exchange through the crack.

"You want something to drink?" Tara asked. Her voice quavered. She strode to the moonlit island, not stopping at the light switch.

"That beer looks pretty good," Baler said.

He didn't look a thing like her father, Charlie, but it was *him*, as plain as the toes on her feet. Ursula began to knead at the hem of her dress, reaching for the double braids she hadn't worn in half a century.

"Oh, yeah!" Tara said, as if she'd just noticed the brown bottle resting on the granite. She reached for it and held it out to him, the cool glass sweating in her hand. "I'm sure it'd be fine for you to drink it. And eat some pie, too."

Baler moved so quickly that he was a blur. In less than a second, he went from being just inside the kitchen door to standing beside Tara inside the salt circle. He fisted her hair with one hand and forced the bottle of beer to her lips with his other. Ursula inhaled sharply.

"Would it be fine for *you* to drink it?" he rasped, tipping the bottle so the beer ran down Tara's face.

Tara gagged, but bless her, she wrested the bottle from his hand as if it were nothing and took a deep swallow. "Sure," she said, covering her cough with the back of her hand. "You don't need to be a weirdo about it."

Baler seemed surprised, then suspicious. He glanced around the room, his eyes lingering on the crack Ursula was peeking out from. She knew he couldn't see her, but his glance in her direction stripped her bare. She was glad she was the only one who was witnessing Tara with this beast. Jasmine and Katrine wouldn't have been able to stomach it. She uttered a courage prayer for the others, those waiting for the signal.

"Aren't you going to drink some?" Tara offered the bottle to Baler, who still held her hair. The grip looked painful.

He took a swig, still staring angrily at the corners of the shadowy room. Ursula watched. He could have drunk every last drop. There wasn't poison in there. That hadn't worked before and wouldn't work now. The magic was in the pie. She reached for the basement doorknob, her heartbeat crashing in her ears. She had one chance.

"You've never looked better," Velda crooned from across the kitchen as she sashayed through the rear door.

Ursula's stomach pushed into her throat and she was forced to pause, her hand on the door she'd been about to step through. She'd been explicit. Everyone was to stay hidden until Ursula called for them. The fewer people involved, the fewer people hurt. Of *course* Velda had ignored the instructions, and now she was going to ruin everything with her selfishness, her need to face her husband! Ursula stood paralyzed, unsure how to pull this back or if such a thing were even possible.

Baler turned to Velda, a lazy, sexy smile breaking across his face as he released Tara. "Why, Ms. Velda." He strolled out a light Southern accent that hadn't been there moments earlier, a little bit of Mississippi honey. "You *do* recognize me. You didn't say a peep at Christmas when I came to shovel."

The cadence chilled Ursula. She recognized it as her father's.

Velda stepped farther into the room and flicked on the light. She wore the same blue dress she'd shown up in tonight, her hair in the same disheveled white curls, her peach lipstick hastily applied, but she blazed with the glorious beauty of her full power, temporarily pulling the best of everyone in the room to herself and reflecting it back. It was like staring into the sun. Ursula leaned forward, nose to the crack, choosing to sear her eyes rather than look away.

Baler's jaw dropped. "I forgot how good you could look, baby."

A secret smile curled at Velda's mouth. She swept forward, eighty years old, stunning. "Did you forget anything else I can do for you?"

Tara stumbled away from Baler, her own jaw slack. She'd witnessed her great-grandma's magic plenty before and thought she'd seen the full extent of it.

Not even close.

Velda glittered and preened, taking Tara's place in the salt circle and standing so close to Baler that she could touch his shirt. He ran his free hand lovingly up her neck, cupping her chin, leaning in for a kiss.

Ursula held her breath.

Velda's eyes were half closed. "Charlie," she whispered. "I've missed you."

His face was an inch away from hers before his intent became clear. He grabbed her by the throat, swiveling to shove her head onto the table, taking up the beer bottle like a hammer. The knife she'd been concealing in the folds of her dress clattered to the floor. It happened so fast there wasn't even time to gasp.

Baler hovered over Velda, his hand in the air, his voice a razor. "You've forgotten that your goddamned magic doesn't work on me, witch."

Ursula's body responded before her mind. She found herself shooting forward, lunging at Baler, clinging to his back. A growl rose from deep within her as she scrabbled for the bottle with one hand and scratched his face with her other.

He pushed Velda out of the circle as easily as tossing a sack of potatoes, then crouched to grab her knife. Blade in hand, he yanked Ursula off his back and tossed her onto the ground, face up. He knelt on her hips, holding the glistening blade to her neck.

Tara screamed.

Xenia, Helena, Katrine, Jasmine, Dean, Audish, and Leo rushed into the kitchen, raw panic in their eyes.

Baler addressed them all at once. "Stop. Or I'll slit her throat."

It was a fact rather than a command. He swiveled to pull Ursula up and against his chest, facing her out like a ventriloquist's dummy, the knife drawing a lick of blood from the cream flesh of her throat. He used his free hand to take a pull from the beer bottle, his lazy smile growing broader.

"How many people do you have here, and just for little ol' me? Oh well. I always have enjoyed an audience." He nodded toward Velda, who was wheezing, unable to catch her breath since he'd thrown her. Katrine knelt at her grandma's side. "That's one thing we always had in common, Mama," he said to Velda.

"You won't hurt her," Katrine said, trembling. "Not with us as witnesses."

Baler threw his head back and laughed, a hollow sound that injected ice into Ursula's blood. "I think I'll be heading out after today anyhow, since the snakes are about done. Not much fun for me without them around, though I've enjoyed watching you all for the past several months." He made a sideways Elvis thrust with his hips. "After I hit the road, you can do what you like with this bluesman's body."

He dug the knife deeper into Ursula's throat. She would not let the tears fall. She would not let her daughters see she was scared. Helena and Xenia held each other. Leo was frozen in place. Jasmine grabbed Tara's hand and pulled her daughter to her, away from the salt circle. Dean threw his arms around them both.

The standoff lingered in the air, thicker than oxygen, not quite solid, tasting of blood.

"This isn't what I thought I'd be getting today," Baler said, reaching up to take a final pull from the beer. "You were a good time, for sure," he said, nodding at Katrine. "Though a bit of a tease."

Her face burned.

"Your sister, too, from what I recall," he grunted.

Jasmine's skin turned the same color as Katrine's. Dean squeezed her tighter.

"But I was hoping for a little younger meat." He leered at Tara, chuckling at her horrified expression, never letting up on the knife at Ursula's throat. He shrugged. "But you can't always get what you want." He leaned forward to kiss Ursula's hair. "And so, I'll have to settle for paying you back that favor from fifty years ago, eh, Ursula? But since it'll be a while before I return, I wouldn't mind a taste of that apple pie."

The room held its collective breath.

"It smells sweet enough to wake the dead." He dropped the beer bottle to the floor, shattering it, and dug his fingers into the pie, the soft apples oozing through his fingers, bleeding brown sugar. "Still warm. You shouldn't have."

No one moved.

He'd either eat it or he wouldn't. If he didn't, it'd be the end of Ursula. But that was okay, wasn't it? At least he hadn't hurt her daughters, not this time. It was only right that if one of them had to pay, it was her.

Baler had the dripping apple flesh to his lips before he paused, shoving it toward Ursula's mouth, chuckling darkly. "I'd slap my knee if I had a free hand. Fool me once, right? Dear daughter, if you don't mind, would you have a taste of this? Wanna make sure it isn't poisoned."

Everyone's eyes widened in horror. This wasn't how it was supposed to happen.

Ursula opened her mouth, and Baler shoved the pie in.

She closed her eyes and chewed.

She swallowed.

A tear ran down Velda's cheek.

Chapter 55

Ursula

Baler glanced around the room and snorted. "You all should see yourselves! You look like you're at a surprise funeral." He jiggled Ursula. "No worries! She seems no worse for the wear. As such, I do believe I will enjoy myself some pie."

He nodded in satisfaction and popped an oozing chunk of dessert into his mouth. The cinnamon sugar drooled down the side of his face. He closed his eyes in ecstasy. "If that isn't the most delicious thing I've ever tasted, then butter don't melt in July. It's like heaven and sex met to share a secret."

He reached for another scoop.

Jasmine cocked her head, watching with the detachment of a scientist.

Baler was just beginning to chew on his second mouthful when his eyes bulged.

He staggered backward. Katrine lunged for Ursula and pulled her away from Baler, who was now scratching at his own throat, his mouth opening and closing like a landed fish. He spit the masticated pie on the floor and choked out, "Poison! How?"

Jasmine shook her head, her smile a grim soldier. "Not poison. Not even a potion. It's a pie I baked, just plain old apple pie."

Baler's eyes grew tighter, his skin shading blue.

"With one tweak to the recipe," Jasmine continued. "Whoever eats the pie has their greatest wish turned against themselves."

Baler may have been trying to make sense of her words, or he may have just been busy fighting for his life. In either case, he appeared frightfully confused.

Jasmine explained. "You wished for Ursula to be poisoned eating it. You ate the pie, and so now *you're* being poisoned." She shrugged as if she'd just told him he'd forgotten to take his B vitamins for the day.

Baler began laughing maniacally in between bursts of painful hacking. "Damn straight you witches are a lot of work. Just when I think I have it figured out. But I'll just come back. You know I'll be back. Not one of you can stop me."

"That's where I come in," Velda said, struggling to her feet and stepping forward.

"And us." Katrine kept her arm around Ursula.

Dean took a step. "And me."

Jasmine beamed at him, not letting go of his hand or Tara's. "And me."

"Me too," Leo said, moving to stand beside Katrine.

"Me three," Audish said.

Once everyone in the room had spoken, they merged hands to form a circle around Baler. While he writhed on the floor, they chanted the curse-breaking spell. Ursula led the words, and everyone but Baler repeated them.

> With the power of my blood,
> And the strength of my verse . . .

Each syllable hit him like a kick, bubbling his flesh. He writhed in agony. The Blackthorn women felt the pain, too, but they held each other, passing the burning between their hands, taking as much as they could so no one had to bear it alone.

I reclaim my own path,
And I destroy your curse.

Baler screamed, his face contorting and melting so he was no longer recognizably human. The air reeked of sulfur. Snakes began to flow in through the cracks, but they didn't come to his aid, never had helped him. The snakes didn't take sides. They just pulled secrets into the sun.

Air. Earth.

Baler spasmed with such force that a bone broke through his skin. He lifted off the ground and hovered inches from the floor, and then dropped, completely motionless. A hazy silhouette hovered above his flesh, a suggestion of a memory, the handsome, angry face of Charlie Tanager. He reached toward Velda, his expression pleading.

"Velda," he begged. "I love you."

She spit at the image.

The silhouette laughed and roared up like a flame, then was sucked back into Baler's body. He started writhing anew.

Water. Fire.

Green liquid leaked out of Baler's eyes and nose, and he retched violently. The churning neon bile burned and sizzled on the floor. Still, everyone chanted, though Dean was as green as the vitriol leaving Baler. Only two lines remained.

As these words are spoken,
Your spell is forever broken.

Baler's body exploded, a wet rain of oil and filth that turned to gas before it hit anything solid. Charlie's molasses laugh echoed, quickly replaced by a scream. Katrine wiped her eyes. Ursula stared. Jasmine appeared to be in shock.

Time stopped, momentarily trapping each person inside the shell of their minds.

Then, with a roar, a reconstructed Baler fell from the ceiling, free of the curse that'd been driving him and as naked as the day he was born. He landed in the middle of the salt circle, whole, shivering and crying.

It was done. Charlie would not be back.

The weight of this knowledge quilted the air, welcoming confession.

"I was raped," Jasmine said, pointing at Baler. Dean didn't know, and he deserved to. "I was a child. My family would have helped me, but I was too ashamed to tell them. I used my magic to cook a meal that would make them blind to my pain and that would send Katrine away, and then I never used my magic again."

Tara squeezed her mother's hand. The air crackled as they all bore witness to her pain. Ursula could see the shame pulsing through her daughter, not nearly as strong as the first time she'd confessed but still there, gliding up and out, but sticking, expanding, crowding her throat. Just when she looked like she would choke on it, Katrine grabbed her sister's free hand. Grateful tears coursed down Jasmine's face.

"I went home with Baler when I didn't want to," Katrine said. She kept a firm grip on Jasmine. "I let him do things to me because I was scared to ask him to stop. Also, my husband cheated on me and I convinced myself that I didn't know about it, but really, I'd known from the beginning that he wasn't the right man for me. Oh, and my sister recently informed me that I was wrong about my gift." She tossed Jasmine a tremulous smile. "I'm not a spotty mind reader, like I've suspected my whole life, or at least that's not all I am. I'm also an empath who makes people better at whatever they want to be better at."

The others nodded, lost in their own birthing secrets.

"As you all apparently know, I had my daughter mix a potion that I used to murder my husband," Velda said, drawing all attention to her with a snap. "I'm sorry, Ursula."

Ursula considered her mother, not sure if she'd heard correctly. "Sorry you killed him?"

Velda shook her head. "I'm sorry I brought you into it. It's my greatest regret. But sorry I killed your father? Not for a second. He was an absolute bastard. I miss him, though, every day of my life." She stepped into the circle and prodded Baler with her toe. He moaned pitifully. "Or, at least I used to. Also, I know what you think of me. Ursula mostly, but Helena and Xenia, too." Her eyes landed on each of her daughters, a sad smile on her face. "You think I'm vain and useless."

Helena began to step forward.

"Now stop it," Velda said, putting out her hand. "You don't need to comfort me. I know it's true. So you can say that I'm selfish, on that you're right. But you can't say that I don't love my girls, because I do. I love you so much that to protect you, I killed the only man who could see the real me."

The constriction she'd carried since she was thirteen fell away from Ursula's throat, and the glass jar encasing her heart finally shattered into a glorious blue rain. She gasped as she took her first clean breath in nearly fifty years. It was guilt and shame, not the curse of her father or the promise to her mother, that'd kept her silent all this time.

The air was simmering. "I'm afraid I can't live without Helena," Xenia said. A burner on the stove flashed into life, sending glowing orange sparks to her feet. She stomped them out without glancing down.

The warm tears burbling up in Helena's eyes doubled, and she grabbed her sister's hand. "I'm afraid I can't live without you, too."

"My power allows me to read your loose thoughts and see the pain in each of you," Tara said, smiling shyly at Leo. She paused before continuing. "It lets me see what you all look like naked, too."

A few legs were discreetly crossed. Jasmine's cheeks burned bright red. It was Katrine who caught the lightness in her niece. She started laughing.

“Just kidding,” Tara said. “About the naked part.”

From the outside, the house glowed like a firefly, and as far away as Battle Lake, people forgot why they were fighting or remembered why they’d fallen in love as every one of the Blackthorn women’s power was restored.

Chapter 56

Tara

Helena and Xenia checked Ursula all over, looking for more wounds.

"Baler wished for you to be poisoned when he ate the pie," Xenia said, disbelief written across her face at Ursula's wholeness. Other than the bleeding at her neck, she seemed fine.

"What was *your* greatest wish while eating it?" Helena finished.

Ursula kept blinking. "For you all to forgive me," she said, appearing so whisper-light she might begin floating. "I thought I was going to die. It never occurred to me that the spell would allow me to forgive myself." She patted her own arms and glanced around her kitchen, muck splattered against the walls, sizzling green liquid on the floor, Baler sitting in the middle of it looking terrified. "We have some cleaning to do."

They filled buckets with hot soapy water and got to work. Audish offered to take care of Baler. Tara asked if she could come with. She was sure her mom and dad would be against it, but it was actually Jasmine who said that it would be fine.

Audish got Baler a towel to wrap around himself and then led the perplexed man out to his car and drove him and Tara to his place. There he found an old pair of pajamas and told Baler to put them on. They were about three sizes too small, but they'd work.

You don't beat up a naked man was Audish's reasoning, and Baler was a man who needed to be beaten up.

Once Audish had a confused but clothed Baler on his feet, he engaged him in an old-fashioned fistfight. Baler didn't know what he was swinging for, couldn't remember anything that'd happened in the past year, in fact, but he'd lured enough teenage girls and married women backstage to assume he had this coming. Still, he fought back. Too bad for him Audish was the 1948 Beaver Tail County bantamweight boxing champion and hadn't forgotten what he knew back then.

He beat all the fight right out of Baler.

While Baler was on the ground flirting with consciousness, Audish leaned over to whisper something into the vast ketchup of his brain. No one would ever know what he said, not even Tara, but it was no coincidence that Baler gave up music that very night and took up telemarketing three states over, forever honing his communication skills.

Part 5

The Healing

The Blackthorn Book of Secrets: Inertia Antidote

While it is commonly understood that an object in motion stays in motion, most folks are less comfortable acknowledging that a passive person stays inert unless a powerful-enough force dictates otherwise. If you know it's time to act and would rather not wait for the 2 x 4 solution the Universe is sure to provide, follow this spell:

Act.

Chapter 57

Ursula

A few weeks later, Ursula stepped tentatively across the threshold of Immanuel Lutheran Church, her sisters by her side.

"We didn't burst into flames!" Xenia said, grinning. "How about that?"

Ursula appreciated the attempt at humor, but she couldn't match it. She was here for one reason.

Dagmar Baum.

The woman was up front, sitting with the choir. It pained Ursula to see she wore dark sunglasses. She imagined Dagmar must be entirely blind. Yet the woman maintained an attitude of arrogance somehow, her nose in the air even now. Ursula knew what it was like to confuse distance for protection. She wished Dagmar peace.

She also knew she owed her an apology. She sat through the most boring sermon of her life, and then, while her sisters waited near the exit door for her, she rushed to where Dagmar was seated.

"Good morning, Dagmar," she said. "How are you?"

Dagmar's head turned sharply. Her lips were pressed into a thin red line. The dark glasses hid her eyes, but her rigid posture exuded pride. Yet her hands fidgeted, the missing pinkie joints stark against the jar she held. Had she been gripping it the entire sermon?

"Ursula," Dagmar said, offering the jar. "I was hoping you'd come today. I brought you something."

Ursula was wondering if Dagmar had some magic of her own—why else would she possibly think Ursula would visit her church today?—when the smell struck her. Her hand flew to her nose.

"It's surströmming," Dagmar said, still holding out the jar. "Pickled herring. I made it myself. It's a family recipe, brought over from Sweden by Albrikt Gottfridsen, my great-grandfather a few times removed."

The jar appeared sealed, but still, the smell was overpowering, like rotting fish and hot eggs. "Thank you?" Ursula said, taking the jar.

"I know it smells like shit," Dagmar said, the corner of her mouth twitching. "That's the point. Albrikt said it was strong enough to knock you into a new attitude." Her chin tipped, her glasses pointing at Ursula. "Thought you could use it."

"Thank you," Ursula said, sincerely this time. Something that smelled this bad couldn't possibly be food, but she was happy for what it represented between her and Dagmar. She cradled the jar, its stench blooming between them. She didn't know how to start.

"I was cruel," she said finally. "I took what wasn't mine." Her voice, as always, stayed measured, but the truth in it burned her throat. "I never respected what it would cost you, or any of the women whose husbands I slept with."

Dagmar gave no indication she was listening. She stared straight ahead, that stiff posture still soldiering.

"I don't have an excuse," Ursula continued, softer now. "Just regret, and a promise that I won't ever do it again. I also want to help you heal your eyes. I fear I may have accidentally contributed to your growing blindness."

The silence between them held weight. Ursula wasn't sure what she expected—insults, silence, the jar ripped from her hands and hurled at her feet—but not what came next.

Dagmar reached up, slow and deliberate, and removed her glasses.

Her eyes were clear. A little red at the edges, perhaps, but unclouded.

"You're not the only one who's been waking up," she said. "After you carried me into my house, I had my own come to Jesus"—here she crossed herself—"which involved some long talks with my husband, who after all was the one who was cheating. The more we talked, the more my eyes healed." She shrugged. "I can see better than I have my whole life. Figured I'd keep the glasses on till someone gave me a reason to take them off, though." Ursula opened her mouth, but Dagmar raised a hand, forestalling any reply. "Don't mistake this for forgiveness," she said. "You've made terrible work for me. But it's better than living in darkness."

She popped the glasses back on and stood to walk away, trailing her hand on the pews. Ursula thought she heard her say "thank you," but she couldn't be sure.

Audish had joined her sisters at the back of the church. He seemed to be around all the time now, he and Helena close as a hand and glove. Ursula didn't mind. She made her way to them.

Audish tilted his head at the jar Ursula held. "Fermented herring?"

Ursula nodded. She still wasn't sure what she was going to do with it. "Dagmar gave it to me just now. Said it was a gift, an old family recipe that she'd made just for me."

Audish didn't hesitate. He reached for the jar and screwed off the lid. To Ursula, the wash of air smelled like an aquatic corpse.

"You have to eat it," Audish said.

Ursula shook her head, her hand over her nose. "I don't think I can."

He stepped closer, holding out the jar, gray lumps glistening on the surface of a filmy liquid. "This is old-country kitchen magic. You don't turn from that when it's offered in love."

Ursula knew he was right. And what was the worst that could happen? She'd throw up in church. "Fine," she said. She gripped a slimy hunk and popped it into her mouth before she could change her mind. Once she got past the smell, the taste was interesting. Umami, with a tingle on the edges of her tongue. She was thinking she was glad she tried it once but that was enough when the strangest sensation rippled across her body, like every cell had opened its window and shaken out its musty carpets, letting in spring.

She couldn't help it. She laughed. Dagmar *did* have magic. "Strong enough to knock you into a new attitude indeed," she said.

The Blackthorn Book of Secrets: Old-Country Magic

When you must leave your home, either through force or choice, you have a careful moment to bind the good of the place and bring it with you to your new location. Simply select the food that most reminds you of what you're leaving behind. Write down the recipe, even if you think it would be impossible for you to forget, and whisper the following over it:

hearth, come with me
hope, come with me
roots, come with me

Remember that the power of the recipe is not in the food, but in the way it connects hearts and histories.

Chapter 58

Katrine

The next week arrived like a fever dream, bringing with it the official declaration of drought across all of Beaver Tail County. First the snakening, and then this. The earth cracked open, thirsting, while Faith Falls baked under a relentless sun. People had to blink to see where they were going. Fires were forbidden. Moods were tight. The generosity that had accompanied the unusual spring warmth was replaced with a peevishness, as if people could hear the screech of parched electrons rubbing up against one another.

"Watch where you're going!" snapped Michael Baum, his fist in the air before he saw it was Bradley Willmar who'd bumped into him on the corner of Lake and Elm Streets. In other parts of town, the fights were impossible to stop. The unrelenting nature of the wind drove the townspeople to the edge, and then past.

Katrine sat at a corner booth of Perfume River, feeling a little nervous. It'd stung to see that Ren and Heidi were together that night, but she'd decided she wasn't going to let it come between her and Heidi's friendship. She'd invited her here to confess that she'd harbored a crush on Ren but that her relationship with Heidi was more important to her than that silliness.

"Sorry I'm late." Heidi slid into the Naugahyde booth across from her. Her red hair was a flawless helmet, her makeup thick enough to remove with a smack to the back of her head. "Are you getting the buffet?"

Katrine had believed, before she'd learned of her true power, that her gift had never been as useful as her sister's or Ursula's, or even Xenia's or Helena's. It was unreliable, for one, as her reads often got muddied by her preconceptions. In fact, she was better at reading someone she didn't know than a person she was close to, and even then, their thoughts came to her sporadically. For another, if her gift revealed what she didn't want to discover, she was liable to override it, and nothing retaliated like a gift ignored. Thanks to Jasmine's revelation about her true power, though, she realized she'd been seeing who the person *could* be, not who they were.

Despite all this, she could still lift random thoughts from a person, and since the Blackthorns had broken the curse, her magic had become more reliable. Heidi's thoughts shot at her like arrows. She was as nervous as Katrine, her extra makeup a shield. She was also lonesome, tired of raising two kids by herself, and hungry since five days ago she'd begun a low-carb diet that included skipping breakfast.

"Why are you looking at me like that?" Heidi asked. "Having another Kat Attack?"

Katrine had forgotten the nickname they'd given her back in high school when she was reading people. Adam had told her she looked like she was power daydreaming, except that her pupils dilated. "Nice."

"I'm sorry." Heidi's cheeks flushed. "I shouldn't have said that."

Katrine shrugged. "It was high school. Jasmine and I were odd ducks. I get why we would have been targets."

"We were all weird in high school," Heidi said. "But not everyone was mean. So I'm sorry."

The owner stopped by the table. Katrine saw that she still had the blue glow from one of Ursula's spells. It must have been a strong one. Her name tag read DIANE.

"Buffet?" Diane asked.

"Just tea for me," Katrine said. "And seaweed salad. Do you have that?"

She shook her head. "No seaweed salad. That's Japanese. You want the buffet?"

"The buffet will be fine."

"Me too," Heidi said. "With a diet cola."

Heidi was sliding out of the booth when her eyes widened toward the front of the restaurant. "Oh!"

Katrine turned to see what Heidi was staring at. There stood Ren with his daughters. He was tall, self-possessed, his smile easy. Katrine felt her heart skip its track for a moment, but she shut down that emotion before it went any higher *or* lower. She was going to respect Heidi's relationship.

"Ren Cunningham," Heidi whispered. "He is such a doll. And don't stare now because he's coming over."

Katrine shot Heidi a confused look, but she didn't have time to question her because there was Ren, smelling of fresh-washed sheets hung in the sun to dry.

"Hello, ladies." His smile reached his eyes, which were locked on Katrine. "Heidi, of course you know Joanie and Clara. Katrine, these are my daughters. I never got a chance to introduce you at Christmas or Sadie Hawkins."

Both girls smiled. One was shorter and round, presumably taking after her mom, and the other had Ren's lanky build. "Nice to meet you," they said in unison.

Katrine smiled back, trying not to focus on Ren. He had so much presence that it unsettled her. "Pleased to meet you both, too."

Heidi cleared her throat. "Ren, you know that Katrine is the best reporter the paper's ever had. I was thinking she could write up a story on your store." She winked at Katrine with all the subtlety of a hand grenade.

Katrine's mouth swung open. She realized Heidi was nudging her toward Ren. Had they broken up?

"That would be wonderful," Ren said. His deep voice traveled straight into Katrine's heart. "If that's okay with you."

"Sure," Katrine said, pulling her attention back to the conversation at hand. "Should be fun. When works best for you?"

"We'll be in the store all day tomorrow," Joanie said shyly.

Diane appeared with two large carry-out bags. "Your food, Mr. Ren."

"Thank you. I . . ." He turned toward Katrine. Whatever he was going to say seemed to desert him. "It was nice to see you."

Their eyes met, and it was all laid out for her to see: his magnificent heart, his talent, his intelligence, his stability, his honesty. It was too much. She looked away, catching a parting glance of him laughing at something one of his daughters had just said.

Heidi leaned over the table and smacked her arm. "I pass you the ball, and you take a dump on it? What was that all about? He likes you!"

"But *you're* dating him!" Katrine said.

Heidi snorted. "I wish. Do you know we ended up at the same spot one of the nights we were looking for Tara? Apparently my mom sent us both, probably trying to set me up with him. But I couldn't even get him to kiss me! I only got a hug because I said I felt faint. Guy must be a priest." She waggled her eyebrows. "Or into someone else. Don't tell me you can't see how Ren looks at you. He's got it bad."

Katrine replayed that night. She'd ended up at the church because Dagmar had sent her there. The woman must have staged the scene, forever hunting for ways to get back at Ursula until she could strike her directly. It was hard to feel mad, though. She was too busy being overjoyed at finding out Ren was single.

And because she felt it so strongly, everyone in the restaurant felt it. Such was her gift. It lifted them higher, encouraged them to reach across the table and hug the person they were with, to put down the fried meat and go for steamed vegetables.

The rush of happiness was so powerful, in fact, that Diane stopped pouring Heidi's diet cola, strode to her car, retrieved her karaoke machine, and slammed it dead center on the one free table in the entire restaurant. Customers glanced up, startled by the sound. The cord barely reached the outlet.

"I sing!" she declared.

She didn't need to search for the song. She'd chosen it years ago. She selected the ninth track on the disk, tapping her feet to the infectious beat. Everyone in the restaurant stared at her, and she stared right back, even though her heart was beating so loud she could no longer hear.

When it was time to sing the lyrics, she nailed it, belting out "I Will Survive" as if she'd been born with the words in her mouth.

Chapter 59

Katrine

A short time after their meal at Perfume River, Heidi called Katrine into her office and asked her to sit. "I've got something big for you," she said, grinning. "Something huge, in fact."

Katrine and Heidi had continued to grow close since Katrine had found out that Ren and her editor were not dating. That didn't mean Katrine was dating him either—she'd been focused on healing family wounds and growing a happiness that could never be stolen from her—but at least it was a possibility. Her interview with him had gone well, and she'd taken his girls and Tara shopping in Fargo at Tara's request.

She'd also contacted worried friends back in London, started taking walks at night with her mom, and gone to Jasmine's house for meals, where she found, to her boundless joy, that her sister was cooking fabulous food again. To everyone's surprise, Dean even preferred it to the processed stuff. Katrine'd also—with Jasmine's permission—brought Tara along on some of her interviews. The girl had a real knack for journalism, and her enthusiasm was reminding Katrine of what had drawn her to writing in the first place: connections.

"Something huge," Katrine said to Heidi, rolling her eyes. "Let me guess . . . Bradley Willmar has secured funding to outfit all the beaver statues with bronze skirts?"

Heidi's eyes twinkled. "Better."

"Spill!" Katrine said, sitting up straighter.

Heidi sat back, feigning concern. "I don't know. It might be *too* massive for you. I don't wanna blow your mind."

"Stop teasing!"

"Don't say I didn't warn you." Heidi pretended to stare at her fingernails before leaning forward in excitement. "Aw shoot, here it is, and tell me if it sounds stupid. What do you think about writing a history of Faith Falls? The good, the bad, the ugly. We'll serialize it in the paper, running a chapter each week. When you're done, you'll have enough to take to a publisher if you want."

"The history of Faith Falls?" Katrine turned the idea over in her mind.

"It'd be about our families, ultimately. A portrait of small-town America. Well, our version of it, anyhow. I'd particularly love to find out what happened to your great-grandparents. My mom still talks about them, you know? But no one knows their story, where they came from, why they ended up here. You could be the one to research it and tell it."

The more Katrine handled the idea, the more she liked it. No, the more she *loved* it. Thoughts floated like dandelion fluff as she considered all the directions she could take this, all the stories she could tell. "It's fantastic, Heidi. Really. Thank you."

"Thank me when you're done," Heidi said, patting her hair. "I think this is going to be more work than either of us imagines."

They beamed at each other across the desk for a full minute, two ex–beauty queens tumbled around by life, the pressure leaving them both stronger and lovelier than they'd been in their youth.

"Not me," Katrine said.

Heidi's face accordioned in confusion. "What?"

"You asked, 'Who would've thought we'd end up friends?' I sure wouldn't have, especially after I stole Josh from you in eleventh grade. I didn't like him, by the way. I just wanted to get back at you for telling Mrs. Mocek that I cheated on the algebra test. Can you believe how immature I was?"

Heidi was pulling back. "I didn't say anything of the sort, though I had just *thought* it."

Katrine drew up, realizing she'd accidentally read Heidi's mind. "Must have been a lucky guess."

Heidi's eyes narrowed. "I recommend you either get better at lying or better at sharing. The town would be less scared of you Blackthorn women if they could make their own magic. In the meantime, can you teach me to read minds?"

Katrine sucked on her teeth. "You sure you'd want to?"

Heidi laughed. "Maybe not. If people waste even half their thoughts like I do, I'm better off sticking inside my own head." She seemed to consider. "But things are changing in town. Even my own mother has started to let down her hair. Literally and figuratively. She's actually taken up hobbies other than hating your mom. I even saw her—gasp—laugh the other day." Heidi grinned. "So let me think about learning how to read minds. In the meanwhile, don't you have work to do? I'm not paying you to sit on your butt."

"You're barely paying me," Katrine said good-naturedly, standing. She stopped in the doorway. "Heidi?"

"What?"

"I'm glad we're friends."

Heidi winked. "I bet you are. I'm pretty cool, you know."

Katrine left, walking on bubbles as she thought of researching and writing about this strange, backward, magic little town. She was on her way to Seven Daughters to share the exciting news with her aunts when a hot gust of wind sprayed her face with grit. She covered her eyes, trying to wipe away the stinging dirt, and felt along the storefronts with her free hand until she came to a doorknob. She pulled it open.

Her ears were filled with the muffled clicking of time.

"Katrine?"

She recognized the deep voice, even though she could not yet see. "Ren?" She panicked for a moment, blind and alone with him, and reached out mentally from habit. He was there, concerned, steadfast. She stopped rubbing at her face and stood straight, eyes shut tight.

"Some dirt blew in my eyes," she said. "I can't see where I'm going."

"Wait a minute," he said.

She heard receding footsteps, a drawer sliding open, water running. In a moment, he was next to her.

"I have a warm washrag," he said, placing it in her hand.

She patted at her lashes with the rag, blinking a few times before opening her eyes. She looked around. It was exactly as it'd been when she'd come to interview him, one large room, timepieces in every size and shape arrayed on the floor and the walls: grandfather clocks, wall clocks, a Betty Boop lamp clock, watches, all ticking in perfect harmony.

"Thanks," she said, handing him back the washrag. "I can see again."

He wore blue jeans and a crisp white T-shirt below blue flannel. A dried leaf was stuck in his curly hair. Katrine thought his strong nose lent him an air of distinguished authority, balanced by a mouth that hinted at both kindness and mischief. But it was his ears, large and slightly comical, that were her favorite. Well, next to his hands.

"I'd like to take you out on a date sometime," he said. His ocean eyes were wide, his expression hopeful.

Her breath stopped for a moment. "Why today?" she asked.

"What?"

"Why are you asking me out today?"

He shrugged. "It's the first time you've come to me on your own."

She smiled a secret smile. Faith Falls had nudged her into the watch store, and it occurred to her that writing the town's history was going to be even more interesting than she could have imagined. She nodded at Ren.

"That's a yes?"

"Yes," she said.

She drove toward Jasmine's with a silly smile on her face, realizing her sister was the one she most wanted to share all the good news with. She'd catch her own goofy expression in her rearview mirror, scold herself, grimace, but the smile would pop up again. She almost didn't recognize the hope, but there it was.

Her bliss was such that she didn't notice she'd received a text until she pulled in front of Jasmine's.

I'm flying to Minnesota, the message said. I need to see you. Love, Adam

Chapter 60

KATRINE

Adam's text had angered Katrine when she read it, but elation quickly replaced the wrath, then came confusion followed by more anger. Their divorce was not yet finalized because of a paperwork mix-up. She'd been waiting to scratch final signatures on the new form and send it to her attorney in London but had gotten too busy. At least that's what she'd told herself. Was that what he was coming to talk to her about?

A follow-up text from Adam confirmed that he would be arriving in Minneapolis later that day and hopping a local flight to Alexandria Municipal Airport, forty miles from Faith Falls. Katrine didn't know how to respond to either message, so she didn't. She hadn't even been certain that she'd meet him when his plane was due, not until she found herself behind the wheel, navigating back dirt roads with corners so sharp that she considered signaling.

The spring air was hot. She passed abandoned farmhouses left to the moth and rust, shocking next to fields full of bright green, the sprouts of irrigated corn.

Adam is coming for me.

The thought was tinged with pride and pain so sharp that it pierced her right behind her eyes. Had Adam broken up with Patsy? He must have. He must have realized that he'd made a mistake, and now he was coming for Katrine to rebuild their marriage. She hadn't told anyone where she was going or why. Would she be bringing Adam back to Faith Falls to meet her family?

She recalled Ren swaying with her at the Sadie Hawkins dance and how relaxed and natural she felt with him, how he treated her with tenderness and respect, of the warm green light that always seemed to surround him. Tonight was supposed to be their first date. It was funny like poison ivy that Adam had reached out to her now, just when she believed she'd finally found a good man.

Adam was a known, though, familiar.

And wasn't a marriage something worth fighting for?

The car left the gravel roads, dust clinging to it, and lit onto tar that shimmered like a mirage in the heat. Her windows were rolled down, and the wind blew her loose hair around her shoulders. She was wearing a simple cotton sundress and cowboy boots, no makeup. She didn't want to seem desperate. But she was, wasn't she? Her husband had cheated on her, and now he was giving her a second chance.

She pounded the steering wheel. Why was she going to meet him? Because she had to, that's why. She wanted to see his face, to hear that his infidelity hadn't been her fault. There'd been so many good times, and that counted for something. It had to.

In the distance, a small plane began to descend toward the local airport. Adam's, certainly. She drove the last few miles and pulled into the parking lot. The airport was modest, designed for hobby pilots, with two runways and a main office, no security. She stayed in her car until the plane touched down and began taxiing toward the office. The shimmer of the sun's blaze looked like it was cooking the tiny aircraft. The plane came to a stop five hundred yards from the parking lot.

Its propellers slowed.

Its door opened.

A man stepped out.

It wasn't Adam. Katrine released a held breath. She checked herself for disappointment and found none. That first passenger turned, talking to someone in the cabin, and then a second person appeared.

This time, it was Adam.

He really was here, in Minnesota.

He took the plane's attached stairs and stood on the tarmac, carry-on in hand. His expression was tentative, she could see that even from a distance. Her heart tensed. She stepped out of the car and began walking toward him. He strode toward her. She had dreamed of this moment a thousand times since returning to Faith Falls last August.

His steps grew easy, confident. The closer he came, the more she could see of him. He was wearing the verdant-green button-down shirt she'd bought him for his last birthday. The sun glinted off a watch, maybe the silver TAG Heuer she'd gifted him on their third anniversary. The hand that gripped his suitcase was the same one that had held her while he listened to her secrets. He was smiling, his light-brown, wide-set eyes fixed on her.

"Katrine."

She stopped. Two yards of space lay between them. He tried to step closer, but it was as if an invisible wall had appeared in front of him. His brow furrowed. He appeared confused.

"I missed you," he said in his charming Chelsea accent. "It's over with me and Patsy. I realized you're the woman for me. I ended it with her, darling. I never should have let it happen in the first place. I was a fool. A complete and utter fool. Please forgive me. I love you so much."

He sounded sincere. She smiled. The smile turned into laughter because she realized he *was* sincere. He wanted her back in his life. She'd given him security, love, respect, admiration, money. She'd handed over everything, and then she'd scrabbled for more to offer to him. She couldn't control her bubbling laughter, and it rose into the air and took flight on happy wings, because she *finally* saw Adam exactly as he was:

intelligent, selfish, handsome, unfaithful, funny, immature, and cruel. It was all there.

What was better, she recognized who *she* was.

She turned and never looked back.

Katrine didn't reveal to Ren how she'd spent that afternoon. That story would unfold as their connection grew. For now, it was enough to be with him in the sultry night, the breeze lifting her hair and kissing her behind the ears.

"You know that fireflies act as a metronome, right?" he said, pointing out the blinking flashes of light along the riverbank.

She smiled. That'd happened a lot this evening, first at dinner, then during the street dance, which they'd left to enjoy this quiet walk along the Rum River. The water was low due to the drought, but it was happy to see them. The dry grass underfoot crunched like straw.

"Really," she said. The sound felt drowsy. Ren's strong hand was holding hers.

"If, by chance, a few males flash in unison," he continued, "others will see it and adjust their own flashes. Soon, the entire firefly chorus is putting on a synchronized light show with no clear leader." He leaned over and pointed. "See that?"

A copse of oak trees sheltered the edge of the river. Three tiny lights flickered at the base of the largest. Two responded. Soon, as if heeding Ren's instructions, they began to blink like a thousand twinkle lights to music only they could hear.

"It's lovely," she said.

More than lovely, it was the vision she'd had when they first touched—secrets like stars dropping from the sky, surrounding them, dancing like fireflies. It was everything that had happened since she'd come home, wasn't it? Ursula and Jasmine had spoken their secrets out loud, robbing them of the toxic power they'd had over the family all these years. As a result, Katrine had her sister back again, and Ursula, Jasmine, and Katrine were building a new kind of relationship, one based on honesty. Dean had moved back home, Audish was dating Helena, Xenia was dating Cleo, and Jasmine had even allowed Leo and Tara to go on chaperoned dates. Katrine was writing. Jasmine was cooking. Ursula was forming friendships, all because the curse had been broken.

Katrine realized Ren was staring at her. She turned, and in his eyes she saw all her beauty reflected back to her. He brushed his hand against her cheek. She closed her eyes. The heat of him was palpable.

Before she could stop it, the confession erupted. It wasn't about her magic, or even her divorce. It was about Baler Trempeleau, the man who'd tricked her body in a way that shamed her.

Ren stiffened as her words poured out. Before she was done speaking, he held her close, gently, his heart beating under her cheek. When she stopped talking, when every bit of shame lay in front of her, he spoke softly into her hair.

"I'm sorry that happened. So very sorry. What do you need to feel safe?"

She tipped her face up to him, because she did trust him, had from the moment she'd first bumped into him outside of Seven Daughters. "Kiss me," she whispered.

He leaned in, but before his lips could touch hers, something warm moistened her cheek. Startled, she opened her eyes.

"Rain!" It'd been weeks since a drop of moisture had fallen.

Ren glanced up. In the yellow circles of the city park lights, tiny drops fell to earth, raising miniature dust storms. The sparse rain began to thicken, and then it started to pour. He grabbed her hand and they scampered through the warm rain, splashing in baby puddles and smelling the richness of thirsty earth.

They ran until they reached the Queen Anne, and then they snuck in through the back door, exactly as Katrine used to do when she crept home past curfew. It wasn't necessary—Ursula, Xenia, Helena, Velda, and Audish were at the movies, and the two of them had the house to themselves—but it was fun.

She stopped just outside her bedroom door, Ren holding her, both of them dripping on the hardwood floor. She stood on her tiptoes, pulled him close, and kissed him passionately. His mouth traced a hot arc to her ear, and he whispered something.

She said, “Hmm,” and the words curved up like a smile.

She led him inside her room and sat him on her bed, slowly slipping out of her clothes. Her wet dress fell to the ground like a seal skin. She was down to her bra and panties when panic overtook her. It lasted only a moment, a petrifying eternal second where she wanted to leave her own body. He reached out to her, but she shook her head. He was so bright, so calm, so open. She could do this. She stripped, standing in front of him fully unclothed, at first defiant and then, finally, letting her defenses down, truly naked.

He stood and pressed his body into hers. She was suddenly starving for him. She yanked open his shirt and pushed him into the bed. He met her desperation with warm, steady kisses, stopped her, and made her look him in the eyes.

“Do you want this?” he asked. She could see the throbbing of his pulse in his neck. His passion was as powerful as hers.

She nodded. “More than anything.”

His entire body shivered. He pulled off his shirt, exposing broad, strong shoulders and arms, a chest covered in soft hair, and a heart that beat just for her. He covered her body in kisses that brought her to the edge of absolute pleasure before pulling away, returning to kiss her mouth and whisper in her ear all the ways that he loved her.

The fruit, when it was finally ripe, was delicious, decadent, full of honey and life. Katrine’s heart hummed with a sweetness like the moment just before tears, stretched out forever.

Everything would be all right.

She was home.

Epilogue

The warm days of April and May eased into a milder June and then July, with highs in the lower 80s and enough rain to turn the entire state of Minnesota into a quivering wilderness of greens, yellows, purples, and reds. The air itself cleansed people like a medicine, a balm to tender tissues, broken hearts, and ill thoughts.

That paved the way for August to stride into town like a wise woman with strong arms, holding them all. With her came a blue moon, a second full moon in a single month, exactly as it had the previous August. Since blue moons normally occurred only once every three years, the lunar anomaly was recognized for the miracle it was, and folks joked that they'd have to update their vocabularies: "once in a blue moon" if it was rare, "twice in a blue moon" for a true miracle.

The Queen Anne felt the enchantment of it, but then, she always felt that way. There was magic in every season, even the darkest. She'd keep that one to herself, unless someone came looking for it. The house had a hunch that Katrine might, now that she was writing again. The Queen Anne had even put aside some pages for her in the *Book of Secrets*, which was, after all, a palimpsest.

On this gorgeous August afternoon, the Queen Anne's kitchen was full of cooks crafting a feast to end all in honor of Katrine's anniversary of coming home, Helena and Audish's engagement, and all the other magnificence that'd built the year.

Jasmine inhaled the scent of the orange-and-lavender sauce that Tara was spooning over the crackling duck skin. They were both wearing Xenia dresses, Jasmine's a dusty rose, calf-length with cap sleeves and a gathered bodice, and Tara's a black shirtwaist dress that her friend Brittany swore was the coolest thing she'd ever seen in her whole dang life.

Jasmine blew on the steaming sauce, grazing it with her pinkie and bringing a taste to her tongue. "It needs a little brightness," she said. "A dash of vinegar should do it. What do you think?"

Tara thought that if she got any happier, the top of her head would fall off for smiling. Her mom still moved like a patient who'd recently had a cast removed, but she didn't seem always afraid anymore. And she was teaching Tara *to cook*. No more prepackaged dinners at their house, or sauces in jars. They ate splendidly, richly, every meal connecting them.

"I think that's a great idea, Mom. What about a little bit of cumin, too?"

Jasmine nodded her approval. Tara wasn't a natural, but she was learning.

"So, that divorce final?" Velda asked Katrine on the other side of the room. They were sitting in the breakfast nook, watching the bustling cooks. Ren had his arm draped around Katrine's shoulders. Leo sat on the other side of Ren, a spot he'd been banished to after Helena had caught him trying to sneak a bit of piecrust.

"Yeah," Katrine said, as Ren squeezed her shoulder in support. Velda had never been famous for her subtlety.

Near the kitchen door, Audish watched his fiancée lovingly as she dipped rose petals into crystallizing simple syrup. Earlier, when the cooking was just getting underway, he'd taken Ren, Dean, and Leo on a walk. Ren's girls had stayed at the house, where Helena was teaching them how to make divinity. Ostensibly, the four men were going to the store to pick up fresh dill and capers, both of which Jasmine swore were crucial to the meal, but Audish had another motive.

"So," he said, breaking the companionable silence. His voice was gruff, almost embarrassed. "I don't suppose I'm telling you anything you don't know when I say a complicated woman is the only woman worth giving your heart to."

Ren, Leo, and Dean nodded.

"Helena Blackthorn is the most amazing, complex, loving creature I've ever met, which is why we're going to be married." He shoved his hands into his pockets. "I was hoping the three of you would stand up with me in the church, if that's where she decides she wants to hold it, or strapped to the top of the Empire State Building, if that's where she'd rather. I'm determined to spend the rest of my life meeting her every need."

"I'd be honored," Ren said.

"Me too," Leo promised.

"Thirded," Dean said.

The wedding was planned for December. It had already been decided that Helena would remain in the Queen Anne, and Audish would move in after the honeymoon. The men shared their visions for the future, bought the herbs and capers, and returned to the house.

The dinner, when it was ready, was amazing. The dining room table creaked under lavender-infused duck à l'orange covered in crispy, sweet-salty skin; tiny quails stuffed with sage dressing; wild perch drizzled with onion jam; roasted garlic soup with poached eggs; fresh-dug garden potatoes in browned parsley butter, their skin so tender that it melted when you bit into it; haricot verts in a lemon-almond sauce; roasted butternut squash; delicate mushroom caps filled with salty bacon, wild rice, and poached raisins; fresh spinach dressed with poppy seed vinaigrette; a wild lettuce salad speckled with sunflower nuts and bits of bright, fresh orange; platters of grapes, apples, nuts, and cheeses; and two loaves of oatmeal bread and another two of crusty French, all four loaves steaming. For dessert, Helena had prepared fresh strawberries with lemon verbena pudding, crystallized rose petals, wild angelica meringues, cherry, apple, and banana cream pies, divinity with the help of Ren's girls, and quarter-size violet and hazelnut cakes.

Conversation flowed as sweetly as the wine. Ren and Katrine couldn't stop gazing at each other, and neither could Audish and Helena, Dean and Jasmine, Cleo and Xenia, nor Tara and Leo.

Velda wasn't buying into it, but she did squeeze Ursula's hand.

The house was so happy that it felt like the color pink.

Afterword

The Blackthorn Women was inspired by genetics professor Bryan Sykes's nonfiction book *The Seven Daughters of Eve*. In his fascinating account, Sykes describes how, through mitochondrial DNA, every person of European descent can trace their common ancestry to one of seven primeval clan mothers, whom he calls the seven daughters of Eve. He bestows on them whimsical names: Velda, Ursula, Xenia, Helena, Katrine, Jasmine, and Tara. His thesis is that we are all connected, and he uses science to prove it.

I use fiction.

Discussion Questions

1. Throughout this book, you enter the minds of four of the Blackthorn women: Ursula, Jasmine, Katrine, and Tara. Which character did you most identify with, and why? Would you have liked to hear the perspective of any other characters? If so, which ones and why?
2. The mystery explores generational trauma—how unresolved pain passes from parents to children, and to their children in turn, until it's acknowledged and healed. What other themes stood out to you?
3. Identify and discuss some of the reasons the inhabitants of Faith Falls might be uncomfortable with the Blackthorns throughout their history there.
4. Velda created a family culture in which everyone kept secrets. What do you think motivated her?
5. In what ways did Katrine and Ursula have a typical mother-daughter relationship? If there were exceptional aspects of the relationship, to what do you attribute these?
6. Why didn't Ursula confront her mother and tell her sisters or daughters that she had helped to murder her father much earlier? Could she have prevented what happened to Jasmine by doing so?
7. Discuss Jasmine's role, if any, in what happened to Katrine the night the snakes rose. Would it have ended any differently if

she had confessed the full story of her assault? Does it matter if it would have? In other words, is it ever your duty to share secrets before you're ready?

8. What do the snakes in the book symbolize?
9. Audish, Leo, Dean, and Ren are all good men who love Blackthorn women. Do you believe it was Charlie Tanager's curse that initially keeps the men from getting and remaining close to the Blackthorns, or was it something else?
10. Do you believe in everyday magic, like the power to make people feel something when they eat food you've cooked, or the ability to sense when someone is dangerous?
11. Is there ever a good reason for family members to keep secrets from one another? If so, what would the circumstances be?
12. Would you want to read a prequel to this novel, one in which we learn the story of Eva and Ennis Blackthorn? Why or why not?

Acknowledgments

I began writing this book in 2002, shortly after my husband unexpectedly died. It was a painful time, but I found comfort in the words and the possibility of magic. As the mother of two small (at that time) children, I found life soon took over. I stuffed away the sixty or so pages that I'd written and didn't rediscover them until a decade later, when I was cleaning out my computer files. Falling right back in love with the words, I cozied up to my computer to type out the rest of the story.

That was 2012, and I'd already published eight novels. Writing this one was different, though. Rather than directing the plot as I typed, I found myself listening for stories and weaving them together. The result was unlike anything I'd written before.

The novel has taken many evolutions since then, including three rounds of professional editing. Traditional publishers ultimately turned it down, but I couldn't let it stay only on my computer. I felt like there was a message in the world of these women, and it wasn't meant only for me. And so, with the support of many wonderful people, I decided to create a Kickstarter campaign to self-publish. It was successful beyond my wildest dreams, and those contributors will always have a place in my heart (starting with Stacy Reller, who was my first donor and so forever gets to run the bead store in Faith Falls).

Thanks to them, this story lived a nice life as *The Catalain Book of Secrets* for a decade or so. Still, it sometimes felt like the redheaded stepchild of my writing career, always sort of in the background. That's why I was over the moon when Jessica Tribble Wells, my beloved editor at Thomas & Mercer, agreed to pick up the book and help it find a larger audience. That meant it got to go through the Magical Editing Machine (starting with Jessica and Charlotte for the big stuff, then handed off to Miranda, Jon, and Kellie for the tightening and polishing). After that, it got a new cover and a new title.

Thanks to them, *The Blackthorn Women* came into being.

Much gratitude also to the strong women in my life, now and past—Bernie, Suzanna, Kiara, Zoë, Christine, Erica Ruth, Kristi, Sarah, Cindy, Shannon, Berns, Carolyn—who taught me about kitchen magic, the power of a good red wine, and the healing spell of female friendship.

A final big thanks to you, the reader. May you find the comfort, hope, escape, and healing in this story that I did.

There's magic enough for all of us.

About the Author

Photo © 2023 Kelly Weaver Photography

Jess Lourey is the Amazon Charts bestselling author of *The Quarry Girls*, *Unspeakable Things*, *Litani*, and *Bloodline*, as well as the Steinbeck and Reed thrillers, the Salem's Cipher novels, and the Murder by Month rom-com mysteries. Lourey writes about secrets, fosters kittens, and travels. She's surpassed a million readers; been short-listed for the Goodreads Choice Awards and the Edgar Award twice each; and won the International Thriller, Anthony, and Minnesota Book Awards. She also has an active reader group on Facebook called Lourey's Literati. For more information, including a link to her TEDx Talk, in which she discusses the surprising inspiration behind her writing career, visit www.jesslourey.com.